PRAISE FOR AL.

Praise for *WOULD YOU RATHER*

"Ashley makes favorite rom-com tropes feel new again with a pitch-perfect friends-to-lovers story . . . The all too real motivation for the pair's fake marriage makes the trope sing, and Ashley surrounds her characters with supportive friends, family, and colleagues, grounding the story in community and heart. Mia's struggles with chronic illness are similarly well handled, capturing both the physical and emotional toll it takes on her day-to-day life. Readers won't want to put this one down."

—*Publishers Weekly* (starred review)

"A love story readers will thoroughly enjoy."

—*Library Journal*

"A pitch-perfect mix of all the best romance tropes, *Would You Rather* is what happens when friends to lovers, fake-dating, and mutual pining are elevated to perfection. Allison Ashley gives me all the feels, and I love every one of them!"

—Ali Hazelwood, *New York Times* bestselling author of *The Love Hypothesis*

"*Would You Rather* is a dynamic page-turner from the very first chapter. Allison Ashley has a masterful way of lighting the kindling in a slow, deliberate burn between two stubborn best friends who refuse to admit what everyone else sees clearly. I laughed out loud as Noah coveted the way Mia looked at chicken wings—any partner would be so lucky to receive such a longing gaze."

—Taj McCoy, author of *Savvy Sheldon Feels Good as Hell*

"Allison Ashley absolutely delivers with this swoony friends-to-lovers romance. The pining and the yearning and the kisses swept me off my feet, and I couldn't help falling in love with Noah and Mia. I loved every second of this book!"

—Falon Ballard, author of *Lease on Love*

"A sparkling, warm romance that reminds us why the friends-to-lovers trope is superior! Allison Ashley skillfully delivers a chemistry-filled, happy hug of a book set against the backdrop of real-life struggle. It's the kind of story I've been waiting for!"

—Sarah Adams, author of *The Cheat Sheet*

"*Would You Rather* made my heart burst in the best way. It hits every emotional high note with moments of laugh-out-loud humor, scenes that will bring you to tears, and cuteness that will make you squeal out loud. Allison Ashley will charm you with this affecting and engrossing love story."

—Sarah Echavarre Smith, author of *Faker, Simmer Down*, and *On Location*

"From stolen glances to the sweeping euphoria of the first kiss, Allison Ashley writes love stories you feel in your soul. *Would You Rather* is a masterful mix of adorable, heart-wrenching, hilarious, and unforgettable. Make sure you have caffeine for the morning, because you'll be up late, unable to put down this incredible book."

—Denise Williams, author of *How to Fail at Flirting*

"Sexy and sweet, with a fresh twist on friends-to-lovers, *Would You Rather* is the type of romance I wish I could read again for the first time. Allison Ashley draws the reader in and holds tight with a carefully woven story, sparkling chemistry, and unforgettable characters. It's pure swoony, flirty, romantic bliss."

—Lauren Accardo, author of *Wild Love*

IF TOMORROW NEVER COMES

OTHER TITLES BY ALLISON ASHLEY

IF TOMORROW NEVER COMES

ALLISON ASHLEY

Montlake

Text copyright © 2025 by Allison Ashley
All rights reserved.

Published by Montlake, Seattle

www.apub.com

Amazon, the Amazon logo, and Montlake are trademarks of Amazon.com, Inc., or its affiliates.

ISBN-13: 9781662527272 (paperback)
ISBN-13: 9781662527265 (digital)

Cover design by Ploy Siripant
Cover image: © irynaalex / Adobe Stock; © clairevis / Getty; © Design_Landsi / Shutterstock

Printed in the United States of America

To the Nebraska Medicine Pharmacy Residency class of 2011.
Best. Year. Ever.

CHAPTER ONE

Elliott

On the evening before her untimely demise, Elliott Holland went on someone else's date.

Okay, *possible* demise.

The mortality rate for what she was about to do was around 30 percent, so her odds were decent. Still, people rarely walked around knowing their exact chances of being alive three months from now, so it was hard not to ruminate on it, at least a little.

Tomorrow morning, she'd show up to the hospital at eight o'clock sharp for a week's worth of massive doses of chemotherapy. Enough to completely obliterate her bone marrow, which would kill her if some Good Samaritan hadn't donated their stem cells to repopulate her body's blood supply.

It had sounded scary at first, but her innate bone marrow was complete shit. Had gone haywire twice and would likely progress to leukemia a third time if she didn't go through with a transplant. The goal was to get rid of her own marrow, like digging deep to scrape out the roots of a dead tree, then refill it with someone else's healthy cells.

It still sounded scary, honestly. But she had no choice. If she didn't go through with it, she'd probably die of leukemia, and she wasn't about to go down without a fight.

She also wasn't about to walk into that mess without a little fun first, which was how she ended up in a cooking class, making a fancy soufflé with a hot stranger named Jamie. An hour ago, she'd been at a bar in the Old Market district of Omaha, wearing her cutest jeans and holding a cocktail in her hand. She'd be wearing a glorified sheet with her ass hanging out for the foreseeable future and wouldn't be able to drink alcohol for even longer, so . . . priorities.

"You sure you don't want me to come?" her mom had asked earlier that evening, lounging on the hotel bed while Elliott swiped mascara across her lashes.

"If this will be anything like the other times I've been hospitalized—and I'm expecting it to be worse—I won't have a moment of peace for the next few months." She wouldn't so much as fart without someone seeing it on a monitor. Even if things went well after the first few high-risk weeks and she was allowed to go back home to Lincoln while she recovered, her parents would hover like teenagers with backstage passes at a Harry Styles concert. "This is my last chance for some alone time."

Her mother, bless her, though clearly disappointed, didn't argue.

Once Elliott exited the hotel lobby and crossed the street, she passed several restaurants and wine bars with lilting music and muted conversation. A couple of them had potential, but she ultimately kept walking until drawn by the sound of laughter.

Tonight, she needed happiness and distraction, not solitude or a quiet that would lead to introspection. She'd have plenty of time for that.

She landed in front of a swinging wood door with the word TAVERN etched across it. Single scraps of paper littered the window just to the left, blocking her view inside but advertising live music, trivia nights, and other themed events.

She pushed through the door, her eyes going wide with wonder. She'd expected a dim dive full of dark wood finishes, leather booths, and an impressive line of draft beer behind an oak bar. Instead, a trio of chandeliers sparkled back at her, casting starlight across the long, narrow space. Several customers sat at a sleek black bar top with bright teal and gold tiles cascading to the floor. Dozens of tiny alcoves lined the wall behind the bar, each filled with bottles of liquor and wine. A white ledge bordered the ceiling, and lush green leaves spilled over from colorful pots harboring several types of plants her mother probably would have known the names of.

The vibrant atmosphere was perfect for tonight. She considered claiming a two-top table, just to see how comfortable those emerald-velvet-covered armchairs were, but opted for the bar. Better for a single, and better for people watching.

She took her time perusing the cocktail menu and ultimately ended up asking the bartender, a burly man named Gus with full-sleeve tattoos and a bright-red beard, to surprise her with something floral and sweet. Her hopes weren't high since he seemed more like the kind of man who knew his way around bourbon rather than vodka, but he flipped her unfair stereotype on its head when he brought her a beautifully concocted, pale-pink cocktail with a sprig of lavender.

She took a sip and stared at him. "This is the best drink I've ever had."

He graciously ignored the surprise in her tone and swiped a towel across his side of the bar top. "It's all in the garnish."

The room filled quickly, and by the time she'd made it halfway through her drink and started on a plate of hummus and pita bread, a band began warming up on the stage in the corner.

Her phone buzzed and she smiled at the candid photo on the screen before putting it to her ear. "I wish you were with me right now."

"Ooh, where are you?" her best friend Yuka asked. "I expected your mother's sobbing in the background, but I hear music. Ergo, I wish I was there, too."

"'Ergo'?"

"It felt right."

"I found a bar near the hotel. You'd love it, even if it's way too cool for me. Mainly it just met priority number one in that my mother isn't here." She loved her mom, truly. And Elliott would never be able to repay everything she and her dad had done for her during her diagnosis (both of them) and everything that came with it. Some days she got the feeling being the parent of a child with cancer was worse than being the patient.

Other days she called foul, believing nothing could be worse than the hand she'd been dealt.

"Fair." Yuka knew better than anyone how suffocating parents could be. When Elliott first met Yuka in the pediatric cancer ward at the tail end of her successful neuroblastoma treatment, Yuka had never been unaccompanied. One or both of her parents had always been around. "A bar, though? Proud of you. Any cute men?"

"I don't know. I haven't really looked."

"I'll wait."

Elliott snorted. "What would I do if there was? You know what happens tomorrow."

"Yeah, *tomorrow*. You've got all night to be something other than a cancer patient for once. What have you got to lose? Live it up, honey."

Some days Elliott wished she had Yuka's devil-may-care attitude. But be something other than a cancer patient? She wouldn't even know where to start. "Not likely."

"Could you try to surprise me just once, Ellie? Literally, all I want in this life is for you to call me one day and tell me you did something completely wild. Threw caution to the wind and let the chips fall where they may."

"Like the time you snuck into that exclusive club in Denver and ended up in a six-week whirlwind romance with a guy who played for the Rockies?"

"God, yes. Ten out of ten recommend."

"Not gonna happen. And it's not my fault you're impossible to shock."

"That's not true. Remember the time you told me you think cheesecake is pie, not cake?"

"Cheesecake *is* pie." She'd die on this hill.

"We're not having this conversation again."

"You brought it up," Elliott said, smiling even as she shook her head. Yuka would arrive next week to spend a few days at the hospital, and it couldn't come soon enough. She missed her laugh already. "Was there a reason for this call?"

"Is there ever? Just calling to check in. How are you feeling? Nervous? Excited? Did you forget anything? I can run by your house before I come up on Friday."

Nervous? Yes.

Excited? Not quite.

"I think I got everything, and honestly, I'm just ready to get it over with."

"I get that. This time better be the last with this bullshit, yeah?"

"So they say." She'd been in remission before, and it hadn't panned out. Despite better odds for a transplant to finally cure her for good, it wasn't guaranteed. Her hopes weren't terribly high.

"Worth a shot and better than dying." Only a fellow cancer patient would speak so candidly. "I'll talk to you or your mom tomorrow, and see you soon?"

"Yep."

"Hey," Yuka said. "Do me a favor before you go."

"I've already told you I'm never getting a tattoo."

"Scan the room. Just once. Check out your options."

"Yuka."

"I'm not hanging up until you do."

Elliott rolled her eyes. She stared at the bottles lining the wall behind the bar and took the final sip of her drink. "Fine, I did it. No one to write home about."

Yuka sighed heavily. "Damn."

"Bye, friend."

Elliott ended the call and set her phone down, regarding the darkened screen with a small smile. Cancer sucked on virtually every level, but it had led her to a lifelong friend all those years ago. There were some things outsiders would never understand, and while Elliott would never wish the disease on anyone, sometimes it was nice to have someone around who knew exactly what she was going through.

"Sorry to eavesdrop," a deep voice said from her right, bringing Elliott out of her thoughts. "But did I just hear you say cheesecake is a *pie*?"

It took her a second to process they were speaking to her, and she turned to regard the person two seats over. She went still, breath catching in her throat. A very, *very* attractive man with wavy, dark-blond hair and light-colored eyes looked back at her. Thick-framed tortoiseshell glasses perched on his nose, and a slight smile curved his lips.

Well. She'd just told a big fat lie because she'd 100 percent write home about this man.

She blinked, recovering. "I did."

The man's expression transformed to something with mock severity, but one corner of his mouth twitched. "You're wrong."

Her eyebrows shot up. "Sorry?"

"Cheesecake isn't pie."

Her spine straightened. "It most certainly is."

"How do you figure?"

She'd have been thrown off by the conversation if she hadn't argued it repeatedly with Yuka over the years. "I don't care if it's in the name; it's not a cake. Cakes are bread-like and have batter that rises. Cheesecake is neither of those things."

"You're right," he conceded, but before she could say *I know*, he added, "It's not pie *or* cake."

She opened her mouth, then paused for a second. "What is it, then?"

"A tart."

"A what?"

"Tart." He grinned then, transforming his face into something even more beautiful, which was really saying something. He seemed pleased with himself in a way that, strangely, didn't seem arrogant. He just looked . . . happy.

Elliott couldn't help but smile, but narrowed her eyes and crossed her legs. His eyes dropped briefly as she did. "Do tell. How did you come to that conclusion?"

She tilted her head as she half listened to his monologue about pastry shells, custard, and a lack of pastry layering on top, inconveniently cataloging details of this man to memory. He looked to be around thirty, give or take a few years. His hair was slightly disheveled in that I-know-it-looks-good-and-I-don't-care-enough-to-fix-it kind of way, and on closer inspection, his eyes were a muted green, like the needles on the pine trees at her parents' house. Hazel, maybe? His nose was straight and speckled with a few tiny freckles, and his cheekbones sloped to an angular, defined jaw. A tiny dimple dented his skin on the left side of his mouth as he smiled and took a pull from his beer, waiting for her response.

For a second she thought he might have bested her, which she'd never admit, but then something came to her. "What about pecan pie? It doesn't have a pastry layer on top. No one questions its identity as pie."

"Ah, but pecan pie isn't filled with custard."

"What about pumpkin?"

His expression faltered for a second. "Pumpkin pie may be in question, you're right. Maybe it's a tart, too."

She cocked a brow. "Or they're both pies, like I said." *But none of them are cakes,* she wanted to tell Yuka.

Also, who was she right now? Elliott wasn't shy, per se, but she wasn't normally the type to kick off an argument with a complete stranger. Yet here she was, and thoroughly enjoying herself, too.

"Jamie, are you mansplaining cheesecake to your date?"

Elliott startled at the boom of the bartender's voice. His eyes were on the stranger beside her, arms crossed and one eyebrow raised.

Her seatmate darted a glance at her. "Damn, Gus. She's not, um—"

"He . . . Jamie?" She paused in question; was that what the bartender called him? Gus nodded. "*Was* mansplaining. But we're not on a date."

Gus blinked at her, then frowned at Jamie. "When we talked earlier, I thought you said . . . ?"

Jamie's neck flushed. "This isn't her. I think I got stood up." He checked his watch. "Twenty-five minutes is late enough to call it, yeah?"

Elliott winced and Gus nodded sagely. "Probably. Sorry, man."

Jamie shrugged, draining the final drops of his beer. "It's fine." He slid his bottle forward. "Give me another on the house, will you? Now that you've embarrassed me in front of a pretty woman."

Smirking, Gus took the bottle. "I think you were embarrassing yourself, but okay."

He stepped away and Jamie turned to her, a sheepish grin on his face. "I wasn't trying to be a dick. It's just, my sister owns a bakery, and she has strong opinions about cheesecake. She's made me listen to that speech five times at least, and apparently I'm carrying on the torch."

His voice was appealing, too. Deep and smooth and . . . *Dammit.* She ignored the dimple and the flutter it caused in her belly. Forced her brain to blow right past the *pretty woman*, too. "How often do you strike up random conversations about dessert?"

"This is the first," he admitted. "But I gave up on my date ten minutes ago and had been trying to work up the nerve to talk to you, so when the opportunity came, I went for it."

She dropped her gaze for a beat, cheeks heating. Despite it being impossible, she was inclined to think Yuka had something to do with this. Elliott wouldn't put it past her to light some sort of enchanting incense. "I'm sorry you got stood up."

"Eh, it was someone from a dating app, and we haven't talked all that much. I wasn't too invested."

She nodded as if she knew what he meant. In reality, she hadn't been on a date in years, and the total number she could count on one hand.

Cancer was a real cockblocker.

"Honestly, I'm more disappointed about missing out on dessert than anything."

Dessert? Elliott side-eyed Gus as he tipped a clear glass underneath a spout several feet away. "Do they have a secret menu here I didn't see?" She'd be interested . . . The hummus had been damn good. Something sweet would be even better.

Jamie laughed. "No. My sister told me about a place a couple doors down that does baking classes for date nights, so I made reservations. First dates are so awkward, you know? I figured as long as the first half-hour wasn't a crash and burn, we could go make French vanilla soufflé while we got to know each other."

Elliott put a hand to her chest, unable to stop the moan that slipped from her throat. "I *love* soufflé."

"God, me too."

Gus brought Jamie a fresh, hoppy-scented beer, and Elliott eyed the large man standing across from her. "Got any candy back there? It's kind of an emergency."

The bartender squinted, stroking his beard. "Candy? I have a stout on draft that's heavy on the chocolate, but it's so thick you can basically chew it. Jamie'd probably like it, but it's a far cry from that cosmopolitan I made you."

She made a face. "Never mind."

Gus chuckled and disappeared to serve a trio of middle-aged women chatting at the other end of the bar. A warm sensation shimmered along her collarbone, and she turned to find Jamie's attention squarely on her face.

He regarded her thoughtfully. "Would you—" He stopped suddenly, shaking his head. "Nah, too weird."

"What?" she pressed as he took a long drink. *Curious E*, her dad had dubbed her as a kid. Always asking why, pressing for more information. Never letting anything go.

"I was going to ask if . . ." He passed a hand across his jaw. "The cooking class. Would you want to come with me?"

CHAPTER TWO

Elliott

She blinked. "Go with you?"

"Yeah, so those reservations don't go to waste. If, you know, you didn't have other plans tonight?"

A swirl of excitement burst beneath her ribs, and she almost said yes on the spot, if only because there was something about this man that made her wish their time wasn't over just yet. She probably should have been apprehensive about the prospect of going somewhere with a strange man she'd exchanged no more than a few sentences with.

But,

1. This kind of thing never happened to her. There was something inherently flattering about a man like Jamie asking her on a date. Or technically, someone else's date, but she wasn't in a position to be picky.
2. French vanilla soufflé.
3. She might die tomorrow or shortly thereafter.

And most importantly, if Number 3 came true, she'd love nothing more than to have her last act be something that would shock Yuka.

"Sure," she heard herself say before she'd consciously made a decision.

He straightened, his torso tilting back in a surprised gesture that made him even more adorable. As if he had no idea how tempting those glasses and that dimple were, and had thrown out the invitation fully expecting a gentle letdown. "Really?"

"Yeah, it sounds fun. And you made me crave dessert. It's basically your duty now to deliver."

His lips spread into a broad smile—*Hello, there*—flashing impossibly white teeth. "It starts in ten minutes, so we'll need to get moving." He downed his beer and gestured to Gus. "Close us out, will you? Just put both on my tab."

Reddish-orange brows rose, but Gus said nothing beyond, "You got it, man."

Jamie stood—damn, he was tall—and Elliott grabbed her phone before sliding off her own stool. His hazel eyes were bright and happy, lips pressed together as if he was trying not to smile. "I just realized I don't even know your name."

"Oh. It's . . ." Elliott paused, Yuka's words flashing across her brain. *You've got all night to be something other than a cancer patient for once. Live it up, honey.*

Elliott's life had been full of the unexpected. When she was seventeen, she'd gone to the ER for a paper cut that wouldn't stop bleeding and, within twenty-four hours, had started urgent chemotherapy for a leukemia diagnosis. At nineteen, she'd almost died from a virus most people don't even know they've had. And at twenty-four, her previously cured disease that was supposed to have stayed that way came roaring back with a vengeance. It had lain dormant for a few years, just long enough to give her a false sense of control over her life again before pulling the rug out from under her.

Tonight, though? Finding this adorable bar, drinking the best cocktail she'd ever had, randomly sitting beside a man who'd struck up an argument about cheesecake, and filling in on another woman's date . . . It was all unexpected, too.

But in a *good* way. That never happened, and a thrill shot through her at the realization, a high she hadn't known since before her diagnosis.

Be something other than a cancer patient for once.

She swallowed, offered her hand, and blurted out her middle name. "May. My name's May."

They were late to the baking class, which normally would have made Elliott antsy to the point of distraction. She knew all too well how it felt to be kept waiting. Sitting in the lobby for two hours for an appointment booked six months prior, staring at the phone and wishing for good biopsy results, living on edge while waiting for the chemotherapy side effects to rear their ugly, unpredictable heads.

It always sucked; it never got easier.

She couldn't control any of it, but she could make sure she was never responsible for causing someone else to wait for her. She was punctual to a fault, if such a thing could be considered a negative.

But tonight, and for the first time ever, she didn't regret her tardiness. Not even when the instructor at the front of the room shot them a pointed glare and informed them, in front of everyone, that they'd need to read the recipe themselves because she wasn't going over everything again.

In fact, Elliott would have taken another lap around the block and settled for a candy bar from a convenience store if it meant she could keep talking to Jamie. The man was kind, funny, and the perfect amount of flirtatious.

"Quick, tell me everything about you," she'd said as they stepped out of the bar and entered the cool May evening—arguably the best month to be outdoors in Nebraska. She hoped to keep him talking, mostly because she was genuinely interested, but also because she avoided sharing personal details about herself at all costs. Being her never-cancer alter ego tonight meant a large chunk of her life would be off-limits for conversation. She just hoped there was enough of her left to stay interesting.

"Wow, everything?" He puffed out his cheeks, stepping closer as a large group passed them on the sidewalk. "I'm Jamie, twenty-nine years old, certified arborist in this grand city of Omaha, where I was born and raised. Played baseball, loves dogs, hates cats, and has a hard time saying no to anything."

"Arborist?" she asked. "Like a tree surgeon?"

"Sure, you can call me Dr. Jamie if you want to." He winked at her then, which coming from some men would be creepy as hell. But he'd laughed right after, almost like he was embarrassed he'd done it, and landed himself firmly in the Charming category.

"Okay, Doc. Do you believe in horoscopes?"

"Nope."

"Me either." Yuka'd gone through a phase a couple of years ago where she'd chalked everything up to "the stars," and Elliott had damn near taken a friendship sabbatical. "What's your most useless talent?"

"Huh. That's a good question." His tongue pushed against his cheek. "I can drink or eat anything cold without getting a brain freeze. Chugging slushies was my eighth-grade party trick."

"Wow, did that get you all the girls?"

"Not a one."

She laughed, and the way he looked at her made her feel as if he thought making her smile was the best thing he'd ever done. Her stomach tightened at the same time her brain warned her to tread carefully.

"What's yours?" he asked.

"I can fold a fitted sheet so well you can't tell it apart from a flat one."

His jaw dropped. "How?"

"Come on, Baseball Guy. You should know practice makes perfect."

"While I'm impressed with you, I'm not sure I care enough about that to perfect it."

"I don't blame you—most people don't." He didn't need to know the time she'd had on her hands over the years.

She learned they both loved to read, his favorite author was Andy Weir, and he had a yellow Lab. She told him about her parents' German shepherd and how jealous her dad had been when Dodger suddenly switched allegiance and chose her as the family favorite. He still wasn't over it, and she teased him every chance she got. They talked about running, which, when she felt up to it, was her favorite method of stress relief.

In a stroke of good luck, Jamie asked what she did for a living just as they arrived at their destination, and she'd gotten away with a vague reply about working on her degree in graphic design.

Any concerns he might ask more about her life disappeared after they arrived and received their public reprimand. Jamie didn't seem fazed and slipped on the sole remaining apron—a pink number with an obnoxiously loud floral print—without batting an eye. He tied the strings behind his back as they walked to their assigned station, briskly rubbed his hands together, and took a deep breath.

"Okay. We're already behind, but we can do this." With a straight face and sudden intensity that seemed more appropriate for a contestant in the final round of *The Great British Bake Off,* he pointed to the open shelves beneath the counter. "Grab the sugar, bowls, and measuring cups while I read through the recipe. My sister taught me to always read the whole thing and measure all ingredients before you start. Be prepared, pay attention. No Rachael Ray shenanigans."

Elliott knelt down to follow his request. "No Rachael Ray what, now?"

"You know. No estimating ingredients." He trailed his finger along the page as he read, gripping his chin with the other hand. "She just pours stuff in without measuring, like she can eyeball a quarter tablespoon or half cup exactly. It's a recipe for disaster, especially when baking. Precision is nonnegotiable."

"Wow." Elliott hugged the bowls to her chest and rocked back on her heels.

"What?"

"Recipe pun aside, you're taking this super serious."

He jerked his head toward her, glasses askew. "Baking is serious business."

She tucked her lips between her teeth. God, he was cute.

He dropped his head forward with a sigh. "I should kill my sister for doing this to me."

"She's like this, too?"

"Worse."

That was terrifying.

She gathered the rest of the things he'd asked for, lining up all the bowls, measuring cups, and spoons by size in descending order.

"Preheat the oven to three fifty," he ordered. Then, as if he heard himself, sheepishly added, "Please."

"What would you do if I told you that when I make ready-to-bake sugar cookies, I put them in while it's still preheating?"

Jamie gasped.

"Thought you'd say that."

He just stared at her. "Don't they burn?"

"Sometimes."

"And you still eat them?"

She shrugged. "It's still a cookie." She nudged him with her shoulder and grinned. "Don't worry, I'll follow your lead tonight. What's next?"

It took him a moment to recover; then he read the instructions for the custard mixture.

"Start with the egg yolks and sugar. Whisk constantly until thickened, and slowly add the cornstarch and milk. Keep whisking, about ten to fifteen minutes."

"Did you just say whisk constantly for *fifteen minutes?*" she cried.

The instructor, a severe woman with gray hair pulled back into a tight bun, appeared at their table. "Do you *want* a lumpy soufflé?"

Jamie, whose back was to the woman, bugged out his eyes at Elliott and mouthed, *No.*

Elliott blinked, meeting the woman's steely gaze. "Um. No, ma'am."

Jamie covered his mouth with his fist, turning a laugh into a cough.

When the woman walked away, Elliott glared at him. "I don't know why you're laughing; you've got the same energy going on. Let's take it down a notch."

He nodded. "Right. Sorry." Then after a few beats: "You called her 'ma'am.' Like she was your seventh-grade math teacher."

"Well! I respect my elders."

Jamie shuddered. "Don't let her hear you call her that."

Elliott huffed out a breath. "Can we move on? We were at the prolonged whisking." She pulled one arm across her chest, twisting this way and that.

"Whatcha doing?"

"Stretching."

He grinned at her, again.

The dimple popped, again.

"I don't remember the last time I smiled this much."

She smiled back at him, fighting to keep the emotion from her voice. "Me either." The mixture of elation and sadness his words brought were way too much for the moment, but she couldn't help the rush of hopelessness. If she ever laughed again after tonight, it would be so far into the future she didn't even want to guess when.

Jamie grabbed the small saucepan and turned on the burner while she measured the ingredients. She whisked the yolks and sugar while he slowly poured in the milk.

He leaned in close and whispered, "Nice form."

Wow, that did things to her insides. Things she had no business indulging tonight. "So, what's next?"

"Let's see. Now we beat the egg whites until you get stiff peaks."

She stopped whisking and let a moment of silence pass. "Beat until stiff. Got it."

His shoulders pitched forward as a snort-laugh burst from his chest. The room went silent, and every head turned in their direction. Elliott spun around to face the wall, grinding her molars together to keep from laughing.

"Sorry. Excuse us," Jamie muttered before he turned to her and stepped close to her body, bringing along a clean scent of masculine bodywash. A flush had spread up his neck, but his eyes were bright with mirth. "Maybe this was a bad idea."

"I think this was a great idea."

The heat of his body surrounded her, but he said nothing for a long moment. Finally, she tipped her head up and met his gaze.

"Yeah, you're right," he said in a low voice. Her stomach fluttered at the way his eyes tracked a path across every inch of her face, from her hairline to her lips. "I'm starting to think this was the best idea I ever had."

Same.

His arm brushed hers, his skin warm and smooth. "You're not whisking," he whispered.

"Shit." She moved her attention to the saucepan as she pushed him away. "Stop distracting me with . . ." She trailed off.

He arched a brow. "With?"

She made a frustrated noise in the back of her throat, flapping her free hand in his direction without looking. "You know. Everything you've got going on there. The glasses, the hair, the dimple. It's distracting."

"The only thing distracting over here is you."

This was bad. "And now, with the flirting. Save it for later. I want to eat a soufflé before I go back to my hotel."

"You flirted firs— Wait. Hotel?" His entire torso faced her. "Do you not live here?"

She kept her eyes on the thickening sugar mixture. "Oh, um, no. Just visiting."

Please leave it at that.

"I didn't realize." The disappointment in his tone was unmistakable. "Where are you from?"

"Lincoln." She probably shouldn't have even given him that much, but she was a terrible liar. Avoidance, redirection, and vague responses were no problem, but a direct question like that was hard to sidestep.

Lincoln and Omaha were barely an hour apart, so that perked him up a little. "Oh, cool. Are you here for work? Fun?" When she hesitated, he added, "Sorry. Too nosy? You don't have to answer that if you don't want to."

She never hated cancer more than at times like these, when she had a glimpse of what her life could be without it: a date with a handsome man whenever she wanted, with butterflies in her stomach and stars in her eyes. "I'd rather not. I'm sorry. It's just . . . the reason I'm here isn't pleasant, and you're doing a wonderful job of distracting me from it."

The quiet air around them turned somber, and she chanced a glance at him. He looked stricken, standing stock-still. "Is everything okay?"

"Hopefully."

He opened his mouth and then closed it, as if unsure how to respond. She couldn't blame him, and odds were good he wouldn't know what to say if she'd told the truth, either. "Is there anything I can do to help?"

"No." Suddenly antsy, she dipped her head to rub her cheek against her shoulder, just above the port implanted in her chest. Her arm was getting tired, and she switched sides. The thought of explaining her sore arm to the nurse tomorrow brought an unexpected smile, though. "Actually, yes." He swayed toward her, waiting. "This. You can beat those eggs, make me laugh, and feed me a delicious soufflé to keep my mind off what happens tomorrow."

After a few moments, the intense Jamie from before returned, and he nodded. "I can do that. Just wait. I'll make the stiffest fucking egg whites you've ever seen."

CHAPTER THREE

Jamie

Twenty minutes later, four ramekins were in the oven. The remainder of the process had gone relatively smooth, save another fit of laughter when the recipe instructed them to fold in the egg whites, for which they'd simultaneously slid into character as David and Moira Rose without missing a beat.

"Stop peeking."

May shot up from where she'd been crouching at the oven window. "Why?"

"There's nothing we can do now but wait. They'll rise or they won't. We succeeded or we failed, and it's time to let them go. What happens, happens."

"Extreme Baker Jamie is back, I see."

He held back a grin. "Who-Cares-If-We-Chill-the-Batter-or-Not May is suddenly very interested in the outcome."

"Fine." She pursed her lips and leaned back against the counter, crossing her arms. "I won't peek if you give me a secret."

"What kind of secret?"

"Whatever you want to tell me."

Her beautiful gray eyes were steady on his. He moved his glasses higher on his nose. One of his nervous tells, according to his sister. "I kind of think I might tell you everything if you asked."

Her cheeks flushed a soft pink. She dropped her gaze to the floor, but her lips tipped up. "Probably don't have time for that."

"Yeah." He rubbed a palm across his jaw. There wasn't much he'd say he intentionally hid from people, but one thing he'd always sort of kept to himself came to mind. "Okay, I've got one. Don't judge me, though."

"No promises."

"Every Monday, I bring home a fresh bouquet of flowers. Just for me." She didn't laugh, so he kept going. "It might sound weird and not typical for a guy, but plants are my life's work and they're beautiful. It makes me happy to walk in and see them."

Heat crept up his neck when she didn't respond right away. Probably the only other person who knew this about him was Ian, his buddy and the owner of the nursery where he worked. But Ian loved plants even more than Jamie, so he'd be the last person to give Jamie a hard time.

Unlike Jamie's dad and brother, who had stopped by unannounced a couple of months back. Jamie'd barely had time to process the fact that they'd stepped out of their ivory tower downtown to slum it with him, so it was even more impressive that he'd managed to stash his bouquet in the cabinet under the sink before they came in. He wasn't embarrassed, exactly, but he didn't need to hand his dad more ammo than the man packed on his own.

He was seconds away from assuming she was a woman who preferred a man more stereotypically masculine, and who was now wishing this date was over, when an unguarded smile spread across her face. "That's . . . one of the best things I've ever heard. That would make me happy, too."

"Yeah?"

"Absolutely, yes. Though, I don't know how you afford flowers every week. That's some expensive happiness."

"Nah, I get them at cost from the nursery I work for. You wouldn't believe floral markup. I get them for next to nothing."

"Oh, I believe it. Capitalism at its best, right?"

"Yep," he said with a dry laugh. "Your turn."

She wouldn't meet his eyes. "Hmm?"

He cocked a brow. "To tell a secret."

"I don't have any," she said with a shrug, picking at her thumbnail.

"Liar."

Her hands dropped to her sides, and she let out the most adorable growl he'd ever heard. "Okay, fine! Give me a second." She tipped her head back, thinking, then settled her gaze back on him. He waited patiently, enjoying the excuse to just look at her. A few seconds passed, and he realized she seemed to be doing the same.

"Is the secret on my face?" he ventured.

A breathy laugh escaped her, and she hesitated a beat before she said, "Maybe I just like looking at you."

Her words sent his stomach falling like an elevator that just dropped two floors. Which was kind of ridiculous, right? It was simple flirtation.

But when had anything in his life ever felt this real, so soon? Normally he'd try to play it cool, at least through the end of the first date and probably the second, too. But something about this woman's charming vulnerability obliterated any bid for pretense. "I like looking at you, too."

She bit her lip and glanced away again. She seemed comfortable with him, and as far as he could tell, she was having a good time. But there were moments, like now, where she seemed almost . . . shy. Inexperienced, as if some of her bolder statements had surprised even her. She was so pretty and funny that it was impossible she wasn't turning away interested guys at every turn.

Had she had a bad experience? Did it have anything to do with why she was here? The protectiveness that filled his chest the moment she'd said she was dealing with something unpleasant had already alarmed him. He didn't need to add any more fuel to that fire.

God, he hoped he'd see her again after tonight.

She spoke again, her voice so quiet he almost missed it, and it took him a few seconds to realize it was her secret. "Sometimes I feel like no one really understands me."

Her tone was matter of fact, as if it was something she'd been dealing with for a while and had resigned herself to a lifetime of being misunderstood. Jamie had good friends he could be himself around, but when it came to his family, he knew exactly where she was coming from.

A long, quiet moment passed. When she let out another sigh and her shoulders dipped under some unseen burden, he took two steps forward. Sidling up beside her, he slid one arm around her shoulders.

A friendly side hug, that's all.

But then she leaned in and snuggled closer, resting her head at the edge of his collarbone. The temptation to turn and wrap her up in a full embrace was strong, but he forced himself to stay put.

He spoke into her hair. "I feel that way sometimes, too."

"You do?"

"Yeah."

She didn't elaborate on what she'd meant. Neither did he.

They remained that way until the timer dinged, and Jamie pulled out their soufflés—two of which had risen to glorious heights.

"Those two were mine," May said immediately.

"The batter was the same. There's no 'yours' and 'mine.'"

"I poured those two. I'm sure of it."

He pinched the bridge of his nose. "I want to argue, but the gentleman in me is pushing back hard."

She grinned and grabbed a spoon, but he held up a hand. "Wait, there's one last step in the recipe. There should be a chocolate bar and a peeler around somewhere so we can add shavings to the top."

He looked around for a few seconds before realizing she hadn't moved, and then he noticed her scrunched nose and pursed lips. "What? What's wrong?" Did he have something on his face?

"Do whatever you want to yours," she said, gesturing to the sad, sunken soufflés. "But that would completely ruin this for me. I hate chocolate."

He stared at her. Blinked.

Stared some more.

Her expression transitioned into an eye roll. "It's not that weird."

"Hold on. I think I'm dissociating."

"Stop it."

"Are you serious? You don't like chocolate?" He'd once eaten four of his sister's chocolate-mousse brownies in a single sitting. No regrets.

"*Hate's* a pretty strong word and one I rarely use, but in this case it's warranted. I can't even stand the smell of it."

"*What?*"

She put the spoon down and put a few fingers to her forehead. "God, you're acting like I just grew a second head."

"That would be less shocking. I can't even wrap my mind around this. People who don't like chocolate don't exist."

She looked like she was about to argue, then stopped and cocked her head. "Does that mean I'm like . . . a unicorn?"

He laughed, the image of her with a golden horn popping up unbidden in his brain. "Or a narwhal."

She laughed a little, too, but regarded him with a slight frown. "The fact that you basically just compared me to a whale aside, you know narwhals are real, right?"

"What?"

"Narwhals aren't mystical creatures. They actually exist."

Okay, he wasn't falling for chocolate aversion *and* narwhals. "No way."

The delighted smile on her face was so charming, it simultaneously made him second-guess himself and want to kiss it off her face. "I swear." She pulled out her phone, tapped a few things on the screen, and handed it to him. "Look."

He took her phone and saw a search page with several narwhal hits. He swiped through slowly, looking at images that did look awfully legit . . . but the things people could do with Photoshop and AI these days was wild. But, oh God, there was one from *National Geographic*. And the World Wildlife Fund? With *actual videos* of these huge beasts with massive spears sprouting from their foreheads. What did they do with the horns? How did they not poke each other or get them tangled up in seaweed all the time?

He had so many questions.

Too amazed to be embarrassed, he handed her phone back. "I wonder what else is real?" he said more to himself.

She leaned in as if to impart some great secret. "People who don't like chocolate, that's what."

The happy, carefree look on her face was such a one-eighty from moments ago after she'd told her secret that he'd repeat looking like a fool a hundred times over just to keep it there. "Fine, I believe you. Since we're skipping the chocolate shavings, can we eat now?"

May clapped and picked up a spoon. She scooped a healthy serving, watching the steam rise. She gently waved the spoon between them, blowing on it. Finally, she lifted the spoon and stopped an inch from his mouth.

His brows rose. "For me?"

She nodded.

He grinned and closed his lips around the spoon, his eyelids falling closed in an instant. The rich vanilla flavor and spongy texture were absolute perfection. "Oh my God."

"Good?"

"So. Good."

She went back and took her own heaping bite. Her chin tipped back as a groan slid from her throat. He clenched his jaw at the sound, frustrated his body immediately assumed the sound was directed at him. It only got worse when she gently placed her hand on his chest, nodding.

"We're real good at this. We win for sure."

He swallowed. "I, uh, don't think it's a competition."

"No?"

"Nah. It's just a class for fun."

She didn't seem to hear him as she went for another bite, more sounds coming from her lips that had his chest rising a little faster. He took in the very public space around them and scooted back a step, muttering to himself, "This was definitely a bad idea."

CHAPTER FOUR

Jamie

May was staying at the Embassy Suites a couple of blocks away, so Jamie asked if he could walk her back. She agreed, and their conversation flowed easily over the next twenty minutes as they slowly, *slowly* made their way. Did she want to prolong this evening as much as he did? She'd reached over to thread her fingers between his within seconds of stepping into the evening air, so he thought she might.

They arrived at their destination too soon. They could have walked around this town for days, and still, it would have been too soon.

She paused at the side of the building, which was partly shrouded in shadows and around the corner from the hotel entrance. It was almost eleven, and across the street several establishments were still going strong, music filtering through the doors as patrons came and went. His sister's bakery was dark, having closed a couple of hours ago—but Frenzy, the brewery next door to it, would be serving into the early-morning hours.

On their side where they stood on the empty sidewalk, they were in their own little world.

He nodded his head across the street. "That's my sister's place, over there."

"Yeah?" May squinted, probably trying to read the darkened sign, then burst out laughing. "Melt My Tart?"

He grinned.

"I never stood a chance during that argument, did I?"

In truth, he saw her point about cheesecake, even if he'd die before admitting it. He was just glad as hell he'd found an excuse to talk to her at the bar. "Would we call that an argument?"

"Discussion, then."

"Maybe you should stop in tomorrow and hear my sister's pitch. You'll see it our way in no time."

She offered a noncommittal smile. He resisted the urge to fill the next few moments of silence, hoping she'd do something with the ball on her side of the court. Like offer a number, an Instagram handle . . . anything. He wanted to see her again, but the way she'd deflected about the reason she was in town made him hesitant to ask for much. His brain had gone through all sorts of scenarios, including dark ones where she might want to remain somewhat anonymous.

Not to him, though, surely? Not after tonight?

"Thanks for walking me back," she said. "And for keeping me company tonight."

"That was the best evening I've had in a long time," he said simply.

"Me too."

He smiled and her gaze dropped to his lips. When she swept her eyes back up to lock with his, the longing in her expression sent a flare of heat beneath his skin.

They stood so close their breath mingled, the air stretching thick between them. She smelled enticing and sweet, some mixture of her citrusy scent, fresh air, and a hint of vanilla. Would she taste as delicious as she smelled?

More importantly, would this be his only chance to find out?

Before he'd consciously decided to lean in, she reached for his arm, her cool fingers wrapping around his skin, and gently pulled him closer.

His heart stuttered when her body came flush against his. They'd connected on so many levels tonight—easy conversation, humor, feeling a little out of place in this world—that it seemed impossible they wouldn't here, too. With lips and hands and eyes closed.

He curled his fingers through hers and lowered his head, dragging in a shaky breath. He paused at the last second with a squeeze of her hand, making absolutely sure she wanted this, and she tilted her chin to close the final distance.

Her lips were soft and pliant, brushing against his in gentle exploration. His free hand curved around her neck, brushing the soft, short locks at her hairline. A shiver passed through her, and she grabbed a fistful of his shirt to pull him even closer.

A groan slipped from his throat, and when she opened her mouth to allow his tongue entrance, he released her hand to wrap his arm around her waist, the kiss going from sweet to filthy in seconds. She arched into him and pulled him with her against the wall as his thigh found its way between her legs. Her thumb traced the shell of his ear as she slid a hand into his hair, sending a bolt of heat down his spine. He dropped his head to her neck, needing a minute to breathe, and pressed his lips to her skin.

Her head fell back against the bricks as he slowly trailed kisses up her neck. She turned and caught his mouth just as he reached her jawline, like he'd been away too long. He smiled and their teeth clashed, and they both took a moment to laugh at their momentary insanity before diving right back in.

"Where," he breathed into her. "Where have you been?"

"Lincoln," she said on a moan when his hand slid under her shirt and to the sensitive skin of her waist.

Never.

He'd *never* felt like this.

"Mmm," he murmured, pressing his thigh more firmly against her when she tugged at his hips. "But you're here now. For tonight. Come home with me."

He sensed a change in her immediately. She'd gone still, eyes snapping open.

Shit. He immediately lifted his head and pulled his leg back. "I'm sorry, I didn't mean to—"

She shook her head, cutting him off. She slid out of his grasp and moved sideways. "It's fine, I just . . . I should go."

"Okay. I'm sorry if I misread something, I . . ." He trailed off, gripping the back of his neck with one hand. Disappointment flooded his system, which still reeled from that kiss.

She touched his hand. "You didn't. I just . . . I can't. It's complicated."

Couldn't what? Complicated how?

He wanted to ask again why she was in town, how he could help—*if* he could help, and if everything was okay.

But she'd already deflected those questions once, so instead he asked, "Please, can I see you again?"

"That won't be possible. I won't be around."

"But Lincoln's not that fa—"

"I won't be in Lincoln."

She no longer met his eyes and didn't offer more information.

"I guess exchanging numbers is out of the question?" Did he sound completely pathetic? It was hard to believe everything between them could have been so one sided, and he wondered if her ambiguity had to do with whatever she was going through. He hated it for her, most of all, but he selfishly hated it for himself, too. Did she really mean to leave everything here? Was tonight really it?

Her gaze dropped to the ground, as if she needed a minute. Then she looked back up at him with glassy eyes. Her voice wobbled. "It will only make things worse for me."

He balled his hands into fists to keep from reaching for her. He was at a complete loss.

She sniffled and began backing away from him. "Thank you for tonight. Really. I'll never forget it."

He lurched forward and grasped her fingers. "Wait. Please, don't go yet. Can we maybe sit for a little while? Just talk?"

She rocked onto the balls of her feet and swiped her forearm across her eyes, and he prepared himself for her to pull away. But then she swayed toward him and nodded. "Okay."

They sat down next to each other on the sidewalk, backs up against the brick wall and legs extended. He said nothing for a moment, relieved she was still in his space and terrified of scaring her off again. Even though he was pretty certain her exit attempt was more about whatever she was dealing with than about him, he still wanted every single second she'd give. Things had felt so comfortable before, and he wanted to get back to her smiles and laughter.

"I hate cucumbers so much I tell people I'm allergic just so one never gets anywhere near me," he blurted out.

She let out a sort of single-snort laugh. It was loud and ungraceful, and he adored it. "Seriously?"

"Seriously," he confirmed. "I don't even think my own sister knows the truth."

She jutted out her lower lip gave him an impressed nod, like, *Nice*. "Maybe I should try that the next time I'm around chocolate. I bet you don't get unhinged side-eyes when you say you're allergic to cucumbers."

"Yeah, avoiding vegetables . . . avoiding chocolate. Those are the same."

Smiling, she rolled her eyes, then looked up at him thoughtfully. "Isn't cucumber a fruit?"

He frowned. "Is it?"

"I think so, but I feel like we're not the best people to discuss food categories. That could go south again real quick."

He laughed. "Good idea."

They fell silent for a few moments, watching the activity across the street. She tapped his shoe with hers and then offered up, "I was voted Most Likely to Quietly Take Over the World my senior year of high school."

It was his turn to grin and say, "Seriously?" Then he added, "That's the best thing I've ever heard. Also, now I'm a little intimidated."

"Me too," she said with a laugh. "Like, how was I ever supposed to live up to that?"

He hadn't known her long, but for some reason he could see it. "You've still got time."

She went quiet and looked down at her hands, and he almost asked if he'd said something wrong. But she leaned her head on his shoulder and asked, "Did you have a superlative?"

"No, my school didn't do those."

"If they had, what would yours have been? Biggest Heartthrob? Beauty and Brains? Most Athletic?"

"Wow. I love this game. Keep going."

She pinched his side, and he caught her hand. He couldn't tell who initiated it, but their fingers intertwined and came to rest together on his thigh.

"Honestly, I have no idea. How about Worst Case of Senioritis? Was that a thing? Because by the third day of school senior year, I was over it. I wanted to be outside or playing baseball, with nothing in between."

They went back and forth like this for another two hours, sharing pieces of themselves on every topic imaginable.

Jamie: "I've never seen a single Star Wars movie."

May: "I love escape rooms. Best modern entertainment idea of all time."

Jamie: "I started drinking coffee when I was ten, because my grandpa was a navy man who drank it with every meal and I thought he was a total badass. I didn't actually *like* coffee until I was sixteen."

May: "If a song has an acoustic or stripped version, that one will one hundred percent be my favorite."

Jamie: "My favorite word is petrichor, because it sounds cool and there's nothing better than the way the earth smells after it rains."

May: "Before tonight, I hadn't kissed a guy in more than two years."

She'd tilted up her face when she said that one, her head still resting on his shoulder, and after wondering what the fuck was wrong with men in Lincoln, he'd acted on impulse. He leaned down and kissed her, soft and slow and deep, careful not to get carried away.

At some point he'd pulled her into his arms as she dozed against his chest, her palm resting on his stomach. After the bars across the street closed and the lights shut off, Jamie held her, trying to force his body to stay awake and soak up every second of this woman that he possibly could.

The last time he checked his watch was at 2:17 in the morning, and when he woke up with a start at 3:02, he found himself slouched against the wall of the Embassy Suites hotel.

Alone.

CHAPTER FIVE

Elliott

One year later

"I miss you already."

Elliott laughed and flipped on her turn signal. "It's been two days."

Yuka's gasp echoed through the car speakers.

"Correction: I miss you, too."

"Better," Yuka said. "How's your new place?"

"So great. Tiffany was right—it's perfect."

"Perfectly close to the downtown nightlife?"

"Apparently, which is why it's a miracle there was a unit available. You know that's not why I wanted to be here, though." The only thing Elliott cared about was the complex's proximity to Nebraska Medicine's hospital.

It was probably a little scary for anyone to live on their own for the first time, but Elliott's fears went well beyond the usual hangups, and she wanted to be near the hospital in case something went wrong. Tiffany, her transplant-nurse-turned-friend who'd kept in touch after Elliott was discharged, lived in the complex to be close to work. Evidently the place was almost always fully rented, but Tiffany had been on a few dates with a girl who worked in the office and had gotten a heads-up when someone was moving out.

"You say that now, but I'm banking on you coming out of your shell. I give it three, four weeks, tops, before you're the life of the Omaha party scene."

"You hear yourself, right?"

"I gotta send Tiffany a fruit basket or something. I already loved her for taking such good care of you last year, but getting you an apartment? Actually, a fruit basket isn't enough. Monthly wine subscription? Stripper?"

Good Lord. "I already promised to take her to dinner tomorrow. I'll make sure she knows how grateful I am."

"Lemme know if you change your mind." Before Elliott could say anything, Yuka barreled on. "So Saturday, right?"

Elliott turned into her apartment entrance and nodded. "Saturday."

Three o'clock. Green Tree Coffee Shop. Elliott would meet Carly, the woman who'd donated the stem cells that had saved her life.

Elliott had learned during the transplant process that her donor lived in the same state, but that was it. She hadn't asked for additional details until after—until she was on the other side of the riskiest first few months, post-transplant. During the first one hundred days, things still could have gone very, very wrong.

But she'd finally felt comfortable enough to ask, and in a twist of fate, it turned out Tiffany knew the donor. When Elliott asked what her options were if she ever wanted to get in contact, Tiffany was primed and ready with Carly's email address.

"I didn't want to bring it up before, but I'm actually friends with your donor. Sort of. We have some of the same friends, and I see her out sometimes. Anyway, it's okay if you decide never to use it, but feel free to reach out to her if you ever want to," Tiffany had said. "She doesn't expect anything, but she'd love to hear from you. For your privacy I didn't tell her much but said I'd be happy to pass on her contact information if you ever wanted to connect."

Elliott hadn't used it right away. The anxiety, even after returning home to Lincoln, had been significant, despite being in familiar surroundings and under the watchful eyes of her family. But as she began to feel normal again and considered moving to Omaha to finally start life on her own, she'd sent an email, asking if Carly would be interested in meeting.

Saturday. Green Tree Coffee. It was finally happening.

"Excited?" Yuka asked. "Nervous?"

"All of the above."

"Want me to FaceTime in? Be a buffer?"

"I love you, but pass." Elliott frowned. "Also, do you think I'm that socially inept?"

"I just know how you are when you're worried about something. Awkward." She drew out the *r* for several seconds. "Also, you just used the word 'inept.'"

"Says the woman who won the spelling bee every year in high school."

"You're still not over 'gazpacho,' are you?"

"No tenth grader wants to eat it, let alone spell it." Elliott pulled into a spot right next to Building C. "On that note, I just pulled in and need to take some groceries up. Talk to you later?"

"Obviously. I'll be heckling you nonstop until you suck it up and go back to that bar."

Elliott groaned. "Let it go."

"I will if you will."

"Yuka."

"I'd bet ten cosmopolitans you've thought about it at least once since you got there. If I'd had the perfect evening and an erotic kiss with a hot guy, I'd go back and look for him, too."

So she'd thought about Jamie once or seven times since arriving. "It wasn't *erotic* and I'm not here for him."

Would the moment live forever, rent-free, in her brain? Yes.

Still.

Elliott could practically feel Yuka's eye roll through the speakers. "I know you're not, but that doesn't mean it's not totally normal to wonder if he's still around—and single—now that you live in Omaha."

"He might not even be here anymore."

"Or he is, and he's been thinking about you since that night, too. That's not the kind of thing you just forget, you know."

"Clearly."

"I'll check back tomorrow. Or in an hour. Who's to say? Love you and miss you."

Elliott sighed, realizing just how much she returned the sentiment. Two days in and she'd already considered giving up on this whole endeavor and moving back to Lincoln. To Yuka, her parents, and everything comfortable and familiar.

She'd been seconds away from a panic attack her first night here and had spent most of the day yesterday with the music so loud in her apartment she could barely think, let alone worry.

You promised yourself you'd at least give it three months. Don't turn back now.

"Yeah. Same."

Elliott checked the address on her phone one last time before entering the shop. The pleasant aroma of freshly brewed coffee greeted her as she quickly scanned the room, looking for a woman with dark hair and a white shirt. Not finding anyone matching that description, she sat at a table near the window, avoiding the urge to pull out her phone, and took in the room instead. Bright light filtered in through floor-to-ceiling glass windows, falling on mismatched tables, benches, and a few scattered armchairs. Baristas chattered behind the counter as the low rumble of a coffee grinder filled the air, and two men hovered near the register, discussing the chalkboard menu posted high on the wall. Seeing how she'd barely slept since the move, she could probably use something with obscene amounts of espresso right about now.

A glass-front pastry case extended past the coffee bar and register, full of fluffy croissants, cookies, overfilled sandwiches, and every variety of brownie imaginable—plain, peanut butter, salted caramel, gluten-free. Yuka, who had a more serious chocolate addiction than anyone Elliott had ever known, would be in heaven. The way Jamie had responded to her chocolate aversion indicated he might have given Yuka a run for her money, but Elliott hadn't stuck around long enough to find out.

Just outside the window, cars traveled down Farnam Street toward Old Market, the entertainment district she'd thought about often over the last year. It was where she'd gone the night before her transplant, and the place she'd met Jamie. Annoyed that she was still thinking about him after her conversation with Yuka several days ago, Elliott tried to focus on something else.

Easier said than done, especially since memories of that night had gotten her through some of the worst days in the hospital room just a few blocks from where she currently sat. She knew it; Yuka knew it.

Tiffany knew it, though Tiffany had no idea who the guy was. The first few weeks after the transplant had been rough, Elliott's body reeling from the chemotherapy and cell transfer, and she'd been half out of it from pain medication and nausea meds. Around four weeks in, she'd started to feel some semblance of normalcy, and one morning while hanging a bag of fluids, Tiffany had asked who Jeremy was.

Elliott had frowned, confused. "Jeremy?"

Tiffany lifted her brows. "You mumble a lot when you're asleep. You keep talking about some guy named Jeremy. At least I think that's what you're saying."

Elliott's cheeks had gone hot. She'd remembered little of the prior few weeks, which was probably for the best, but she'd dreamed often of Jamie. Sick and drugged, Elliott must not have been the best enunciator.

"Oooh, you're all flushed," Tiffany had said with a grin. "Boyfriend?"

So Elliott had told her the whole story about the fun, kind, and handsome man she'd spent one magical evening with. She told Tiffany how Jamie made her feel, how perfect it was to kiss him, and the way she'd felt as if a weight had lifted from her shoulders during those hours they'd spent together.

She never corrected Tiffany on his name, though. Maybe she'd wanted to keep him all to herself, or maybe she'd had some tiny fear Tiffany might know him. Which wouldn't have been a bad thing, necessarily . . . But less than a month after her transplant wasn't the time to attempt any reconnections with the guy, and it felt safer that way.

Nearly a year later, it was true she hadn't come to Omaha for him, and she'd made her peace with the possibility she might never see him again. But she'd be lying if she said she hadn't been on the lookout for a tall, blond, hazel-eyed man with glasses since arriving almost a week ago.

How did he usually spend his Saturdays? Was he always outdoors, surrounded by the trees he loved so much, or did he occasionally settle into a place like this with an Andy Weir book under one arm and that dimple on display for all the world to see?

Had he ever been in this coffee shop? Sat in this exact chair? Ordered a drink and a pastry to go? Or was he so loyal to his sister's business that he never stepped foot inside another place like hers?

Did he, like Elliott, ever find himself wide awake at three in the morning, unable to turn off the thoughts racing around his mind?

A hesitant voice broke through her thoughts. "Elliott?"

Elliott jerked her gaze from where she'd zoned out to find the woman she was meeting today. Her hair was a rich chestnut color and her eyes a dark brown. From the start Elliott figured her donor was around her age—she'd been told they tried to match donors to be as close to the same age as the recipients as possible—but had no idea how else to picture the woman who'd saved her life.

She was gorgeous in a simple white oxford shirt and jeans. Elliott shouldn't have felt instantly frumpish in comparison, but something about how this woman wore them reminded her of a pop star out for a weekend stroll, paparazzi lurking behind every corner to snap a candid.

"Carly?"

The woman smiled and nodded.

A wave of emotion suddenly crashed over Elliott, and tears abruptly pricked beneath her eyelids. Without conscious thought, she came to her feet and threw her arms around Carly's shoulders.

"I'm sorry," she said on a quiet sob. "I thought I'd be cool, but . . ."

Carly hugged her back, the intake of air through her nose sounding suspiciously like a sniffle. "You don't have to be cool. I'm not gonna be cool."

Elliott tightened her hold. "Thank you."

Carly seemed to know Elliott was thanking her for more than excusing her show of emotion. "I'm happy I was a match."

They separated and sat across from each other, wiping their eyes.

"Thanks for meeting me," Elliott said. "I can't imagine not being able to thank you in person."

Carly shrugged. "It's so weird—I don't feel like I did anything. I told Tiffany the same thing when I donated. It was pretty simple, actually." She winced. "Well, on my end. It was almost just like giving blood. I know it probably wasn't the same for you."

Elliott dropped her eyes to the table. "No, it wasn't easy. But I got through it, and I'm here now. Because of you. So thank you."

"That's the last time you get to thank me, but you're welcome."

"Can I buy you a coffee?"

"I won't say no to that."

Once they'd settled with their drinks, Elliott asked how Carly had ended up in the bone marrow registry.

"It was for this honor society I was in during college, Beta Alpha Psi. Basically a fancy name for an accounting club." She laughed lightly. "Every year they have this big philanthropy event where people came to get swabbed and be put in the registry. To be honest I'd forgotten all about it until they called me about you."

"Registering for something like that wasn't even on my radar until I needed one myself." Elliott reached up and absently rubbed the raised area under her skin where her port remained. She was in complete remission and was likely to stay that way, but . . . she wasn't comfortable getting it removed yet.

Just in case.

"You just moved here, right?" Carly asked. They'd briefly emailed back and forth about meeting, and Elliott had mentioned her relocation from Lincoln.

"Yeah, just about a week ago."

"What brought you here?"

"Cancer treatments and the transplant sort of put me behind with school, so I just finished my graphic design degree. For years my dream has been to help small businesses find footing with the chaos of social media, and to help with branding and graphics, that sort of thing. So that's what I'm here to do. Start my own business to help others get theirs off the ground."

"Really? That's fantastic. Small businesses have been my jam ever since my college roommate opened a jewelry shop in Little Bohemia." Carly thumbed the gold bangles on her wrist. "I watched her spend hours in our apartment making each little piece by hand, trying to make a name for herself."

Elliott nodded, loving that Carly shared her enthusiasm. "It changes your perspective when you see someone start from scratch, doesn't it? I think my love for all things local came from my parents. They own a bookstore in Lincoln, and I basically grew up there. I shared everything I learned with them as I pursued my degree, and I've seen their business flourish because of a few strategic events and social media updates. I had so much fun with it and realized I want to do that all day, every day."

"Did you already have clients in Lincoln, then? Other than your parents' place?"

"Not official ones, no. Everyone I love is there, but we both know Omaha has more opportunity for this kind of thing. Less college town, more distinct neighborhood districts, young professionals just starting out, and locally owned businesses. I got a job at Starbucks to support me while I build it up." She'd have loved to find work at an independent coffee shop but couldn't pass up the insurance benefits that came with even a part-time gig at the major coffee chain. "I'm not very familiar with Omaha, though, so getting the lay of the land is first on my list."

"Well, you're talking to the right person. I'm not from here originally, but I've been here since college. And I'm out and about so much I became the unofficial social chair in my circle of friends. I know almost everything about this town. Where you should go, where you shouldn't, and—oh! You should come out with my friends and me tonight. I'm sure you'd like to meet some people, too."

"Really?" Elliott had slept terribly last night and had planned on trying to turn in early tonight, but she could squeeze in a nap later this afternoon. Lately she'd had better luck sleeping during the day, anyway. "You wouldn't mind bringing a stranger? I could be super awkward or a total weirdo."

"Normal's boring."

"Boring" was probably the best word to describe Elliott. Except for that night with Jamie, when she hadn't been. "Boring's worse than weird," she ventured.

"Nah. You just need a little fun, which is my specialty." Carly cocked a brow. "Are you single? I have a hot guy friend who's unattached. He's a photographer. He might look intimidating at first with the long hair and tattoos, but he's the sweetest guy you'll ever meet."

Elliott wasn't quite ready to be set up on Day Six of her independence, but Carly looked so excited she couldn't help herself. "I don't have a boyfriend."

Carly grinned. "You'll come, then?"

"Sure." She wasn't mentally prepared for a night of making small talk with a bunch of people she didn't know, but she'd need to get out at some point. It was better than sitting around with loneliness and anxiety as her only companions.

Yuka would be proud, and she definitely needed to have some fun.

And maybe, just maybe, meeting another guy would finally help her think about something other than Jamie.

CHAPTER SIX

Elliott

At eight o'clock that evening, Elliott walked up to The Patriarch, an old home that had been converted into a craft beer house. She smiled at the Victorian-style architecture, loving the idea of repurposing the building for something so fun. She hadn't drunk much since the transplant, but it didn't matter. As soon as she walked in, she knew this place was her style. It was low key and mellow, with a few long, heavy-looking wood tables and benches in the main room and leather couches and chairs dotting the smaller rooms that seemed to shoot off in every direction.

Yuka would love it, and Elliott could bring her dad when he came to visit. The man knew more about beer than anyone she'd ever met and would fit right in at a place like this.

The hum of conversation and a song by an indie rock band Elliott saw in concert a few years ago filled the air, and the planks of the hardwood floor creaked as she walked, searching faces for the only one she'd recognize. Just as she was about to pass another doorway, someone suddenly walked out, and she slammed into a hard chest.

"Oh my gosh, I'm so sor—" she started as she took a step back, but when she looked up, the words died in her throat.

Jamie stood in front of her, as tall and imposing as ever, staring down at her as if she were a ghost.

It sort of felt like she was. She hadn't hit him that hard, but seeing him knocked the breath straight out of her. A stiff breeze would have carried her away, shifting and swirling like the curls of excitement building in her stomach.

A healthy layer of scruff covered his jaw, and his hair was a little longer and still insanely perfect. His eyes were the same hazel, still behind a pair of black-framed glasses, which looked way hotter on his masculine, angular face than was necessary.

"May?"

Oh.

That voice. She closed her eyes for the briefest second, savoring that deep rumble she remembered so well. She'd loved his laugh and the effortless conversation from that night, but this husky tone reminded her of the words he'd rasped against her ear, his hands wrapped around her waist and his large body pressing her back against the wall. *Come home with me.*

She'd almost forgotten she'd given him her middle name.

"Is it you?"

She was staring at him like a complete fool, but she couldn't seem to grab ahold of a single thought racing around the track in her mind. She vaguely registered one questioning her choice of outfit this evening and wishing she'd gone with something a little sexier. Another had something to do with narwhals, but she didn't trust herself to land a joke right now.

"Elliott!" A feminine voice came from somewhere. "You made it!"

It took physical effort to tear her gaze from Jamie's face. Carly had come to stand next to Jamie, a smile on her face, and she wrapped her arm around his waist and pressed her body against his in a manner that spoke of more than familiarity.

It spoke of intimacy.

Elliott blinked. *He can't be.*

As Elliott processed the couple before her, the room threatened to spin around her, and she took several deep breaths, willing her heart to slow down. She was no stranger to emotions that bordered on overwhelming and had gotten pretty decent at keeping them under control.

"Um, yeah, I just got here," she managed to get out.

"Did you meet Jamie already?" Carly asked, casting a fond look at him.

Jamie glanced between them, confusion marring his features.

Elliott hesitated, unsure how to answer the question. He had to be Carly's boyfriend, but for how long? Had they been together the night she met him? Unlikely, since he'd been waiting to meet someone from an app that night . . . But in that case, surely it would be okay for Carly to know they'd met before. He hadn't seemed like the kind of guy who'd get with women on the side if he was in a relationship, but how well did she really know him? She didn't want to look at Jamie again right now, but she had to, hoping he'd give her some signal for how to handle this.

She slid her gaze to his face, gritting her teeth against the onslaught of sensations skating across her skin and gathering in one suspicious cluster inside her rib cage.

Tell her you know me.

"No, we didn't officially meet. I just came around the corner and ran into her. Literally." He frowned slightly when he added, "*Elliott,* was it?"

Okay, so they both had some explaining to do.

Oblivious, Carly laughed and lifted a brow at Elliott. "You okay? He's not a small person."

"I'm fine."

"Well, Jamie, this is Elliott, the one I told you about who got the bone marrow I donated. Elliott, this is my boyfriend, Jamie."

Understanding drifted down his features, and he swallowed as he held out his hand. His voice came out softer, somehow. "It's nice to meet you."

She cleared her throat and shook his large hand, pulling away from the contact as quickly as possible. "Likewise."

She looked up to find him unsmiling. It had been a year since she'd seen that dimple, and it didn't appear that would change anytime soon. What must he think of her, knowing she'd lied to him?

It occurred to her she could turn around and leave. Fake illness or text Yuka, asking her to call with an emergency. This was a lot to deal with all of a sudden—seeing Jamie again so unexpectedly, learning he was in a relationship with her donor, of all people . . . and wondering if it was possible that on the best night of her life, she'd been the other woman.

There was also the fact that something in the vicinity of her pitiful heart ached with the realization Jamie hadn't been pining for her this past year. He'd moved on and was happy with someone else.

She could go back to her apartment and process this information with a massive bag of chips and Yuka on speakerphone. Maybe do a little recon with Tiffany in a few days, because if she knew Carly, she definitely knew Jamie. She'd know how long they'd been together. Thank God Elliott hadn't given Tiffany Jamie's real name that day in the hospital.

But then she thought of Carly, the woman she'd spent an hour with this afternoon. More, the woman who had literally given up a part of her body to offer Elliott a new chance at a full, cancer-free life. They'd talked about silly things like where to shop and get pedicures, and the terrifying center lane on Dodge Street that switched directions depending on the time of day. Carly was sweet and kind and had just wanted to offer Elliott friendship. She'd seemed so excited when Elliott agreed to come, and Elliott hated to disappoint her. She owed her everything.

Literally.

This evening wasn't just the three of them—there would be more people for her to talk to. Maybe even enough that she could avoid Jamie for the rest of the evening. Part of her worried he might try to get her alone to talk, which probably needed to happen at some point, but that was *not* something she'd do while Carly was around. For some reason he'd wanted to pretend they didn't know each other, so that's what she'd do.

For now, he was nobody.

Besides, hadn't she been promised a hot guy with tattoos?

"Sorry this place is a little shabby. If it were up to me, we'd be somewhere with high-top tables and cosmopolitans, but it was Jamie's turn to pick," Carly said with a good-natured eye roll. She released Jamie and tugged on Elliott's arm, completely unaware of the tension snapping between them. "Come meet everyone. They asked how I knew you, so I went ahead and told them, like you said I could."

"That's fine."

Jamie didn't follow them into the side room and instead continued to wherever he'd been headed when Elliott ran into him. Carly introduced Elliott to four additional people—two women and two men, one of whom was exactly as Carly had described him. She caught his name, Stephen, because she'd been expecting to meet him, but forgot the rest as soon as she heard them. Her brain struggled to focus after what had just happened.

"You don't look like a cancer patient," one of the women said after Elliott sat down.

"Tara. Fuck." Stephen shot Elliott an apologetic look.

"What?"

"I'm not technically a cancer patient anymore," Elliott said mildly. "Thanks to Carly, hopefully it will stay that way."

Tara nodded thoughtfully. "I didn't mean it in a bad way. I just meant you're really pretty, and you look . . . normal."

"Not helping." Stephen shook his head and regarded Elliott from beneath ridiculously long lashes. His eyes were warm and kind. "Sorry, she has zero filter."

Elliott smiled. Cancer was an uncomfortable topic for some people—she'd seen every reaction in the book. "She called me pretty. I'll allow it."

He laughed and tilted his head. "She's not wrong about that part."

He had jet-black hair that was pulled up in a tight bun, tanned skin, and striking blue eyes that contrasted sharply against the rest of his features. He was slender, his body completely opposite of Jamie's behemoth form, and had a full sleeve of tattoos along both arms. He wasn't her usual type, but then again, she hadn't dated all that much. Did she even have a type?

"Carly said you work at Starbucks? Which one?"

"The one off Seventy-Second Street." One of the four streets she knew in Omaha.

Jamie returned to the table, a beer glass in each hand, and slid into a chair directly across from her. Carly immediately tucked herself close to his side and grabbed one of the beers.

They were an attractive couple.

Elliott forced herself to focus on Stephen, who gave her an easy smile. "Really? You can't have been there long. I'm in there at least once a week, and I'd have noticed you."

Why didn't Stephen's flirting hit the same way as when Jamie'd done it? It was damned inconvenient. "I haven't—I'm still in training. Just started last week."

He took a pull from his beer. "Maybe I'll stop by twice this week."

"I'll probably be there," was all she could think to say. Yuka would have had some fun, flirty response if she liked the guy, or a firm and effective deterrent if she didn't. God, Elliott wished she was here. "And you're a photographer, right?"

His blue gaze reminded her of a clear summer sky. "Yeah, that's right. Officially I work at *Enjoy Omaha* magazine, doing headshots and stuff, but that's only so I can afford to travel and build my portfolio in nature and wildlife photography. Nebraska doesn't have the most diverse scenery, so I've gotta go elsewhere when I can."

"Nature photography . . . is that like *National Geographic* kind of stuff?"

"That's the dream, yeah. Not that I expect to ever hit that level. Hell, I'd be happy for my shots to be on postcards at random truck stops across the US."

She grinned. "Next to the personalized pocketknives and key chains?"

"I'd rather be between the novelty lighters and dream catchers, but I'll take what I can get."

Elliott laughed, and a tingling sensation shimmered down the back of her neck as she sensed Jamie's attention on her. She did her best to ignore her body's insistence that they not forget his close proximity. *Why aren't we closer to him?*

"What's the coolest place you've ever photographed?" she asked. "Your absolute favorite?"

Stephen put his elbow on the table to face her more fully. From his opposite side, Tara frowned at his back. "No one's ever asked me that before."

"I've barely stepped foot out of Nebraska. I'm hoping to live vicariously."

"In that case . . . Jackson Hole in Wyoming. Since the second I left, I've wanted to go back. The jagged peaks of the Tetons behind the forest were so beautiful I could barely take my eyes off them. I spent hours trying to capture an image that would do them justice."

"Did you?"

"Every time I look at the photos, I want to go back. Which is sort of the whole point, isn't it? If I see a picture of someplace I've never been, and I'm so moved by it that I know my life won't be complete until I see it for myself? That's a fucking great photo."

Elliott couldn't help her smile, nodding in agreement. His passion was infectious. "Now I've gotta see those Teton pictures."

"I can't believe I don't have any on my phone to show you, but yeah—anytime."

"You're making me want to quit Starbucks already, you know."

He raised a brow.

"We're in the same boat with our day jobs funding what we *really* want to do."

"Yeah? What else do you do?"

"Graphic design for small businesses. Sort of how you just said a photo can inspire someone to travel to that exact place? I want to use design and branding to help local businesses do that. When they find that perfect customer or client, everyone's happy. But sometimes they just need a little help finding each other. A logo, brand identity, or website can make or break a business."

Stephen nodded as she spoke. "One hundred percent agree. I randomly listened to a podcast the other day about the best logos of all time, and I'm convinced the hidden arrow in the FedEx logo is the whole reason they're so successful."

"Simple goes a long way. Target, Nike, McDonald's—some of the simplest but biggest logos of all time."

"Well, when I'm ready to get a website up and running, I'm coming your way."

Before Elliott could respond, Carly spoke from across the table. "Wait, you do websites, too?" Elliott turned her head to look at Carly, and for a split second her eyes met Jamie's. "Think you could help with a restaurant?"

She swallowed past the lump of discomfort suddenly lodged in her throat. "Sure. During my internship, I helped rebrand a pho place in Lincoln. We changed their logo, redid their menus, website, and signage—the whole deal."

Carly elbowed Jamie, whose gaze had dropped to his beer. "Did you hear that? She could help Blythe with the bakery." Carly turned back to Elliott. "Jamie's sister has a bakery in Old Market, Melt My Tart. The food's awesome, but the website and brochures could really use a facelift. Blythe was just talking about wanting to find someone to help her with it."

The words slipped out without thought. "I know that place."

"Really?" Carly asked. "Have you been?"

Jamie's glass had been at his lips, and he quickly set it on the table, splashing some over the side.

"Sorry," he muttered, not looking up as he reached across the table for several napkins. Carly leaned away to avoid the mess.

"I didn't go in," Elliott clarified, hiding trembling hands under the table. "I was checking out Old Market. I . . . saw it when I was walking around, and the name kind of stuck with me."

"Didn't I tell you I'd find you some work around here? I'll take you by and introduce you to Blythe. I bet she'd love to work with you. Don't you think, Jamie?"

He kept wiping the table. "Yeah. Sure."

Carly smiled at Elliott. "What do you think?"

Honestly, she should say no. Building on the connection with Carly and Jamie wasn't a good idea. Both for her sanity and because Jamie clearly didn't want Carly to know they'd met, which complicated things.

But this was her first business opportunity, and a successful business in one of the most popular locations in town would be a great place to start. Carly had a lot of friends and could bring Elliott numerous business opportunities just like this, and it wouldn't look great if she declined her very first chance.

Plus, if Blythe hired her and was happy with Elliott's work, she'd spread the word, too.

Elliott smiled at Carly. "Sure. I'd be happy to."

CHAPTER SEVEN

Jamie

Eleven months earlier

Two weeks had passed since May disappeared from Jamie's life, and he was not okay.

He didn't smile as much. Slept like shit. Didn't feel like going out with friends, and even skipped Tuesday dinner with his mom. Regret followed him around like one of those rain clouds constantly hovering over Eeyore, a companion as pitiful as it was unforgiving.

The gravity of losing her hadn't fully hit until the following morning, after the daze of such a perfect evening cleared like fog after the sun came up. He'd replayed the time spent with May with fresh eyes and a clear head, and concluded there was a good chance he'd met—and lost—his soulmate.

Exaggerated? Maybe. He'd have said so if anyone had asked him before that night. He wasn't into fate or horoscopes or love-at-first-sight nonsense. He still hadn't done the latter—hadn't fallen in love with her—but he knew beyond a shadow of a doubt he could. That he *would* fall for her if given the chance.

If they had more time.

He'd found her attractive when he had noticed her at the bar and was obviously interested enough after hearing her laugh to put himself out there and talk to her. He'd had no idea it was only the beginning of something life changing.

In a single evening, she'd teased him, stood up to him, flirted with him, laughed with him, told him something vulnerable, complimented him, let him go first, asked him for a favor, fallen asleep with him, challenged him, trusted him, soothed him, and kissed him like it was her last day on earth.

They'd covered a year's worth of ground in a few hours, and something told him they hadn't even scratched the surface.

He'd never met anyone else like her, and he was desperate for more. The way she'd looked at him and touched him said she'd wanted that, too. Something was going on with her, but the way she'd kissed him . . . He struggled to believe she'd left for any reason other than she'd felt like she *had* to. That she'd had no choice.

He should have asked for her last name, an email address, or given her *his* number. A social media handle . . . For God's sake, something! Because ever since that morning after, he'd been searching and hadn't found a trace of a woman named May in Lincoln, anywhere. It was like she'd never existed.

Three weeks ago she'd been a stranger, and now he had a growing list of questions only she could answer.

What about white chocolate? Did she like that?

Did she have any siblings?

What was her theory about what happened to Malaysia Airlines Flight 370?

Had she ever seen a narwhal with her own eyes?

"Back again?"

Jamie did his best to glare at Gus, which wasn't easy. The man was the friendliest person Jamie'd ever met. "You're a bartender. I thought you weren't supposed to judge people."

Gus snorted. "That's all bartenders do. We just hide it like damned professionals."

Normally, Jamie would have laughed at that. Today, he barely cracked a smile.

Gus sighed and rested his palms flat on the bar top. "Still no luck, huh?"

Jamie shook his head.

"Sorry, man."

Jamie had already asked, so he knew the answer. Still, he asked again. "You're sure you didn't catch her last name when she was here?"

"Since you picked up the tab that night, I never got a card from her," Gus said. It was the same thing he'd said the first time.

"You didn't ID her when she ordered? She looked pretty young." He was grasping at straws, now.

Gus's expression turned a bit pitying, which Jamie ignored. "I thought so, too, at first, and I almost carded her. But then I saw her eyes, and I knew that woman had seen more than twenty-one years of life. Looked like she'd seen a hell of a lot more than she should have by now, if you ask me."

There'd been a few moments where Jamie'd thought so, too. Those beautiful gray eyes had been expressive and so damn pretty, but at times also held a deep sadness he wasn't really sure what to do with.

"How about I get you a beer?"

Jamie nodded.

When Gus walked away, Jamie's eyes slid sideways to the empty chair May had occupied two weeks ago. For a split second he wondered if he'd be better off if he'd never even spoken to her but just as quickly dismissed it.

Even if it made him miserable now, he'd remember that night for the rest of his life. He couldn't find it in himself to regret spending it with her.

He just wished like hell he hadn't let her slip away.

CHAPTER EIGHT

Jamie

Jamie drove home in a trance.

He'd always been the kind of person who needed time to process things and, with the exception of on the baseball field, had never been much of a snap decision-maker. He preferred a slower pace, reviewing all angles and the pros and cons of a situation, and considering the consequences of decisions before he made them.

A trait he had *not* learned from his father.

May—no, Elliott, apparently—had been the furthest thing from his mind as he'd stepped out the door to head to The Patriarch tonight. When he'd agreed to try things again with Carly, he'd firmly shut away the memory of that night in Old Market into a far corner of his mind, well beyond reachable in his conscious moments.

He'd accepted that dreams were out of his control, but even those had become few and far between.

To say it was a shock to see her tonight was like saying Babe Ruth was just an okay baseball player.

He hadn't thought he'd see her again.

Ever.

Didn't think he'd ever know why she disappeared that night, either. Apparently she'd been about to go through a crazy medical procedure, which made sense in hindsight.

Her blond hair was longer now, almost down to her shoulders, and several shades lighter. Otherwise, she looked the same, and he'd known it was her right away. When she laughed at something Stephen said, he'd remembered the first time he'd heard it: sitting alone at that bar, kind of embarrassed he'd been stood up, then brought out of his pity party by the sound of a woman laughing into her phone beside him.

He was glad Elliott had finished her degree. Graphic design suited her. Probably a weird thing to think since he barely knew her, but it seemed to fit her all the same.

He came to a stoplight and gripped the steering wheel tighter. How on earth was *she* the one Carly had met this afternoon? Whose life she'd basically saved?

Seriously, what were those odds?

The situation wouldn't have been so weird if he hadn't kissed Elliott that night. If he hadn't . . . *felt* things that night. He was irritated as hell at the unwanted rush of emotions that flooded him when he'd first set eyes on her tonight—before his rational brain took over.

It had been one night, and it had been a long time ago. It didn't matter now, and he was fine with that.

But even though he had nothing to hide—he'd been single that night, everything was consensual, and he and Carly hadn't gotten back together until several months later—he'd pretended he'd never met Elliott. Wasn't even sure why he'd done it, but the words had come without thought.

No, we didn't officially meet. Nice to meet you, Elliott.

The flash in Elliott's eyes told him she hadn't appreciated the deception, and she probably thought the worst of him for it. Maybe she even thought he'd been with Carly the night they'd met. Which was almost laughable since he was the last man on earth who would cheat on a woman he was dating. He'd watched his dad and brother go through women like toddlers with cheap toys, and he'd vowed a long time ago to never be anything like them.

But it was fucking inconvenient to be blindsided with the woman who'd made him believe in the concept of soulmates while accompanied by his girlfriend, a woman he respected and cared for.

So yeah, he'd panicked.

If it were up to him, he'd avoid Elliott after tonight. Omaha was a decent-size city, and he didn't care for Starbucks. But with Carly's clear intentions to befriend her and asking her to get involved with his sister's business, things weren't looking good. Once Carly decided to take someone under her wing, there was no stopping her.

What would his sister think about Elliott?

He shook the thought away, vowing to deal with that bridge when he came to it.

He arrived at his apartment just as unsettled as when he'd left The Patriarch and walked up to the second-floor apartment. His yellow Lab, Hank, immediately jumped on him in greeting before going straight to the leash hanging by the door, tail wagging.

"Need to go out, buddy?" He tossed his wallet and phone on the kitchen table. "A long walk sounds like a good idea."

Jamie's mood was still shit the next morning. He hadn't slept well and sat at his kitchen table for a good half hour, nursing a cup of coffee, before he finally decided he'd better at least let Hank out to pee and run around a bit.

He pulled on athletic shorts, and soon they were weaving between apartment buildings toward the dog park at the center of the complex. The fenced-in area with a section for large dogs and another for small ones was the biggest selling point for this place. That and the running path that circled the large development, giving him a multi-mile loop when he wasn't in the mood to drive to one of the lakes or trails.

Hank's pull on the leash strengthened the closer they got, and once Jamie slipped him through the fence and unclipped his leash, he was off like a shot toward a group of dogs in the corner. Jamie propped his arms on the fence and grinned. It was impossible to be in a bad mood while watching dogs play.

When he'd run circles to his heart's content, Hank loped back to Jamie, and they made their way back across the grass. A mere ten yards from the dog park, Hank paused and plopped down onto the grass, panting happily with his tongue lolling from his mouth.

Jamie arched a brow. "It's a lie-in-the-sun day, huh? Fine. But just for ten minutes, okay? We've gotta run some errands later."

Jamie sat down beside Hank, propping his forearms across his raised knees. He took a deep breath of the fresh morning air and exhaled, his gaze aimlessly passing around the apartment buildings bordering the park.

That's when he saw her.

On a second floor balcony, not ten yards from where he sat, stood Elliott.

She didn't return his shocked stare, so she didn't appear to have seen him. Her hair was pulled up into a tiny, messy ponytail, not something she'd have been able to do the last time he saw her, and she brushed away a few strands that had escaped in the breeze. She wore a white tank top and jeans, her slender arms resting on the railing. Her face angled toward the sun, and she closed her eyes for a beat, a small smile spread across her lips.

Unbidden, his brain conjured her scent that had surrounded him last night, and the subsequent crackle in his chest made him uneasy. He was in a committed relationship and had never been even remotely tempted by another woman when he had a girlfriend. He'd always figured if he was, something wasn't right.

He wasn't so susceptible that a single reunion with Elliott made him question what he had with Carly, but that tug beneath his sternum, plus the lingering lie he'd told about not knowing Elliott, turned over like hot stones in his gut.

As if he'd called out her name, her eyes suddenly popped open, and her gaze collided with his.

Shit. It had just been a few seconds, but it probably looked like he'd been sitting here staring at her like a total creeper. Reflexively he dropped his attention to the ground, but that made it even worse. He looked back up at her, his face heating, and raised a single hand in an awkward wave.

She straightened, blinking, and though he was a little far away to be sure, her brow furrowed. "Jamie?"

Hank lifted his head at her voice.

"That's me," came out of his mouth, like a complete dumbass.

She said something just as a cacophony of barking chorused from the park, and she repeated herself, louder. "Do . . . do you live here?"

"Yeah." He stood and jerked a thumb behind him. "On the other side, but I bring my dog here all the time."

"Oh. I do, too. Live here, I mean. Obviously?" It came out like a question, and she rolled her lips between her teeth as if telling herself to stop talking.

They regarded each other in silence for a beat, and he wished for something else to say. He hadn't expected to see her again so soon, and definitely hadn't expected to practically be neighbors. There were things he wanted to tell her—things best said without a group of friends or strangers around to overhear.

Should he, though? Was there any point in clearing the air, or was it best to leave her thinking the worst of him, which might encourage her to keep her distance?

A beat of silence stretched for what felt like minutes, and she removed her hands from the railing and took a step back, as if to head back into her apartment.

"Can we talk?" he blurted. "Could you, I mean . . . Do you mind coming down for a minute?"

Her eyes shifted to the sidewalk. "Okay."

Jamie shifted on his feet while he waited, folding his arms and then thinking better of it, eventually sliding his hands in his pockets. Hank, still panting on the bright-green grass, eyed him with curiosity. Or maybe it was pity.

A few minutes later, she appeared around the corner and walked toward them. As soon as Hank realized she was headed his way, he leaped up and took off in her direction. Jamie barely reacted in enough time to grip the leash and avoid his dog bowling her over. He tugged Hank back a few steps, his spinning tail now swatting Jamie on the legs.

She crouched down on her knees and scratched Hank's ears, grinning, and Jamie had never been happier to have this dog as a buffer. "Well, hi."

Jamie relaxed a little, and Hank jerked forward to lick her face, pushing her into the grass.

"Hank!" Jamie tugged him back. "Shit, I'm sorry."

"No, it's okay." Elliott held her hand out as if to say she wanted him back, laughing. "I love dogs. I miss having one around."

Jamie relented, loosening the leash several inches. Hank tucked himself right next to Elliott and rolled onto his back.

"You want a belly rub, huh?"

Jamie registered a feeling of contentment at the revelation she liked Hank and immediately dismissed the thought. He didn't care if she liked dogs or not. He stood beside them for a minute, felt awkward being the only one standing, then sat a few feet away.

As she slid her hand along Hank's soft fur, she glanced up at Jamie. Her gray eyes moved back and forth between his, waiting.

"I just wanted you to know I wasn't with Carly that night." The words tumbled out in a rush, and his neck prickled with heat. "When we first met."

Something flickered in her expression, and he couldn't decipher its meaning. She kept her attention on him as she steadily swept her hands across Hank's fur, listening.

"I've known her a long time and we'd dated before, back in college. But we were one hundred percent not together that night." He gripped the back of his neck. "I guess . . . I needed you to know that."

Her eyes searched his for another moment, then her shoulders seemed to relax, and she nodded. "Thank you for telling me. That possibility crossed my mind, and I couldn't bear the thought of doing that to the one person who gave me a chance at life . . ." Her voice shook and she trailed off.

He could say more. Tell her that he'd looked for her, thought about her for months. But that moment was gone—they were different people and had moved on, and their situation was different now.

What good would it do?

A quiet question drifted to him. "Why didn't you tell her we'd met?"

He'd asked himself the same question. "I don't know. I panicked, I guess. I wasn't expecting to see you, so it was a shock on its own . . . But seeing you with Carly there? I wasn't prepared to handle that. I'm sorry."

"Do you think it would upset her to know the truth?"

"I don't think it would make her happy."

Elliott nodded, accepting the nonanswer. It wasn't ideal, but at this point, it seemed best just to move forward.

Silence hovered between them while the sounds of the outdoors and dog park continued around them. After a moment, he said, "So you got a bone marrow transplant. That's what you were doing last year."

She dropped her gaze to her hands. "I'm sorry I didn't tell you. And that I gave you my middle name and . . . disappeared like that. I was admitted the next day, and if I survived, I knew I'd be in the hospital for months. It's a pretty risky procedure. I didn't know how it would turn out, and it just seemed easier not to say anything."

"What exactly happens, if you don't mind me asking?"

"I don't mind. The cancer was in my blood, so they gave me really high doses of chemo that killed all the blood cells in my bone marrow. So much that my body never would have been able to make new ones.

But that's the whole point, because left to its own devices, my body keeps turning it into leukemia. After they wipe my cells out, they give me fresh, healthy ones from someone else."

"Wow." Even after he'd learned Carly had donated, he hadn't really known what it meant. "So it's literally Carly's blood running through your veins right now?"

"Yeah, I guess you can think about it like that."

"That's so cool." He winced. "I mean, not cool that you had to do that, but it's . . . interesting, I guess." *Stop talking.*

"I know what you mean." He couldn't tell if she meant it or was just taking pity on him, but he appreciated it all the same. "I think so, too."

"And . . . it went well? It, uh, worked, I guess? You're okay now?"

Her gray eyes were gentle and focused. "So far, so good."

"I'm glad to hear it," he said softly.

"How long have you lived here?" she asked, changing the subject. "In this complex, I mean."

"About four years. Ever since I got back from Arkansas."

"Arkansas? I thought . . . Didn't you say you'd always been in Omaha?"

She'd remembered that detail, huh? He stretched his legs out, leaning back on his hands. "I guess I did, didn't I? It's true when I'm giving the abbreviated version of my life story." He gave a humorless laugh. "Or when I'm trying to impress someone, since Arkansas was a failure. My senior year of college I was drafted for pro baseball, but it didn't work out in the long run."

Elliott frowned. "I'm no baseball expert, but my dad's a huge fan so I watched it a lot by proxy. I didn't think Arkansas had a team?"

"They've got minor league. Most players don't go straight to the major leagues out of college, no matter how good they are. The minor leagues are there to prepare us, but even then, a lot of guys never make it big. The Royals Double-A team is in northwest Arkansas. I was lucky and moved to Triple-A pretty quick and got to come back to Omaha to play. I got injured not long after that, though." He'd been disappointed at first, but in hindsight it worked out for the best. "Minor-league pay sucks, so I'd been working at my friend's garden center during the offseason the whole time. When I was cut from the team, I got my certification and started doing it full time."

She paused her ministrations with Hank. "I'm sorry you got hurt."

He shrugged. "It happens. I enjoyed playing, but there's a lot about the pro-athlete life I don't think I would have liked. I was never into it like some other guys were, so it's probably better this way. I climbed trees way before I ever picked up a baseball glove."

She glanced at the midsize maple at the edge of the dog park. "I don't think I've ever climbed a tree."

His mouth dropped open. "Never?"

She shook her head.

"We—" He caught himself. "You should remedy that. If you can find a good one with a spot to sit and just look out on the horizon, there's nothing better."

"I think I might be past my prime for that," she said with a laugh. "I'm more of a ground dweller, anyway."

"Got a thing about heights?"

"If by 'thing' you mean bone-crippling fear, then yes." She looked down and added quietly, "I have several of those."

It was on the tip of his tongue to ask what she meant, but at the last second he went with, "My sister hates heights, too. It's funny . . . That's actually how I ended up in my first tree. We were flying kites as kids, and hers got caught in one, and she started crying because she was too afraid to go after it." He grinned at the memory and that ladybug kite that was too torn up by the branches to be used again anyway, which had caused a whole new round of tears when he'd gotten down. "I should thank her for inspiring my eventual profession, probably."

"You should." She met his gaze for a beat, then cleared her throat and stood. "I'd better go."

"Oh." He scrambled to his feet as well. "Sure." Hank tugged on the leash, and Jamie tightened his grip. "See you around?"

"Maybe," she said with a nod, then disappeared into her building.

Jamie and Hank made their way back home, and he realized after the initial awkwardness, he and Elliott had had a nice conversation, almost like they were friends. His first inclination after seeing her last night had been to stay away, but after that?

Maybe he had nothing to worry about, after all.

CHAPTER NINE

Elliott

The second Elliott was back in her apartment she called Yuka.

"Well?" Yuka demanded by way of greeting. "How did it go? I can't believe you didn't call me last night."

"Sorry, I thought you might be asleep." Elliott, on the other hand, probably only got a total of three hours by the time she'd finally shut her mind off. For once, her thoughts had been consumed by something other than rogue leukemia cells sneaking around in her blood, just waiting for the right moment to explode, but she wouldn't go as far as to say it had been a good distraction. She'd been this close to driving back to Lincoln but somehow talked herself into staying put.

Yuka squealed. "Out that late, huh? Please tell me it's because of a man."

"I did meet a guy named Stephen, but nothing wild happened because it's me. He seems nice."

"And?"

"He's attractive. Very, actually."

"Details, woman. Hair color, eyes, hand size? Don't hold back."

Elliott closed her eyes and leaned her head back against the couch. "Yuka."

"Okay, forget about hand size. Trade for the kind of shoes he was wearing."

Elliott inhaled, her lungs tight and painful. "Jamie was there."

A pause. "Sorry . . . Who was what now?"

"Jamie—*the* Jamie—was there last night."

Yuka's screech was so loud Elliott jerked the phone away from her ear. She would have been amused by Yuka's excitement if the situation were anything other than what it was.

After a few seconds, Yuka seemed to register the fact Elliott wasn't screaming with joy alongside her. "What's wrong? Did he not remember you?"

"He did." Elliott rubbed her palm against her sternum. "But he's . . . um. He's Carly's boyfriend."

Her words hung in the air like string puppets, dancing before her eyes. Saying it out loud was more painful than she'd expected. Which, if she thought rationally about it, was ridiculous. She'd met him once, a year ago. They'd spent approximately six hours in each other's company. Yes, there had been a connection. Attraction. Chemistry. But it had been temporary, and she'd known that from the start.

Just because she'd allowed the memory of that night to carry her through the long nights in that dark, isolated hospital room didn't mean she had any claim on him. Even as her body slowly healed, loneliness was the sickness that festered in the silence, and it was only natural she'd relive those moments of joy to keep herself grounded. It didn't mean they were meant to be, or that there'd been a reason they'd met that night.

The fact that her heart shattered like glass when Carly slid her arm possessively around his waist was an unfortunate side effect of an unusual situation and the unrealistic expectation she'd created in her mind over the past year.

Yuka still hadn't spoken.

"Are you there?"

"Yeah, I'm . . . shit. I'm processing."

Elliott nodded in miserable understanding. The burning sensation of tears built beneath her eyelids.

"That sucks, Ellie. Bad."

"Why, though?" She agreed, obviously, but admitting to it made her seize up with guilt. "The woman who saved my life is happy and with a man who, from what we know of him, is an amazing catch."

"Sure. Good for Carly and all. I owe her big time for what she did for you. But *you're* my best friend. Not Carly. And I know you've been thinking about Jamie this whole time and hoped you'd find him again. I wanted that for you."

I wanted that for me, too. "They're really cute together." A few tears escaped, which pissed her off.

"I refuse to respond to that." There was a beat of silence. "So what did he do? When he saw you?"

"We were only alone for a few seconds before Carly walked up, and then he pretended like he didn't know me."

"The *hell?*"

Elliott grinned despite herself. Ten seconds ago Yuka had been screeching with glee that Elliott had run into him, now she'd probably slash his tires if Elliott said the word.

She was the most loyal friend Elliott had ever had.

"I think he just felt uncomfortable seeing me again. I mean, the last time he had, I'd used a fake name and left him sleeping on the sidewalk. I don't know what I'd have done if I was in his shoes."

Some men might have been pretty pissed at her, under the circumstances. But he'd just seemed shocked and then stayed quiet most of the night. Even this morning when they were alone and he could have let her have it, he'd just been . . . *nice.*

How was it possible they lived in the same apartment complex? Elliott was paying extra to rent by the month, and that decision was looking better by the day. At least she could get out of here quickly if it became too much and she needed to relocate.

Yuka sighed heavily. "I'm sorry, Elliott."

"I am, too. And you're the only one I can admit that to."

"I know. That's exactly why you should. We all need one person we can be totally vulnerable around and not worry about being judged."

Elliott gripped the phone tighter. "I'm lucky you're my person."

"Don't make me cry. I gave you one job when you left."

"Sorry." She traced her thumb along the seam of a couch cushion. "There's, um. Something else."

"That doesn't sound good."

"People were asking about me, and when I mentioned my degree and the kind of design I do, Carly sort of asked if I'd be interested in working with Jamie's sister. I guess she's been looking for help with her business website and stuff."

"Jamie's sister?"

"Yep."

"That's . . . not ideal."

"I don't know why I said yes. Everyone was looking at me, and I'd just told everyone how I wanted to help small businesses. Wouldn't it have seemed weird to say no? And it's a great opportunity, right? The thing with Jamie aside . . . Barely a week here and I already have a client. The sooner I build my portfolio and get established, the sooner I can stop making coffee and focus on what I really want to be doing."

"But . . . can we put the thing with Jamie aside?"

"We can try."

Yuka sighed heavily, then cleared her throat. "You know what? You're right. This is fine, we're fine, you're fine. You'll blow that woman away with what you can do, her business will thrive because of you, and she'll refer you to everyone else she knows. Small business owners stick together. It will be so great."

The temptation to ask *But what if it's not great?* rose up, but Elliott tamped it down.

Think positive. You can do this.

They hung up shortly thereafter, and Elliott sat on the couch in the quiet space for a few minutes. If she was at home, she'd be in the kitchen with her mom or on the back porch with her dad and their German shepherd. Maybe sitting in the café in their bookstore, reading the newest employee-recommended book of the week.

She wasn't used to the silence. Wasn't sure she liked it, yet. So far, all it did was remind her she was here alone. If she got sick or something else happened, no one would know.

Stop. She exhaled forcefully, as if expelling the thought before it could gain a strong hold. *You're fine. You can do this.*

She just needed a distraction.

She eyed the boxes stacked around the living room and stood, hoping that unpacking and organizing would keep her mind busy for several hours.

After sliding on a cloth headband to keep her hair back, she queued up an upbeat playlist on her phone and spent the next few hours emptying every box. Only an hour remained before her Starbucks shift when she lowered herself to the floor with the final box, Books scrawled across the top in Sharpie.

She considered what was inside and hesitated before finally sliding the box cutter through the tape. As a voracious reader, she wanted— *needed*—the books inside this box.

All except one.

Naturally, the book in question was right on top, the pink cover glaring at her from its perch atop her favorite novels.

She stared at it for the span of several blinks, considering. She couldn't return it. No one she knew would want it, and she didn't particularly want to keep it. Maybe she could donate it. Did libraries take random books about baking?

A local culinary school, maybe?

She shoved it onto the shelf with more force than necessary, where it would stay until she decided where to take it, and made quick work of the rest of the box.

"Where did you say you'd heard about the bakery, again?"

"I stayed at the hotel across the street before my transplant, and I noticed it one night. It was already closed, but the name caught my eye." Elliott cast a quick glance at Carly before they crossed the street toward Melt My Tart. For someone who didn't do it often, the lie came out surprisingly smoothly. She was careful not to look across the street to the hotel and the exact spot she'd sat with Jamie for hours, melting into his body as they talked and laughed and kissed, and where she'd dozed off and eventually slipped away like a thief in the night.

"It's so clever, right?" Carly half turned to face Elliott as she opened the door, shaded by a pink-and-white-striped awning. "It's legit, too. Blythe makes a mean lemon tart."

The sweet scent of sugary baked goods rushed to meet them as they walked in, immediately reminding Elliott of the cooking class she'd gone to with Jamie. His sister might be a master of lemon tarts, but Elliott doubted she'd ever find something that hit quite the same as that first bite of French vanilla soufflé. She couldn't recall what she'd had for dinner or the genre of music the band had played at the bar that night, but she knew the perfect, airy texture of a dessert that wasn't too sweet or too savory, and the exact color of Jamie's eyes as he'd watched her.

Her pulse went a little haywire at the memory. She rubbed her hand across her collarbone as she dragged her gaze to the front where the woman she assumed was Blythe finished up with a customer. She looked to be in her early thirties and had the same light-colored eyes and dirty-blond hair as Jamie, the latter pulled back in a tight ponytail.

How far did their similarities go? Did Blythe have his sense of humor? What did she think about his baseball career cut short and pivot into arboriculture (yeah, she'd looked it up while bored out of her mind in the hospital bed)?

Had their night last year meant enough to him that he'd mentioned it to his sister?

Then Carly said, "How cute is this place?" and Elliott remembered she was here for more than reminiscence and what-ifs.

She had a job to do.

The bakery's color theme was clear and unique—lime green and hot pink—consistent with the signage outside. The floor was a light-hued natural wood and the walls a soft white—closer to an ivory or eggshell. White subway tiles lined the customer-facing side of the counter and display case, but that's where the neutral palette came to an end. The bright-colored pastries and desserts popped from behind the clear glass, offering a mouthwatering display of macarons, cupcakes, bars, and what Elliott could only assume were mini tarts. A large pink menu board hung behind the counter, and lime-green chairs framed two-top tables near the entrance.

"It's adorable," Elliott replied, and meant it. She found a menu on a nearby bistro table and looked through it, ideas already forming.

As soon as the customer left, their arms full of boxes, Carly ushered Elliott to the counter.

"Hey, Blythe!"

Blythe grinned. "Is this the girl who's gonna save me?"

"Yep." Carly turned to Elliott. "I already filled Blythe in on everything I know about you."

"Which isn't much," Elliott said with a laugh she hoped came out lighthearted but sounded more nervous-adjacent.

Carly waved a hand. "It's enough. Obviously, this is Jamie's older sister, Blythe. Blythe, this is Elliott."

"Nice to meet you."

"Same to you." Blythe checked her watch. "I've got about five minutes until closing, but I doubt anyone else will come in. Want to sit? I'll be right there."

"Sure."

Carly asked Blythe about some upcoming party, and Elliott took a seat at one of the tables. She pulled her laptop out of her bag and opened it to the bakery website, comparing it with the to-go menu on the table, trying to keep her mind from drifting to thoughts of Jamie.

How close was he to Blythe? Did they grow up racing their bikes down their childhood street? Did he pull immature pranks on her, like leaving a toad in her bathroom, or did they team up and work in cahoots to mess with the rest of their family?

Blythe dropped across from her a few moments later, and Carly stopped at the edge of the table.

"Welp," Carly said. "I'll leave you two to it."

Elliott frowned. "You're not staying?" Carly lived on the west side of town, which meant this was a long-ass drive for a three-minute introduction.

"Nah, I'd just get in the way." Carly cleared her throat and lingered, rocking back on her heels. Blythe seemed to be hiding a grin but said nothing. Finally, Carly glanced at the pastry case. "So, uh . . . got anything that's just gonna go to waste in there?"

Blythe laughed. "There it is."

Elliott couldn't help but smile. That was something Yuka would do.

"Pick whatever you want; just make sure you post a picture and tag the shop."

"I know the drill."

A few minutes later, Carly left, and Blythe locked the door from the inside and flipped off the OPEN sign. She sat down with a sigh, pulling the white apron over her head.

God, she looked so much like her brother.

"Thanks for agreeing to talk to me," Elliott started. Her mentor through internship was big on exuding confidence during client conversations and had forced Elliott to practice often. It would take a while to build an experienced portfolio to impress clients, so for now she'd have to skate by on passion and sincerity. "I'm new at this, but I've got the creativity and skills to do whatever you want. I thought we could just talk through some general ideas about what you're looking for, and I can email you some concepts in a few days. You can decide then if you want to move forward with hiring me. No pressure."

"Sure, that sounds good."

"Carly said you're interested in redoing the website and maybe working on some general brand support?"

"Yes, exactly. I know how important building a brand is, and I want people to see a pink box"—she pointed to the pile of boxes behind the counter—"or a pastry or even an Instagram ad and immediately think of us. I want to be first on their mind when they want to cater a baby shower or birthday or just grab something sweet on the way home from work. It's just that my artistic skills don't go beyond the kitchen, so I'm hopeless when it comes to this kind of stuff. I know how important social media is in theory, but I struggle to have the energy for it."

"It's a lot of work, and always on top of actually running your business. Plus, it's constantly changing, which doesn't help."

Blythe gave an exaggerated, exasperated nod.

"But that's what I'm here for." Elliott spun the computer around so they could both see the screen. "I checked out your website last night, and I have a few ideas."

"Girl, I'm all ears."

They spent the next forty minutes talking through Blythe's thoughts and Elliott's ideas. They went off on a few tangents, laughing about some of Blythe's disastrous baked-goods ideas (black bean brownies when she was on a "fiber kick") and a typo on a batch of business cards that read MELT MY FART in large, bold lettering.

"I'm still not sure that was an accident." Blythe had laughed.

"I'd blame the intern," Elliott had agreed. Blythe was an absolute delight, which was inconvenient. There was no way Elliott wouldn't help her now.

They'd finally arrived at the last few logistical questions Elliott had before she was finished. "Are the hours on your website up to date? You close at six except on Friday and Saturday, when you stay open later?"

"Yeah. At first I wasn't sure about the late nights, but my brother suggested it. Thought it might pick up the late-night crowd down here on the weekends."

"Your brother?" The question just came out, and Elliott could have smacked herself. Bringing Jamie up was a mistake.

"Well, my younger brother. I have two, but only one I like. Jamie, Carly's boyfriend. You've met him, right?"

Oh.

"Um, yeah. Last weekend, actually." Elliott paused, then added, "He seems nice."

That sounded natural, right? That's what someone who hadn't had her tongue in his mouth would say. Someone who'd never felt his hard body grinding against hers would definitely refer to him as *nice*. Full stop.

Her cheeks flushed anyway, and she hoped like hell Blythe wouldn't notice. She didn't seem to.

"He's the best person I know."

From what Elliott knew of him, he did seem pretty great. Great and *taken*.

It was definitely time to get out of here. Elliott closed her laptop and stood. "I'll get to work on this right away. If you approve of the concepts I send and we agree on a brand direction, I can start building some back-end web pages for review. Let me know if you have any additional thoughts in the meantime."

"Sounds perfect." Blythe walked her to the door and unlocked it. "This was great. I think we'll work well together."

Elliott smiled. She agreed, even if she was a little hesitant to remain so connected to Jamie through his family. "I think so, too."

CHAPTER TEN

Jamie

When Jamie stepped out of his apartment to let Hank out, he considered just taking him for a walk around their building to avoid the possibility of running into Elliott. Yeah, he'd felt good about everything after their talk last week, but then he'd dreamed about her. Nothing R-rated, but didn't they say you dream about whatever you think about right before falling asleep? He didn't remember doing that on purpose and didn't like knowing his brain had gone rogue.

But then he decided he was being ridiculous and took Hank to the dog park like usual. It seemed a little overboard to allow Elliott's presence to alter his routine.

On Mondays, Jamie usually hung around in the office at McCormick's Garden Center, finishing paperwork and taking calls from clients. He didn't mind residential jobs—a good thing since that's where he spent most of his time—but his favorite projects were the major commercial developments. He worked with the landscape designers and architects at the Garden Center, and their team was one of the more sought after in the city for simple but eye-catching landscapes: the entrance to Henry Doorly Zoo, the gardens just to the east of Old Market next to the Missouri River, and the trees that lined much of the downtown nightlife area. Not long after he'd met Elliott, he'd done some work at the hotel where she'd stayed.

It was where they'd kissed and fallen asleep under the stars, and in those first few days after she disappeared, he'd watched for her constantly. He'd wanted to see her again so badly it hurt. One day he was so distracted watching the hotel doors he almost lost a finger to his favorite pruners.

As the weeks passed, he'd thought about her less, gave up on finding her, and had finally started to move on. And the day he'd started dating Carly again, he had told himself to stop thinking about that night and about Elliott for good. It worked 99 percent of the time, that stupid 1 percent flaring when he was back in Old Market. Memories from that night would flash through his mind, there and gone, unbidden and without forethought.

Something about Elliott lingered in his subconscious for the longest time, maybe because there'd been no closure. She hadn't slapped him or left him with harsh words. He'd walked away from that moment still wanting her and confident she felt the same. And despite the way she'd left him on the dark sidewalk, part of him had thought he'd find her again. Like . . . like it had been fate that brought them together. He'd had the most ridiculous fantasies, like he'd turn the corner at the grocery store and there she'd be, one hand on her hip as she considered the whole-bean coffee selection.

Nothing about him and Elliott had felt final. Or over. Like their connection was a physical object, suspended and frozen in time, something that wouldn't disappear or float away. He'd shut the memory away when he'd finally decided to close the door on the possibility of ever finding her.

But now that Elliott was back, a small, unwelcome part of him wanted to peek inside that door to see: Had he truly moved on, or was it an illusion? What if everything was still there—the chemistry, the emotions, the laughter? What would he do if they resurfaced, even though he was with Carly now?

That thought disturbed him the most—the possibility that no matter how hard he'd fought against it, he might have inclinations like his father's.

It also immediately strengthened his resolve where Elliott was concerned. He wouldn't throw away what he had with Carly based on a single encounter from a year ago, no matter how intense his feelings had been at the time. A few hours of fun didn't mean he and Elliott would have made it as a couple, even if she'd stayed.

Right?

He startled when his phone buzzed on the desk. God, how long had he sat here, brooding?

Blythe: I can't come to dad's party tonight, so sorry

He groaned, and typed out what? Why not? Stacy, their dad's wife (Jamie refused to call her his stepmom, not only because she was Wife Number Four but also because she was a measly six years older than he was) was throwing his dad a party for his sixtieth birthday. Jamie wasn't exactly looking forward to it.

Blythe: Holden's sick.

Jamie: Is he okay?

Blythe: Yeah. Nothing serious, but sick enough I don't want to leave him. I hate to ditch you with dad and Greg.

Jamie: No worries, focus on my favorite little guy. Carly's coming with me, anyway.

Carly was the perfect buffer at family events, especially those involving his dad. An extrovert and queen of the social scene who could make small talk with anyone, she rarely met someone she couldn't befriend. Even, conveniently, arrogant assholes like his dad and his brother, Greg. Carly made evenings spent with that side of his family easier to swallow.

After the divorce, Jamie and his sister had gravitated more toward their mother, and to this day, Jamie would choose an evening with the women in his family over his dad and brother. But his dad was still that—his dad—and their relationship was just complicated.

In some ways Jamie held little respect for him, the first hit coming after his dad cheated on his mom. Then each accusation of infidelity from subsequent wives chipped away at what little remained. But he'd been a surprisingly supportive father through high school and college, always pushing Jamie to be his best academically and athletically. Not that he would ever ask, but if he was ever in a bind and needed money or help, his dad would do it without question. So while he kept social interactions with his dad to a minimum, Jamie figured a party for a major birthday was something he should attend.

Blythe: I heard Greg is bringing a new girlfriend.

Jamie: Of course he is.

Greg had followed in their dad's footsteps in more ways than one—joining the family business and going through women faster than the cans of Axe body spray he doused himself with.

Blythe: Want me to call around nine with an emergency?

Jamie checked his calendar app to confirm the party started at six. There was no way he'd make it three hours.

Jamie: Better make it 8.

Jamie wanted to leave almost as soon as they walked through the door.

He'd never really liked being in this house. It was the place his father had broken his mother's heart and torn their family into halves: Dad and Greg vs. Mom, Blythe, and Jamie. Those first few years of splitting his time across two houses had sucked, and Jamie had been jealous of kids who didn't commute between bedrooms.

The assortment of guests in attendance was . . . awkward. Several of his dad's work buddies were there, mostly older men. Some had brought their wives, some hadn't, and the ones that hadn't were making quick work of flirting with the other half of attendees: Stacy's young, perky friends.

Then there was Jamie's older brother, Greg, with a woman who looked about twelve years his junior on his arm.

Jamie blew out a breath and tightened his hold on Carly's hand, steering her straight to the bar set up on the patio next to the pool. She'd had an early meeting at the accounting firm where she worked, so he hoped she'd want to lie low, enjoy a drink outside, and pass by his dad in, say, half an hour on their way out to wish him happy birthday.

"Carly!" Stacy rushed over, clapping her hands with a little hop. "You made it."

Carly's hand slipped from Jamie's as she hugged Stacy with an equally enthusiastic greeting. In minutes, Carly was sucked in with a group of young women, giggling and talking.

He'd always admired her ability to fit in seamlessly with any crowd, even an elite, high-profile one like this. Despite being raised by a single mother who was constantly in financial straits, Carly's natural charisma made the men feel important and the women as if she were their confidante and friend. Everyone loved her.

She hadn't always been so extroverted. When he met her that first week of college debate class his freshman year, she'd been friendly but reserved. She'd just moved to Omaha on a scholarship to Creighton University's accounting program, and it was clear she felt out of place in the new environment.

Then when they were assigned to debate a position on dress codes in primary education programs, he'd watched her come to life and gain confidence by arguing a topic she cared about. They'd started dating that year, and he'd watched her come further out of her shell and eventually become the center of their social group.

She'd been happy for him when he was drafted but wasn't interested in the life associated with professional sports. He hadn't faulted her for wanting consistency in her life, and to this day it was the most amiable breakup he'd ever had.

They'd kept in touch as friends while he was in Arkansas. When he moved back to Omaha, he occasionally saw her out and about over the next few years, but it wasn't until a friend's thirtieth-birthday celebration a couple of months ago that they'd ended up back at his place. The next morning while he made breakfast, she'd asked if he wanted to give it another try, and they'd been together since.

Being with Carly was familiar and effortless. His family loved her—all of them—and they mostly had the same friends. They both enjoyed their own space and still led their own lives, which suited them both.

It was hard to imagine anything better.

A familiar voice approached Jamie from behind. "Hey, bro."

Jamie picked up his beer and considered his brother. "Hey."

"Where's Blythe?"

"Couldn't make it," Jamie said. "Holden came down with something."

Greg's face twisted in distaste.

God help this family if Greg ever had children. "How's it going?"

"You know how it is. Work's insane and Dad's been riding my ass."

Jamie took a long pull of his lager, unsympathetic. "You're the one who went to work for him."

"He pays me well."

To Jamie, it still wasn't worth it. He regarded the other partygoers, not interested in talking about money. "Good turnout," he offered.

Greg chuckled. "Most of them are Stacy's friends. I'm not complaining—she set me up with the hot brunette in yellow."

"Lucky you," Jamie said dryly.

"Hopefully."

"Where's Dad?"

"Probably wherever the food is. Kitchen, I guess."

Jamie found his dad exactly there. It had been a few months, and his blond hair was drifting closer to white every day. Even at sixty, he was still a good-looking man and wore it like a badge of honor.

His dad clapped him on the back. "Jamie. Thanks for coming."

"Happy Birthday, old man."

His dad laughed. "You'll be here before you know it." He tipped his chin at a couple walking by. "How's the tree business?"

"Great."

"I always have something for you, you know. If you want a real job."

Jamie stiffened but refused to take the bait. "Thanks, but I have one."

His dad continued on, eyes scanning the room as he spoke. He'd always been a master at remaining in control while feigning disinterest at the same time.

Was it not exhausting? All the facades and pretending?

"Come on. You're my son. Yard work isn't what you were meant to do."

"I *enjoy* yard work, and you know I do more than that." He didn't elaborate. It wasn't the first time they'd had this conversation, and it was useless.

"And I say *you're* more than that." In a rare flash of emotion, his dad's hazel eyes finally met his. "You were a baseball star. People couldn't wait to see you in Royals colors. Working as a gardener was fine during offseason, but it can't be what you want to spend your life doing. There's nowhere to go. No way to move up."

"Not all of us care about being at the top."

"Bullshit. Every man has a burning desire to rule their kingdom."

The toxic masculinity rolling off his skin was suffocating. This was exactly why Jamie avoided coming here.

Jamie took his time responding and surveyed the pristine backyard, thanks to the incredible job his team had done last year. "Now that you mention it, I think I'd better check on that kingdom. I'll see you later, Dad. Happy birthday."

His dad shrugged and pulled out his phone, and Jamie went back outside, regretting having come into the house in the first place. He took a deep breath of fresh air, always happier when he was outdoors.

The yard was the best part of the property, hands down.

Four mature oaks—Jamie's favorite—stood tall and regal across the yard, casting glorious shade from their thick canopies. Last summer, his dad had considered taking two out for a water feature, and Jamie'd nearly had a stroke.

The bright-green grass surrounding the pool was thick and lush, and a stone path led to a pergola surrounded by plant life. Bushes and shrubs of varying shades of green lined the path, with flowers in brilliant purple, pink, and yellow hues arranged throughout. It was beautiful and it smelled incredible—earthy and faintly sweet. Even before the flowers had existed here, this was where Jamie had disappeared as a kid when he wanted out of the house.

He chatted with a few other people he knew and finished his beer. His brother was well on his way to drunk, and when he wandered outside and snide comments about Jamie's failed baseball career started flying, Jamie went in search of Carly.

She smiled when he approached, planting a kiss on his cheek.

"Ready to go?" he asked.

She glanced at the full cocktail in her hand. "Oh. Already?"

"I'm pretty tired. If you're still having fun, feel free to stay, but I'd like to head out. That okay?" They'd driven separately, both having come from work.

She glanced at the women still engrossed in animated conversation. "Sure. I think I will stay, though. I haven't even caught up with your dad yet. Talk to you tomorrow?"

"Yeah. Try to keep these fools in line, okay?"

She laughed and waved him off happily, effortlessly absorbed back into the fray.

Jamie walked outside and closed the front door. He released a pent-up breath, his body loosening with each step he took toward his car.

CHAPTER ELEVEN

Jamie

Three months after Jamie adopted Hank, he'd signed him up for obedience school. Most days he'd say it was the best money he had ever spent, because Hank generally listened and had decent manners.

Except, apparently, when it came to Elliott Holland.

It was Tuesday evening, and he'd just let Hank out of the dog park. When other dogs were around, Jamie usually leashed Hank. But there'd only been one other person there, and their pet was still frolicking inside the enclosure. Hank was good about sticking close to Jamie's side.

Which is why it caught him off guard when his dog took off like a shot across the knoll, nearly knocking a woman off her feet as she came up the sidewalk. Jamie took off after him, apologizing profusely as he approached.

He huffed out a half laugh when he found Elliott kneeling and grinning at Hank as he rolled onto his back and offered his belly, tail sweeping the ground.

"Come on, man." He glanced down at Elliott. "Sorry. He's shameless."

She chuckled and rubbed her hand up and down Hank's fur, completely unbothered. "I love it. My parents have a German shepherd back home, and I miss him."

He remembered. But it seemed like a good idea not to mention he could recall with distressing clarity every single thing she'd said to him that night.

"One introduction and Hank already misses you, apparently. He doesn't normally run off on me like that."

She murmured something to Hank he couldn't make out, and Jamie stood there for a moment, then took a step sideways and leaned his back against the wall of her building. The sun was slowly making its descent past the horizon, cooling the heat and shifting daylight to something softer.

"So how are you settling in?" he asked. "To Omaha, I mean?"

"Pretty good, I think. It's bigger than Lincoln, but it doesn't really feel that different. Starbucks is actually a really fun job, and I've been working on some designs for your sister. I really hope she likes what I come up with."

"She will." The only thing that got his sister worked up was the food itself. She'd never been too picky about things like design and marketing, and even if she was, the little he knew about Elliott told him she wouldn't half-ass the work she did.

Elliott nodded but kept her eyes on Hank so he couldn't read her expression. "There are a few things I'm still trying to figure out around here and there, though."

"Yeah? Like what?" Maybe he could help.

She glanced up, gray eyes meeting his. "Okay, like where's a good place to buy local art? My best friend came to visit over the weekend and shamed me for my bare walls. We took a trip to Home Goods, but those warehouse stores just aren't my thing. Shopping small is. I'd rather find something one of a kind and support a local artist if I can."

"Quick tip? Don't let Blythe hear you trash-talk Home Goods. I'm pretty sure the last time I babysat so she and her husband could go on a date, that's where they went. They were there so long they barely had time to hit a taco truck and eat in the car on the way home."

"She's a small business owner!"

"Sure, but where else can you buy a bohemian-style painting, gourmet pasta, and four dog beds at the same time?"

"Costco?"

He cocked his head. "Isn't Costco just as bad as Home Goods?"

Her shoulders fell. "Well, yeah."

He laughed, feeling a little unbalanced at the smile on her face. "Well, you're in luck, because there's a pretty great art scene around here." His mom was really into that scene and had even dragged him along for some painting classes a couple of years ago (he was worse than terrible). "If you're looking for high-end stuff, Old Market has several galleries. For more of the underground scene, check out Dundee or the Blackstone District. There's a creative co-op in Dundee that has lots of booths for local folks."

His mom knew the owner of the co-op and sometimes helped out on the weekends, and he hoped Elliott and his mom didn't cross paths. It wouldn't be wise to invite any additional connections with her, especially not after he'd heard from Blythe after their consultation.

Unsurprisingly, his sister had really liked her.

What would she say if she knew Elliott was the woman he'd met last year? His sister was the only person he'd told about that night, and after declaring she'd "never seen him like this over a girl," she'd become an amateur detective, scouring the internet for any information on a woman from Lincoln named May. With only that to go off, and the fact May had actually been Elliott's middle name, Blythe had come up empty-handed.

Eventually, like Jamie, Blythe gave up hope of ever finding her.

"Oh, great. Hang on—let me write that down." Hank sat up when Elliott paused her ministrations to reach for her phone and open the Notes app.

When she finished and looked up, he asked, "What else?"

"Know any good places to go running?"

A memory flashed through his brain: a dimly lit street, a warm breeze, and his hand wrapped around hers as they walked.

Sometimes I go for a run when I need to get out of my head.
Yeah? Me too.

He cleared his throat, shifting his attention to Hank, who'd set his paw on Elliott's knee. "The Keystone and Riverfront trails are pretty popular. Lake Zorinsky, too. I wouldn't recommend going alone when it's dark, though. If you ever want to, you'd be welcome to take Hank with you." Hank perked up at his name.

"Really?"

"Sure, he loves running. I take him a few times a week. He knows to stay at your side and not veer off or get caught under your feet. And even though he's just a big baby, he looks scary enough." Elliott wasn't his to protect, but growing up with a sister and, for much of his life, a single mom, his defensive instincts ran pretty deep. If she wanted him, he'd lend her Hank anytime she asked.

"Never hurts," Elliott agreed. "My dad was always trying to get me to take Dodger with me when I ran, too." She tipped her head toward his legs, one foot crossed over the other. "It must be nice to be a giant and not have to worry about people picking on you."

"I'm not a *giant*." Six-three was tall, but not that tall. "Seriously, though, just let me know if you want to take him. Anytime."

"Thanks," she murmured.

A long moment passed before she gave Hank a final pat and stood, as if she was about to head inside.

He should have leashed Hank, said a polite goodbye, and walked away. But that damned memory lingered. Reminding him of everything they'd talked about and how much they had in common.

I always have a book with me.

"Read any good books lately?" he blurted.

Something indecipherable flashed across her features as her eyes went wide and a pink flush spread up her neck.

His brows raised. "Wow, whatever it is, I definitely need to check it out."

Her expression wiped clean. "It's nothing."

"No way—now I'm intrigued. You have to tell me." He had to know what put that look on her face. "I once read a book that involved mutant hedgehogs in space, so it'll be hard to shock me."

She folded her arms and scrunched her nose, regarding him for a long moment. Finally, she said, "Promise you won't make a thing out of it?"

"I promise," he said, even though he had no idea if he'd keep it.

"I sort of got you a book."

She . . . what? "What?"

"God, this sounds ridiculous." She shook her head, rubbing at her forehead. "Honestly, I'd completely forgotten about it, but I came across it during the move. I bought it months ago when I was still living in Lincoln. I was at a bookstore, and something caught my eye that made me think of you and something we talked about . . . um, the night we met. I bought it just in case I ever ran into you."

"Really?" He took in a long breath as a light pressure settled on his chest. "What was it?"

Her lashes brushed her lightly freckled cheek as she looked down. "I, um . . . I have it here. But I'm not sure I should give it to you."

"Why not? It's just a book."

"I don't know. If I had a boyfriend, I wouldn't want another woman giving him a gift."

She had a point. "Right. Good call."

"Sorry, I shouldn't have even brought it up."

He slid his hands into his pockets and smiled, hoping to ease the concern wrinkling her forehead. "No big deal. But can I at least see it?"

"You just said . . . ?"

"I just want to look at it. I'm curious what subject would make a virtual stranger think of me. I'll give it back."

Their gazes collided, and she searched his face for what seemed like forever. She chewed on her lower lip. "I guess that would be okay. But you can't keep it."

"Deal."

He dropped onto the grass beside Hank while she slipped inside the building. He'd half convinced himself to get up and leave—because what was he doing?—when she returned with a large hardcover book. She handed it to him and sat down facing him. He caught a whiff of citrus that he hadn't noticed earlier as he regarded the cover.

The Big Book of Pies. He flipped open the cover and noticed a bright-pink sticky note jutting from the top, marking a page about halfway through. He felt Elliott's gaze on him as he went there.

As soon as he processed what he was looking at, he barked out a laugh. Hank lifted his head and eyed him warily while Elliott just grinned, a hint of satisfaction in her eyes.

Once he had his breath back, he handed the book back to her. "This doesn't prove anything."

Her eyebrows shot up. "It's a recipe for cheesecake." She held it up so the cover was visible. "In a book of *pies.*"

"The author clearly didn't do their research."

She regarded him for a moment. "You'll never let it go, will you?"

"Me? You're the one who planned to prove me wrong the second you saw me again." The pleasure he felt in the fact she'd thought about him—enough to bring something with her to Omaha—filled him with joy and discomfort. "I think you're the competitive one, here."

"If you're not competitive, admit it's a pie."

"Absolutely not. It's a tart."

"You're impossible."

Yeah, Blythe had said the same thing once or five times.

He just shrugged. "If by 'impossible' you mean right, then yes."

Can I come over?

Jamie sent the text within minutes of returning to his apartment. Half an hour later, he was on his sister's back porch with a beer in his hand.

Blythe reclined on a deck chair, hands folded behind her head as she gazed at the stars flickering in the darkened sky, patiently waiting for him to say what was on his mind.

They'd done this more times than he could count, though sometimes their roles were reversed.

He released a long, slow breath. "Do you ever wonder why Dad and Greg are the way they are?"

"No. I hardly think about them at all."

Apparently she didn't share his fear of turning into them. "Must be nice."

"They're driven by loyalty only to themselves. I can't tell if it's in the hope of achieving some illustrious social status or about feeling powerful. Maybe both. All I know is, I'm glad I fell under Mom's influence. That we both did."

"What if we didn't, though? Not completely? What if some sliver of Dad's asshole tendency is buried somewhere?"

"Jamie." She frowned. "Even on your worst day, you're not like him. Like either of them."

Most days, he'd agree with her. Not because he was some perfect moral specimen, but because he'd worked damned hard toward becoming a man of strong character. To the best of his ability, he'd surrounded himself with people he respected and wanted to emulate, like his mom and high school baseball coach. He made mistakes just like everyone else but reflected back and tried to learn from them. His mom had encouraged self-discipline and held him accountable for his actions, expectations he'd carried forward for himself into adulthood.

In his eyes, honesty and integrity were as close to godliness as a person could get.

Which was why the emotional roller coaster he'd been on since Elliott had arrived left him feeling so unsteady.

Maybe he'd never really been tempted before.

"How did you know Jake was the man you wanted to marry?"

When she didn't reply right away, he glanced over at her. She eyed him curiously, as if trying to piece together how the two questions were connected. "Everything was different with him. Better and brighter. After that first date I found myself wanting to be with him, no matter what I was doing. Even mundane errands were better if he was with me. I loved the way he saw the world and how he helped me see it in a new way."

The *Why?* would come soon. She'd try to get to the bottom of why he was asking these questions at some point . . . but until she forced it out of him, he wasn't going there. He didn't even have a full grasp on it himself.

His thoughts and feelings were a shit show.

"Have you ever been interested in another man? Since you realized you felt that way about Jake?"

If the question caught her off guard, she didn't let it show. "Define 'been interested.'"

He almost said *I can't*, because the whole reason he'd come over was to try to figure out where that line was. But he tried for a broad definition to see what she'd do with it. "Interested in getting to know more about them, I guess. Enjoyed talking to them."

She shrugged. "Sure. There was this one night Jake and I went to a bar in Dundee. It was a slow night, so we talked to the bartender for like two hours. The guy had this fascinating life—he'd lived on a boat and made his way through Europe with just a backpack. He was young and super hot. I had a blast, hearing his stories. He was friendly, funny, and passionate about travel and was about to leave on another adventure. I haven't seen him since, and sometimes I think about him and wonder how he's doing and if he's achieved everything he wanted to."

Jamie turned that over in his mind. Was that all this was with Elliott? She was interesting, young, friendly. He definitely found her attractive. She'd been dealt a shitty hand in a lot of ways but still had a lot she wanted to achieve. And the more he learned about her, the more inspired he became.

Was it okay for him to acknowledge those things and think about her sometimes? To wonder if she'd ever get everything she wanted?

Wonder who would give it to her?

"Are these questions . . . theoretical?" his sister asked carefully.

He took a deep pull from his beer. "There's a woman I met. Recently." A partial lie. "She's . . . different from anyone I've ever met." The word felt dangerous, especially with the way Blythe had just used it to describe Jake. But it felt like the only thing that fit. "She's a cool person and I like talking to her. We have a lot in common. She's attractive."

"Have you . . . ?" Blythe trailed off meaningfully.

"God, no. I haven't cheated, or anything close to it. After watching Dad's and Greg's behavior all my life, I'd never do that. But I guess I also want to be extra careful about anything leading up to it. Men and women coexist platonically all the time. I've done it, too. I have women friends and have had no issues maintaining those during the times I've been in a relationship. But this woman . . . Something feels different when I'm around her."

"Different from what? How you feel about Carly? And by 'different,' do you mean better?"

"I don't know," he answered honestly. That's what troubled him the most.

"Is she interested in you?"

"No. I mean, I don't know." There'd been a moment, that night at The Patriarch, when her body crashed up against him, and for a split second everything stopped. He'd cycled through surprise, confusion, then recognition.

And the way she'd looked at him . . .

Shock, but also something like relief. Like he was something she'd been searching for.

Then Carly had walked up, and nothing even close to that had happened again. Elliott had been polite and friendly, if a bit reserved, around him. She paid him the same level of interest someone might pay a distant acquaintance while standing in line at Trader Joe's.

Which, really, was how it should be.

"How much time have you spent with her?"

"Not much." Even if it felt like he'd known her for years. He considered telling Blythe who Elliott was, but it seemed pointless, and he didn't want to make things weird for Elliott or his sister as they began working together.

"It was instant, then? This feeling?"

He didn't answer her right away, wanting to stay away from the first time he'd met Elliott. Away from thinking about it, let alone talking about it. It wasn't what happened that night that was the problem, anyway. He'd been single then. It was the way his body reacted *now* anytime she was near. "Yeah, it was." It is. "How am I supposed to know if this is just a passing interest in something new and unexpected or something bigger? Something I need to address in my relationship with Carly?"

Was the fact he was even asking himself that question a sign something was amiss, either in his moral compass or in his relationship with Carly? "Is it wishful thinking to hope I'll never notice another woman when I'm in a relationship? When I'm married someday?"

"Yes." Blythe sat up and swung her legs over the edge of the chair, resting her elbows on her knees. Her eyes were pointed but kind, without a trace of judgment. "There are hundreds of thousands of people in this town. You'll come across some your own age who are easy on the eyes and have good personalities, and there's nothing wrong with forming connections and friendships with other people. I think when things become risky is if you find yourself wishing you'd rather be with them than with Carly. At no point during that encounter with the bartender did I wish he and Jake could switch places. I had no interest in going home with anyone but my husband. On the contrary, I couldn't wait to get in the car and talk to Jake more about that guy—get his take on what that life might be like."

Jamie set the bottle on the deck and rubbed his eyes. He didn't wish he could be with Elliott instead of Carly, did he? Frankly, he'd flat-out refused to let his mind go there. Emotions rose when he was around

Elliott that he immediately forced down. What would happen if he acknowledged and examined them? Maybe they wouldn't be as bad as he thought, and he'd quickly shift back to his comfort zone with Carly, confident their relationship was right.

It was the alternative that prevented him from doing so. What if he wanted something else instead? What if, instead of comfortable, he leaned into the unrestrained side of possibility?

"If I'm being honest, I've never understood you and Carly together. I love you both separately, but I don't get you together. You two have never seemed—"

"Don't," he interrupted. "I don't need that right now."

Blythe held up her hands. "Okay."

"I just . . . I've always been so careful not to be like Dad. But he crosses the clear line of infidelity. It feels like there's a lot of gray area up to that point, and I don't even want to step foot into that phase, either."

"There is a lot of gray area," Blythe agreed. "And that line is different for each couple, which is where communication comes in. I remember a few years ago when Jake and I were first dating, I came across him having lunch with a woman I didn't recognize. It was a nice restaurant, and they looked pretty cozy sitting in that corner, smiling and laughing. I didn't say anything in the moment, but I stewed over it all afternoon, wondering why they were together, why they looked so close, and why he hadn't told me about her. Turned out it was a business partner he'd had for years, and they'd had a standing lunch at that exact spot for ages, well before he and I had even met. Nothing was, or ever had been, going on between them, and he invited me to their next lunch so I could meet her.

"I was embarrassed, but when I really thought about it, it was the assumed secrecy that had bothered me so much. We talked everything out, and because Jake works with a lot of women and has women friends, we figured out that being open about his interactions with them is how I'd always feel safe in our relationship. I feel included. If I found out he was intentionally keeping interactions with other women from me, that's where it crosses my line and the trust I have in our relationship."

He hadn't needed his sister to confirm that lying to Carly about knowing Elliott was wrong, but her words still hit him square in the chest. Not coming clean right away made this whole thing worse.

"Have you talked to Carly about it?"

He sure as hell should have by now. "I was trying to figure out if this is big enough to even bring up," he hedged. "I guess I keep hoping it will pass."

Blythe leaned back on her hands. "I'm not saying this specifically about you and Carly, okay? But don't forget you're in the dating phase, which involves commitment, yes, but also the understanding that something might alter the course. A major life event, a career move." She paused. "Another person. You're allowed to change your mind. Don't be so worried about turning into Dad that you force yourself to stay in something that isn't right."

"I'm not doing that."

She just regarded him in that quiet, watchful way she sometimes did. He hated it. "Okay."

He closed his eyes. Grit his teeth so hard his jaw ached. "I don't want to hurt anyone," he whispered.

"I know." Her next words were soft, gentle. "But sometimes ignoring something makes it more painful in the long run."

He blew out a breath and stood, then gathered both their bottles. He quietly slipped into the house to toss them and returned.

She was on her feet now, too, and gave him a quick hug. "I'm glad you came over. Even if I'm not sure how helpful I was."

"I'm not sure, either," he said, and in a rare show of grace, she ignored him.

"I could be off the mark, but just in case I'm not . . . I think you need to start here." She put her hand on his chest. "You're so worried about everyone else and what they might think. It's not a bad thing, because yeah, you might need to have a conversation with Carly, or this woman, or both. But it won't do you any good until you know what's going on first in your head. You've gotta figure out what *you're* feeling. You can't have an honest, worthwhile conversation with someone else if you haven't been truthful with yourself."

And with those words, for the first time in forever, Jamie left his sister's house even more conflicted than when he'd arrived.

CHAPTER TWELVE

Elliott

Yuka: Bitch you're famous!

Elliott grinned at her phone, glancing up to make sure no customers waited before she replied.

Elliott: That might be an exaggeration

Yuka: Twenty-three new followers since yesterday!

Elliott had finally tweaked her business website to perfection, so she'd created an Instagram page for her services, too. Carly had shared it to her Stories, and because she hadn't been lying when she said she knew everyone in this town, traffic to Elliott's page had been immediate.

She'd even gotten three DMs from Carly's friends requesting more information, including one who ran a sizeable party-planning business as @ChantalPlans. If her follower count was any indication, she'd be a significant client for Elliott to land.

Elliott: I'M FAMOUS

Yuka: Well, Nebraska famous

Elliott: I'll take it

Elliott: Maybe we should send Carly that fruit basket

Yuka: YES. Please let me write the note

Yuka: You saved my life, and I said thank you

Now I have followers, so here's some fruit, too

God, she missed her friend. Yuka's recent weekend visit wasn't long enough.

Elliott: That's . . . something

Yuka: You're right, I'll keep workshopping

Elliott grinned and tucked her phone back into her bright-green apron. She took a long sip of the coffee she'd poured for herself, savoring the warm, rich flavor. She'd originally picked Starbucks because it seemed like fun and had solid benefits, but the free coffee ended up being the perk she appreciated the most. With sleep being as elusive as the meaning of human existence these last few weeks, she'd latched on to caffeine as if it were her lifeblood.

Which, come to think of it, probably didn't help matters . . . but at this point, it was a vicious cycle she didn't know how to stop.

Last night a headache came on around ten. A constant headache was one of her first symptoms when she was originally diagnosed, so despite knowing they were common and it was probably nothing, they never failed to send her into a spiral of fear. She'd taken medicine and the pain faded quickly, but the same hadn't been true for her nerves. Thank God her mom had been up and sat on the phone with her until almost one in the morning—the only reason she hadn't dropped everything and driven back to Lincoln for the night.

Hence, coffee.

The front door opened and Stephen strolled in, tucking his hands into his skinny jeans and flashing a wide smile as he approached the counter.

Elliott gave an awkward wave because, well, she was awkward. He'd stopped by several times since their introduction, and she'd like to say she was getting better at handling the attention and mild flirting, but honestly, it was hard to know. One of her coworkers, Suzie, mooned over him anytime she was on shift and he came in, and the smooth, sexy way she spoke to him made Elliott feel wholly inadequate.

"Hi," she said, because she couldn't pull off *What's up, handsome?* like Suzie.

"Hey. What time do you get off?"

She checked the clock on the register. "Ten minutes."

"What are you doing tonight?"

Nothing except working on some design stuff . . . How sad was that on a Friday night? She considered what else she could say, not because she wanted to lie and say she had plans, but she just felt exposed as he stood there watching her, waiting. She'd expected him to ask her out eventually, based on the way he'd stood in that exact spot flirting with her on multiple occasions, much to Suzie's dismay.

Elliott didn't object to the idea of going out with him; it just made her nervous. She didn't have a lot of experience with the dating world.

Finally, she settled on the truth. "No plans."

"I'm about to meet some friends for dinner down the street. Wanna come?"

Okay, so maybe it wasn't a date. Or Stephen was more perceptive than she gave him credit for and was trying to keep the pressure low. "Sure. Do you mean, like, right when I get off?"

"If that's okay? I'll just hang around till you're done, and you can follow me, if you want."

She looked down at her jeans and black V-neck. Not far off from what she'd have chosen anyway, but . . . "I smell like coffee."

"Is that supposed to be a bad thing?"

She didn't mind in the least. "If you're good with it, I'm in. Where are we going?"

"It's some horribly pretentious raw-food restaurant," he said, rolling his eyes. "Carly picked it. But don't worry—the hummus appetizer and drinks are worth it, and there's always a taco truck parked right outside. You won't regret coming."

Carly picked it?

Would Jamie be there?

"I like drinks. And tacos."

Stephen grinned at her. "I like you already."

"Hard not to." Had she just made a joke? A flirty one? "I just need a few more minutes to finish up and clock out."

He ran a hand through his dark hair, his eyes happy. "Take your time."

She tried to ignore the nerves fluttering around as she finished up her shift duties. While she'd been committed to moving and living on her own, it hadn't stopped her from bemoaning to Yuka how awkward she could be and how difficult it would be to make new friends.

Yuka had replied with standard-issue brutal honesty. "I won't argue the awkward part, but one, I love that about you, and two, the only way to get better at meeting people is to do it." She'd be so proud when Elliott texted her later and told her what she'd done tonight.

A few minutes later, Elliott hung up her apron and walked with Stephen to the parking lot. The restaurant was only a few minutes down the road, and they parked along the street and went inside together.

Pretentious or not, the place was packed. Stephen stood tall and looked around, jerking his chin up in acknowledgment when he found who he was looking for. "Over there."

Elliott followed as he wove through the room to a group of high-top tables in the back. Tara With No Filter was there, and several other people Elliott didn't recognize. Carly waved, and beside her stood Jamie.

He straightened as soon as he laid eyes on Elliott, holding her gaze for a second. Then Carly said something to him, and he leaned down to listen.

A shriek sounded from behind her. "Elliott!"

She turned and found herself immediately enveloped in a hug. She grinned wide as she returned the gesture. "Tiffany! What are you doing here?"

Tiffany pulled back and elbowed Stephen. "Carly invited me. I told you we had a lot of the same friends, remember? I didn't know you'd be here!"

"I didn't, either, but I'm so happy to see you."

Stephen dropped a friendly arm across Elliott's shoulders. "I grabbed this one from work. Didn't even let her take a breather, but figured she could use some fun after making Frappuccinos for high schoolers all day long. How do you two know each other?"

Tiffany waited, allowing Elliott to decide how much detail to give.

"She was my transplant nurse. Took care of me for months and was the only person I knew when I moved here."

"No way? That's cool."

"Small world, huh?" Tiffany added.

Elliott smiled, ignoring Jamie's large form taking up space in her peripheral vision.

Stephen gestured to the table. "Should we sit?"

"Sure."

Once again, Carly and Jamie ended up right across from them. A server approached the table, and Carly took the lead, ordering several plates of raw-food assortments.

"Oh, but make sure there's no cucumber anywhere. My boyfriend's allergic."

A memory triggered in Elliott's brain. Cool night air against her skin, Jamie's warm body beside her. *I hate cucumbers so much I tell people I'm allergic just so one never gets anywhere near me.*

Did he remember telling her that? She took a breath and chanced a glance at him. His gaze was on her face, handing her a silent reply.

What else did Elliott know about him that his girlfriend didn't?

That was a question she had no business asking, even herself, so she forced herself to concentrate on the conversations going on around her. Stephen's friends (Carly's friends? Tiffany's friends? Whatever.) were entertaining and interesting, swinging easily from topics like sports to pop culture and back to current events.

People periodically snuck away for prolonged periods, returning only for someone else to leave. Tiffany had just drained her second margarita and scurried off somewhere when Elliott leaned close to Stephen to ask what the deal was. In that moment she felt a rush of heat across her skin and darted her eyes across the table.

Jamie's eyes dropped as he stood and walked away.

"Where do people keep going?" she asked.

"Shh," Stephen said conspiratorially. "It's almost our turn."

"For what?"

"You'll see."

A few minutes later, Stephen nudged her shoulder and nodded toward the front of the restaurant. With a frown, she headed that way. As soon as they were near the door, he put a gentle hand on her arm.

"It's our turn for tacos," Stephen said slyly. "Carly gives us a hard time for not giving her food a chance, so we try to be sneaky about it."

Elliott laughed and followed him outside. "You're not as smooth as you think you are."

Sure enough, a bright-orange taco truck was parked a block away. Stephen turned to face her, walking backward as he spoke. "She's probably pretending not to notice. Either way, she hasn't said anything the last two times we've been here, and everyone gets what they want."

That was totally something Yuka would do. "Works for me."

They approached the small crowd of people lined up at the window. Jamie was there, taking his credit card back from the woman at the window and stepping aside. He hadn't looked up yet, tucking his card into his wallet. When he did, his gaze found Elliott and Stephen right away. He seemed to consider what to do, then approached them.

"Not a fan of carrot sticks and celery?" Elliott asked. She hoped it sounded casual.

One corner of his mouth tipped up. "Not as a meal."

"You gotta tell your girlfriend to stop picking this place, man," Stephen said.

Jamie shrugged. "We all take turns. Plus, I think we single-handedly keep this taco truck in business."

"Fair point."

"I thought you said you couldn't come tonight," Jamie said mildly.

"I wasn't planning on it," Stephen returned, then grinned at Elliott. "But I saw this one's car at Starbucks on my way home and thought a change of plans was in order."

Elliott's cheeks warmed, and she looked between the two men. "I'm glad you brought me. Mostly because I love tacos."

Stephen laughed and they took a step forward as the line moved. Jamie stayed where he was.

"I'd better wait over there. See you guys in there." He turned and walked to wait near the pick-up window.

"He's in a weird mood," Stephen muttered, then shrugged. "Anyway, I'm really glad you came."

"Me too. Thanks for the invite."

His blue eyes met hers. "Could I have your number? Maybe we can hang out sometime. Just you and me."

She had the urge to glance at Jamie. Had he heard that?

It doesn't matter, does it? He isn't available.

Jamie wasn't available and she was. Stephen was nice and seemed interested in her. What did she have to lose?

"Sure. I'd like that."

The rest of the night was the best evening Elliott had spent since moving here, until it wasn't.

After dinner, the group had migrated to the patio and continued ordering drinks. Conversation was lively and Elliott finally relaxed, settling in and getting to know everyone better.

Things were in full swing when Tiffany, who was a hilarious and loud drunk, sidled up to Elliott and placed both hands on her shoulders. She'd done the same ten minutes ago, declaring Elliott a striking image of Jennifer Lawrence and how had she not noticed that before, then flitted off to talk to someone else.

"Elliott."

Her face was so serious and wide-eyed as she balanced herself, Elliott couldn't help but laugh. "Tiffany."

Tiffany let out a long, beleaguered sigh. "I have to know. Did you ever find that guy?"

Oh, shit.

"Guy?" Carly materialized beside them. "What guy?"

Shit, shit, *shit.* "No. Um, that's . . . No. It wasn't a big deal." Okay, deflect *better.*

"What guy?" Carly demanded, louder. A few of the others stopped talking.

Tiffany's eyes watered. "Oh my gosh. So when Elliott was in the hospital, she kept talking about this guy. They met the night before her transplant, and it was like love at first sight. She couldn't stop thinking about him. But then she was in the hospital for months, and she didn't have his number."

Carly's jaw dropped open. "No!"

Elliott shook her head, trying to make eye contact with Tiffany in the hope that she'd shut up, but by now everyone was listening, and in her inebriated state Tiffany was oblivious to Elliott's discomfort. She dropped one hand from Elliott's shoulder and dramatically placed it over her heart as she addressed the group. "It was the most romantic thing ever. She said his name while she slept. I finally asked her about it one day, and I swear, Elliott, I've never forgotten the look on your face when you told me about him. Especially the way he kissed you that night."

Elliott wrapped her arms around her roiling stomach. She refused to look at Jamie, sitting at a table nearby. His silence was the loudest of all.

"I would give my left kidney to have someone look that way when they said my name. What was it, again? Something with a *J* . . ."

Words. NOW.

Her brain screamed profanities, but follow-through wasn't a thing Elliott could muster, apparently. Her legs were rooted to where she stood, heart racing. She forced a swallow, and for a second, thought she might choke.

"Jeremy! It was Jeremy." Tiffany finally met Elliott's gaze, triumphant for a beat before taking in and misreading Elliott's expression. Her face fell. "You really never found him again? Did you look for him?"

"I—"

Carly grabbed her hand. "Maybe we could help you find him."

Elliott blinked, a prickling sensation building beneath her eyelids.

"Yeah, I bet between all of us we could track this guy down," Tara chimed in. "I know a Jeremy."

"Me too," Stephen said easily, apparently unbothered at the thought of helping a woman he just asked out find her long-lost love. "Did he work in construction?"

She wouldn't answer that.

"What did your guy look like?"

Her head spun so badly she wasn't even sure who'd asked that last one. Pressing her lips together, she inhaled deeply through her nose, praying she'd stay upright. The sky swirled around her just as a familiar ringtone sounded from her purse.

"I—" She stepped back, away from everyone staring at her. Everyone except Jamie, probably, whom she refused to look at. With a shaking hand she held up the vibrating phone. "Sorry, I need to, um—"

Turning on her heel, she rushed into the restaurant and pressed the phone to her ear. "Yuka. Thank God."

"What? What's happening?" Her best friend's worried voice was the best sound she'd ever heard. "Are you okay?"

"Yeah, just . . . Give me just a second, and I'll call you back, okay?"

Elliott hung up and slipped out the front door, texting the number Stephen had texted to her a short time ago.

Elliott: I'm not feeling well, I'm heading home.

Once she'd made it to her car and had driven two blocks away from the restaurant, she pulled into a vacant parking lot and called Yuka back. She put the call on speaker and set her phone on the console.

"What the hell?"

"Sorry. I was out with Stephen and—"

"Excuse me," Yuka yelled.

Shaken, Elliott rushed to get past that. "He stopped by Starbucks right before I got off and invited me to hang out, but there were a ton of people there. That's not the important part."

"Undecided, but okay. Continue."

"Remember how Tiffany knows Carly? She'd mentioned they run in the same circles sometimes. Well, Tiffany was there tonight, got drunk, and told everyone about Jamie. In *front* of Jamie."

"Oh. Oh, shit. No. That's not good." Yuka paused. "But wait, didn't you give her a fake name back then?"

"Yeah, thank God. No one other than him knew who she was talking about. But the fact that he heard all that . . . Yuka, she went on and on about how in love I was with this guy. I'm mortified."

"What did he do?"

"I have no idea. I couldn't look at him. They'd just asked me to describe the guy when you called." She dropped her forehead to the steering wheel. "This is a fucking disaster."

"It's not great," Yuka agreed. "But let's look at this objectively. You were both there that night; you know how good it was. The conversation, the connection, the erotic kiss—"

"We agreed to strike 'erotic'!"

"We most certainly did not. Anyway, all I'm saying is it shouldn't come as a surprise to him that you were still thinking about it in the days right after. Especially with what you were going through, you know? I'd be shocked as hell if he hadn't felt the same way."

"We'll never know because I'll never ask him. Because he has a girlfriend. Who, as it turns out, saved my life. Which is why this is all so disastrous to come out now, and in front of them, no less."

"Well. Yeah. That part is pretty awful."

"What if someone figures it out and tells Carly?"

"How would they? Jamie's the only one who knows, right?"

"Hell if I know. That group seems more Carly's than his . . . He sort of sticks near her and doesn't talk to the others too much. So I doubt he's close enough with any of them to have told them what happened. But I could be wrong, and it's possible someone knows and will put it together."

"But you said Jamie and Carly weren't together back then, right? Why would it be so bad?"

"Because we've been lying to her by pretending we've never met this entire time!"

"Right." Another pause. "So tell her. Come clean."

"I can't. Not now. It's too late, and I'm not sure it's my place to do that without Jamie on board. I just . . . I don't want to hurt Carly."

"Yeah, okay." Yuka hummed thoughtfully. "We also don't want to make her mad after she promoted the hell out of your business."

Elliott stilled for a beat. She hadn't even thought about that. If Carly suddenly had a reason to hate Elliott, she had the capacity to make a lot of other people hate her, too. Like @ChantalPlans, and every person Chantal could introduce Elliott to.

She wished she could say she didn't care about that part and that the only thing that mattered was being a good friend to the woman who'd given so selflessly to a stranger, but she couldn't ignore the fact the career she wanted was just within reach. "This is just . . ." She crossed her arms over her head and groaned. "I'm a terrible person."

"Don't talk like that. You've been put in a difficult position, and you're handling it as well as you can. There's no perfect way to maneuver these things, okay? You did nothing wrong, except maybe not coming clean about meeting Jamie before, but even that's sticky at this point. You've got Carly's best interests at heart, and that's what matters."

She closed her eyes, suddenly exhausted. "It doesn't feel like enough."

"What you need is to go home, pour yourself a glass of wine, and binge some *Love Is Blind*. Okay? Give yourself a little time to shut off."

"When have I ever been able to shut anything off?"

"I was hoping it was something new we could try. You know, with the fresh start and all."

Elliott snorted. "Some fresh start. You know, I really thought I could do this—be friends with Carly and her friends, including Jamie. Work with his sister, too. But now I just . . . I don't know. Maybe I should give up on this idea of being in Omaha and doing life on my own. Why did I even think it was a good idea? You're in Lincoln. My family's in Lincoln. I'm comfortable there, and I can do this job there. Maybe this is too hard."

"The selfish part of me wants to agree and bring you back home, and I understand why, in this moment, you're second-guessing this decision. But if we remove the situation with Jamie, you're doing everything you ever wanted. You're living on your own, working, building your platform. Making connections and teaching others to grow their businesses. You're pursuing the job you want and having pretty damn good success right off the bat. You're meeting new people and stepping out of the comfort zone you were sentenced to for so long. I'm so damned proud of you, and I'd hate to see you give up so soon at the first bump in the road."

"We're calling this 'a bump in the road'?"

"A big bump, okay? The kind that spills your coffee and makes you yell *shit* so loud the person two cars over hears you. But you keep driving to your destination, right?"

"What if it blew a tire? Bent an axle?"

"Do axles bend? Is that a thing?"

"Hell if I know."

"Well, you call AAA to help you. Or you change the tire yourself because you're an independent woman."

"Like I know how to do that! Does my car even have a spare tire?"

"How far are we taking this analogy?"

"You started it."

"Look, all I'm saying is you're doing something incredible that you've been thinking about for a long time. You want this, even if it's hard to see it through the crap that happened tonight. Don't let this thing with Jamie hold you back from your dreams. No man is worth that, okay? He's not worth it."

Elliott didn't know what to say to that.

"Right?" Yuka pressed.

Elliott frowned, and finally replied, "Right."

But as she restarted the car and made her way back to the apartment, she questioned if she really believed it.

CHAPTER THIRTEEN

Jamie

Jamie's hands shook as he pulled into Carly's driveway and put the car in park.

"You okay?"

Her familiar voice sounded muffled. Far away. His fingers were numb, and he rubbed his palms up and down his thighs, blinking himself back into awareness.

Rational thought was just out of reach, as if his brain could do nothing but man the machinery in his body, directing basic functions like pumping blood and breathing. Single words bounced around his head, jumbled and erratic.

Elliott.

Kiss.

Love.

Carly.

He couldn't seem to grab ahold of any to make sense of them.

"Jamie?" Carly said, probably for the second time.

He looked over at her then, noting the slight frown between her brows. He cataloged her features, ones he'd known for years. He knew so much about her—the good and the not-so-good. Not long ago, he'd have said she knew the same things about him, but that wasn't true anymore, was it?

She didn't know he'd met Elliott last year. That the night he'd spent with Elliott was possibly the best night of his life, and that until the day he *forced* himself to stop thinking about it, he'd replayed kissing her over and over in his head. That he thought he'd moved on and was ready to try again, but that truth was shattered when he saw Elliott at The Patriarch. He'd been fighting himself ever since, unwilling to give in to the selfish, ugly side of his brain he apparently inherited from his father.

Tonight, he'd lost that battle.

Tiffany's words had ripped through him like a shock wave.

She said his name while she slept. Elliott, I've never forgotten the look on your face when you told me about him.

When Elliott, pale and shaken, had walked away, Jamie had desperately wanted to follow her. He'd wanted to ask her if what Tiffany said was true and if even a sliver of those feelings remained.

If he was really, *really* honest, even before all that, when she and Stephen walked in at the beginning of the night? For a split second he'd wished he was the one standing beside her.

It wasn't okay.

He swallowed past the gravel in his throat. "Carly."

The gravity in his voice was unmistakable. She blinked. Straightened.

"I—" he began, but nothing else came. How? How was he supposed to do this? "Shit."

Part of him didn't want to, but if he looked deep down, he'd know it was only because he didn't want to hurt her. Not because he wanted to stay with her. It wasn't enough, and she certainly deserved more than a man struggling with feelings for another woman.

"Are you breaking up with me?" Her bold question startled him.

Fuck, just say it. "Yeah. I think so."

"You *think* so?"

He hated this. He hadn't been in that many serious relationships and hadn't gone through too many breakups, but something told him no matter the number, this would never be easy. Even the first breakup with Carly, which had been mutual and perfectly cordial, had still left him feeling glum for several days afterward.

He gripped the back of his neck. "I'm sorry. I'm fucking this up." His gaze shifted through the window beside her briefly. "I . . . Something just doesn't feel right to me."

To her credit, she didn't seem pissed. Or . . . sad, even. But maybe those would come . . . It had been less than a minute, after all. "What do you mean?"

Even before tonight when Tiffany flipped his world upside down, he'd thought a lot about what his sister had said the other night. About being honest with himself.

He'd also thought about how she'd described her relationship with Jake—which, while only a few years old, was solid as a rock and very different from anything he and Carly had. Comparisons weren't helpful, but when he asked himself basic questions and answered them with the bare truth, the answers didn't leave him content.

Do you challenge each other to be better people? He had no idea but was inclined to say no. He and Carly didn't drag each other into negative habits or anything, but sort of just . . . existed in the same space.

Do you share the same interests and values in life? Interests? Some . . . but they were very different people. He enjoyed time to himself, so he hadn't really considered it a negative before, but from this viewpoint he realized if he was doing something he loved, he felt neutral about whether she was with him or not. Values in life? He didn't know. They didn't really talk about that kind of thing.

Why are you together?

He gripped the back of his neck. "You know how when we decided to get back together, we both agreed to try because it felt so easy? I think you even used the word 'comfortable.'"

Her eyes met his and a hint of defensiveness entered her tone. "It was supposed to be a good thing."

"I know, and it can be. I've always enjoyed being around you. We get along, we're attracted to each other, we both know what to expect. I guess I'm wondering if there's more to it, you know? What if there's a better reason to be with someone than it just making sense?"

She looked at him, expression unreadable. "Where is this coming from?"

"I don't know," he hedged. It was partly true—he was confused as hell about what he was doing. "We're getting older, I guess. I've been thinking about what I want out of life and what my future looks like, and I just want to be honest with myself, and with you, about what we're doing. It feels like we might just be together to avoid being alone, and that's not fair to either of us." He searched her face, trying to read her. When she didn't speak for a moment, he asked, "Am I way off base?"

She blew out a slow breath. "No, I guess not. But relationships don't always have to be about infatuation or overwhelming passion. That stuff fades. Sometimes they're about security and companionship. I thought that's what we both wanted."

"I thought it was, too, but I think I was wrong. I want both. Partnership—and friendship—are important. We have that, and your friendship means a lot to me. Though when I think about it, I'm not sure we ever really had passion. Even at the beginning."

She didn't respond and slowly dropped her eyes to her lap. She wasn't the type to shy away from discussions or arguments when she felt strongly about something, so her calm demeanor in this moment spoke volumes.

Lukewarm wasn't how this should feel.

"I don't want to hurt you, but I just think that maybe this isn't what a relationship is supposed to be. I'm sorry."

"Me too." She turned straight ahead. "But I have to ask, because I didn't see this coming at all . . . Is there someone else you're interested in?"

His heart lurched in his chest.

Yes, having Elliott front and center these last few weeks had thrown him off-balance, and after tonight especially, he finally admitted to himself he wasn't over her. But he had no intention of acting on those thoughts. He wouldn't pursue anything with Elliott. Not for a while, anyway, and even then, who knew if she'd even want to?

"No."

Her chin dropped a fraction, shoulders relaxing.

"Are . . . Will we be okay?" he asked. "After this?"

She grabbed her purse but made no move to get out of the car. "We were last time."

"Yeah. This time it just feels . . . different, I guess." Final.

She glanced over. "I know."

They sat in silence for a few beats. Just as he was debating reaching across to hug her, she opened the door.

She got out and dipped her head down, eyes solemn. "I hope you find what you're looking for."

He swallowed, hoping like hell he'd done the right thing tonight. "I hope we both do."

CHAPTER FOURTEEN

Elliott

Elliott withdrew to Lincoln and worked from her laptop in her parents' backyard over the weekend, wanting to be as far from her apartment as possible.

Under no circumstances did she want to run into Jamie.

Not thinking about it was a different story, especially because she spent most of her time working on designs for Melt My Tart. She'd get in a groove with colors and lettering for a few hours, then something would trip a wire in her memory and there she was, standing in that cooking class with Jamie, warm and smiling as they joked about narwhals.

Which inevitably fast-forwarded her memory to what Tiffany announced and what Jamie must be thinking of her now. Was he weirded out? Did he think she was a stalker? Worse, would he want to talk to her about it?

Tiffany had texted the next day, apologizing for divulging Elliott's personal business that night, and asked if it was the reason Elliott had disappeared. There was no point in making Tiffany feel bad, especially because if Jamie wasn't Carly's boyfriend and they weren't in this situation, Elliott might have appreciated a coordinated effort to locate him on her behalf. So she'd assured Tiffany all was good, she'd just felt off and gone home.

Monday afternoon, Elliott drove back to Omaha and made her way to Old Market for a meeting with Blythe to review design ideas. She'd mocked up a few home-page options she was considering for the website and a basic draft of changes she recommended for the menu. She'd probably gone a little overboard for a client who hadn't officially signed on, but not only did Elliott enjoy doing it, she didn't have much in her portfolio yet. She wanted to show Blythe exactly what she could do.

She slung her camera over her shoulder as she got out of the car, wanting to be prepared if Blythe wanted to move forward and she could take a few fresh shots of the bakery for the website.

Blythe was nowhere to be seen when Elliott walked in, and a young, smiling woman stood behind the counter instead.

"Welcome in," the woman greeted.

Elliott approached the counter, shifting her laptop under her arm. "Hi. I'm here for Blythe?"

"Sure, hang on a sec." The woman disappeared into the back briefly, then returned with Blythe on her heels.

"Hey, Elliott," Blythe said warmly. "Okay if we sit out here? There's a desk in the back, but it's pretty cramped."

"Sure."

She paused at the pastry case. "Can I get you anything?" Waggled her eyebrows. "On the house."

"Oh, that's so nice—but no, thank you. I'm not a big sweets person."

Blythe blinked. "Not even a chocolate chip cookie? Not to toot my own horn, but they're the best in the whole entire world. No wait—the universe."

Elliott laughed. "That's so nice, but I'll pass. I don't care for chocolate."

Blythe just stared at her.

"You don't like *chocolate*?" The other employee sputtered.

"Don't worry—I make up for it in other ways. I could probably eat a whole block of cheese or a gallon of buttered popcorn by myself."

Blythe snorted good-naturedly and continued to a table. "So could I, but I'd finish it off with a brownie."

"Most people would," Elliott agreed and sat across from her. "Before we get started, I wanted to thank you for mentioning me to your friend Jackie. She reached out about help with her logo."

"Oh, sure." Blythe winced. "But we'll see if you're thanking me after you work with her. I figured since you're just starting out you'd want any and all business—I've been there—but she can be a little . . . picky."

Elliott couldn't afford to be choosy right now. "If I made it through working with my parents in one piece, I can handle anything."

"What do they do?"

"They own a bookstore in Lincoln. The biggest fight they ever had was over T-shirts and whether they should use reading puns or not."

"Who doesn't love a good pun?"

"My mother, apparently. My dad and I are with you." Her READING IS A NOVEL IDEA T-shirt was her favorite one to sleep in.

Blythe tapped a finger to her chin. "T-shirts . . . Should I have T-shirts?"

"Maybe. Though I think if you're wanting to consider branded merchandise, other things might be a better place to start, like coffee tumblers or stickers. T-shirts can be hit-or-miss with restaurants."

"Sure, that makes sense. I'm getting ahead of myself anyway." She gestured to everything Elliott spread out on the table. "Where should we start?"

"How about the website?" Elliott flipped open her laptop, multiple minimized screens ready to go. "I have several designs for you to look a—"

Blythe's phone buzzed on the table. She glanced at the screen and grabbed it. "Sorry, it's my brother." She typed out a message and set her phone down again, the screen still illuminated.

Something warm and terrifying twisted in Elliott's chest at the mention of Jamie. The urge to glance at the message was real.

"He's been a little needy this weekend since . . . Well, I'm sure you know about the breakup. Being friends with Carly and all."

Breakup?

"The what?" Her voice came out wobbly.

Blythe winced. "Shoot, I just assumed you'd have heard. I hope they weren't, like, keeping it quiet or anything."

A thread of unease unraveled in her gut. Did something happen after she left the restaurant Friday night? Did Carly somehow find out Jamie was the one Tiffany had told everyone about?

Had he come clean and told her?

Oh God.

"No, but that's . . . I'm sorry to hear that. Are they . . . um. Is he okay?"

"Yeah." Blythe seemed genuinely unconcerned, so it must not have been ugly. "I like Carly and everything, but between you and me, they've always been an odd pair. I think maybe he finally realized they're not the best fit, you know?"

Elliott blinked, unsure how to respond, her thoughts no longer in this room. Somehow she managed to get back to business as if Blythe hadn't just dropped that huge bomb on her, and she made it through the rest of the meeting without incident.

But as soon as she left the bakery, anxiety and frustration rushed in full force, along with a tiny sliver of hope she refused to acknowledge.

Nothing about this was good.

She had to know what happened. Was she somehow responsible?

Blythe said Jamie was fine—was that true? Even if it was, what about Carly? She couldn't bear the thought of Carly's heartbreak.

She had to talk to Jamie.

As soon as she arrived in her apartment she went to the balcony—the exact spot she'd stayed away from all weekend—searching the dog park.

Jamie wasn't there.

She'd have gone straight to his apartment if she knew where it was, but when they first met he'd just pointed in the opposite direction. There were five buildings on that side.

Agitation crept higher up her spine with each passing minute, so she sat down to wait. Took several deep breaths and attempted to calm down. Made a valiant effort to inhale the summer air and enjoy the weather while she waited.

In a stroke of good luck, she didn't have to wait long. A yellow blur moving across the grass half-an-hour later caught her eye, and she lurched to her feet. "You!"

Jamie started and twisted around to look at her. His lips parted but he said nothing.

She jabbed a finger at him. "Wait there."

Less than a minute later, she strode across the sidewalk, heart lodged in her throat. Jamie was rooted to the same spot, hands jammed in his pockets, his expression a mixture of apprehension and melancholy. It was all wrong, the distress in his eyes, and it brought her anger down a notch.

Hank stood beside him, tail wagging, and she gave him a gentle pat of acknowledgment before focusing on Jamie. "You broke up with her?" She tried to minimize the accusation in her tone, but his widened eyes said she was only partly successful. "Why? How could you do that?"

Did he deserve to be interrogated? No.

Was this any of her business? Probably not.

But the guilt simmering just beneath the surface didn't care. Certain she was some kind of homewrecker, she took it out on him.

He said nothing, though his eyes darted across the grass to several other people hovering around the dog park. An older couple slowly made their way toward where he and Elliott stood. He cleared his throat. "Could we, um, maybe go somewhere else to talk about this?"

She sighed and hesitated only a beat before nodding toward her building.

"Okay if Hank comes up?" Jamie asked quietly as she turned on her heel.

She didn't look back and walked to the entrance. "Yeah."

The elevator ride was awkward and silent. Hank seemed to sense the tension and remained close to Jamie's side as they made their way down the hall. Once inside her apartment, she crossed her arms and faced him.

His posture was stiff, a far cry from his usual confident stance as he took in her living room.

Her apartment seemed smaller with him inside. Her reckless heart flickered through the possibilities she'd imagined the first few days living in Omaha—possibilities Jamie might someday be in this space for her. On her couch, in her kitchen, in her bed . . .

All before she'd met Carly. Before she knew who he belonged to.

This time, her voice was barely above a whisper. "Please tell me you didn't break up with her because of me."

His eyes slid closed for a beat, chest rising and falling beneath his gray T-shirt. "I can't."

"Because of what Tiffany said?"

He slowly ran a hand through his hair, leaving it in disarray. His eyes were tired, dark circles underneath. A small piece of her heart went out to him. Most of her concern lay with Carly, but this wasn't easy on him, either.

"That was . . ." He pressed his lips together, and his eyes briefly rose to the ceiling as if he didn't have the right words to say. "Beyond what I could handle."

Her throat closed up, and she took several steadying breaths.

"Did you tell her? About . . . us? That you're the guy?"

Something flared in his eyes when she said *us*. A traitorous part of her relished the word, too.

There is no us *in that sense. There can't be.*

"No."

She expected a wave of relief, but none came. Even if Carly didn't know Elliott was the reason for her ruined relationship, she was the reason all the same. Carly's heartache and tears were Elliott's fault.

"Maybe I should have," he continued. "I don't know. This whole situation was just . . . I didn't see it coming. I didn't expect to still—" He stopped himself, a muscle flexing in his jaw. "I just couldn't continue on like that. It wasn't right and she deserves better."

What had he stopped himself from saying? Continue on like *what*?

Something told her the answers would make this a thousand times harder, so she asked something else instead. "Is Carly okay?"

She watched his face carefully, and strangely, that question seemed to relax him a little. "Breaking up is never fun, but we've been friends a long time. She texted me this morning, asking about some dying plants in her neighbor's backyard, so I'd say we're fine. She's fine."

Only God knew what made her ask the next question. "Are you? Fine?"

He regarded her, eyes searching her face. Maybe trying to determine just how honest he could be. "I'm not sure yet."

She had a disturbing urge to step forward and hug him. This had been a bad idea, inviting him up here. Where it was quiet and they were alone. Where his glasses-framed hazel eyes were kind and gentle and not at all demanding.

Instead, she blurted, "I can't date you. If that's why you broke up with her, thinking we'd, um . . ." She folded her arms across her chest. "I won't do that to Carly."

"I understand," Jamie said, sincerity dripping from his words. He hadn't moved a single step from where he'd stopped when he first entered her apartment. His entire face turned downcast, the cheerful dimple nowhere to be found. "I didn't expect anything from you. I made the choice myself, regardless of whether anything was possible between us or not. I get that the connection you have with her makes this . . ."

"Impossible."

He winced slightly at the word. The finality of it. His mouth opened as if he'd say something, then closed again. He adjusted Hank's leash in his hand.

She folded in on herself. "Part of me wishes I'd never moved here. All I've done is cause problems."

He shook his head, frowning. "None of this is your fault. I made the choice to get back together with Carly when I wasn't ready, and that's on me. You've done nothing but good since you've been here. Carly was so happy to meet you, and you're doing incredible work for my sister. Her business will flourish because of it, and so will everyone else you work with. And you're doing something you've always wanted to. Going after your dreams."

He reached across and gripped one forearm as he spoke. "I made myself crazy last year, wondering what happened to you. Wondering if maybe I should have pushed a little more to make sure you were okay . . . Worried you'd kept yourself a secret because you were scared or sick, or worse. I can't tell you how glad I was to learn you were alive and well and . . . happy. Especially after learning what you'd been through and why you'd come back. So, I . . . I hope you stay. If for no other reason than you deserve something good. No—something incredible. You've been through a lot, and you're just now living the life you want to live, and you should have nothing less."

It took everything in her not to let the tears burning beneath her lids fall. She would the second he walked out that door.

Happy, comforting tears at his kind words and encouragement to focus on herself and what she wanted.

And lonely, brokenhearted tears because she wasn't living the life she wanted to. She wanted him in her life in a way he never could be. How long would she grieve the loss of that particular dream—one she'd held close for an entire year?

Her bones were like iron, her entire body weighing her down. "For what it's worth, I'm sorry I left you like that. With nothing." It was no use thinking about how different things might be if she'd given him a number, an email, something. But she wished she had, all the same.

"You had a lot on your mind."

Hank let out a slight whine, probably wondering why they were all just standing around. Jamie gave him a pat on the head, never releasing her gaze.

"Even if I wanted to . . ." What? Be with him? Try? She couldn't make herself say it out loud. "I'll never do anything to hurt her."

He exhaled an audible breath. "I wouldn't want to, either."

She believed him.

"I'm not expecting, or asking for, anything," he said for the second time.

She nodded. "Yeah. Okay."

Hank stood up and barked impatiently, and when Jamie shushed him, he barked again. "I'd better get him out of here."

"Okay," she repeated, suddenly and inexplicably sad.

"Elliott?"

Her eyes met his. "Yeah?"

"Do you think we can be friends?"

Friends.

She turned the question over in her mind, inspecting it like a pending contract. From the minute she'd realized he was Carly's boyfriend, being friends with Jamie is what she'd tried to be. And while externally she thought she'd done pretty well, deep down she'd crashed and burned.

Could she be in the same room with him and not want to touch him? Catch a hint of his soap and stop herself from leaning in, just a little, for a second hit?

Would she ever stop wishing she was funnier so he'd laugh more and flash that adorable dimple?

Could she voice the hundreds of questions she'd wanted to ask him over the past year without falling for him even more? And avoid answering the same questions about herself so he wouldn't get in too deep? Because she hadn't let anyone inside her head, not really, except for Yuka and her family.

If anyone could get past her defenses, it would be him.

Could she really and truly be *just* friends with Jamie Sullivan without making herself (or them both) miserable in the process?

She didn't know, and despite the hope in his hazel eyes, she said as much, unwilling to sugarcoat it. "I'm not sure."

He flashed a small smile at that, surprising her. "I'm not sure I can be friends with you, either," he admitted. "But I'd like to at least give it a try. If that's okay."

It was possible she'd regret it later, but she didn't stop the answering grin that pulled her lips up.

"Yeah, okay. Let's try."

CHAPTER FIFTEEN

Jamie

When Jamie arrived home the next evening after dinner with his mom and a run to the grocery store, he received a call he wasn't expecting. He was just pushing through the front door of his apartment when his phone rang.

It was his sister.

He slid his thumb across the screen and put the phone between his shoulder and his ear, pulling things out of the bag. "Hey."

"Hi," she said. That was it.

Jamie waited for her to continue. Blythe was a texter through and through, so when she called, it was usually because she had something specific to say. She always got straight to the point and got the hell off the phone.

When she said nothing more, he frowned, pausing with a box of whole wheat pasta in his grip.

"What's up?" he prompted.

"Elliott's her, isn't she?"

It took him a second to connect who she meant by "her." He stopped in the middle of his apartment. "What?"

"Elliott. Yesterday when she was at the shop, she mentioned hating chocolate. I've only heard of one other person who said they didn't like chocolate, and it was that girl you told me you met last year. It suddenly clicked when I got home after work."

Jamie didn't know what to say.

"She's the girl you tried to find."

He released a burdened sigh, his eyes drifting closed. "Yeah."

"She's also the reason you came over that night, asking about connections with other women."

He cleared his throat around the lump forming there. "Yeah."

"*And* she's the one Carly donated bone marrow to."

He opened his eyes. "You're telling me things I already know."

"This is crazy, Jamie. What are the odds?"

He didn't answer that, and instead pulled a beer from the six-pack he'd just bought and slid the rest in the fridge.

"Are you okay?" she asked, tone gentler. "I remember how you were after she disappeared. I can't say I understand being that into someone after one night, but you were totally gone over her. I've never seen you like that."

He had the sudden urge to cry.

He couldn't remember the last time he'd cried. "I've never felt a connection like that."

"She's been back, what, a month now? Do you feel it still?"

"Yes." It was the first time he'd admitted it out loud. "I tried to ignore it at first, but . . . that's why I ended things with Carly. I don't expect anything to happen with Elliott, but it wasn't fair to stay with Carly when there was another woman I kept thinking about all the damn time." He fell backward on the couch and popped the top off his beer. Hank leaped up and stretched out beside him.

"Does Elliott feel the same way about you?"

"I don't know." Sometimes, with the way she looked at him, he thought she might. Hoping for it was pointless, though, and would only make things worse. "But even if she did, Carly saved her life. She'd never do anything to hurt her." He took a long pull from the bottle, then pressed the heel of his hand to one eye to stem the sudden burning beneath his lids. "I don't want to, either."

"You really think Carly would care? The first time you two broke up, I saw her out with a new guy six days later."

"It doesn't matter. I didn't break up with her to pursue Elliott. And Elliott doesn't want me to. Can you just be supportive and let me wallow in what a fucked-up situation this is?"

"Oh, this is definitely fucked up. The woman you basically fell for in a single night and who ghosted you for a year finally returns—but by that point you had a girlfriend, one who saved her life, because of course, so you can't be with her. And because you still had feelings for her and are a decent guy, you ended things with said girlfriend. So now you don't have either one."

He scrubbed a hand down his face. "Appreciate the recap."

"I assume Carly doesn't know who Elliott is to you."

"She doesn't," he confirmed. "That was Mistake Number One, but it's too late now."

"Is it? What if you told her? Maybe she'd understand."

He'd considered that, too, but it didn't seem worth it. "Carly's a good person, but she can hold a grudge. I should have come clean right away, but it's gone too far. If I did it now it would hurt more than just Carly and me. Elliott would get caught in the middle, and she doesn't deserve that, either."

"So you're just going to be miserable, Elliott will be miserable, and Carly will move on and find someone else who probably fits her better because you two never made sense in the first place? All because you don't want to take a risk?"

He frowned. "I don't think Elliott will be miserable."

"Based on what you told me about that night, it's hard to believe she didn't feel the same about you. I wouldn't be surprised if she's just as torn up about this, wishing there was some way things were different." She paused for a second, her tone turning thoughtful. "I could do some recon, you know. I hired her, and I could talk to her—"

Jamie shot forward. "Don't you *dare*. I mean it. Promise me you won't say anything to her."

"I'm supposed to keep pretending I don't know who she is? That I don't know?"

"Yes."

She let out an annoyed sigh. "Fine. I promise."

He sank into the cushions and leaned his head back. A promise from his sister was as good as gold. "Thank you."

Jamie stared at the ceiling as a few beats of silence passed. He'd thought breaking up with Carly would give him a measure of relief from the guilt that had plagued him recently. Instead, his body and his heart just felt . . . heavy.

"I'm sorry you're going through this," Blythe finally said. "I'm here for whatever you need."

His chest squeezed. "Thank you," he said again. He was lucky to have her.

"But can I say one more thing?"

"Depends on what it is."

"I know you're trying to do the right thing here. You've always shied away from things that cause other people discomfort. And if you ultimately decide staying away from Elliott and not talking to Carly is that right thing, I'll support you. But I just want to make sure you know that no matter how you spin it, no one walks away from this unscathed. There's something to be said for considering other people's emotions, but sometimes our decisions are going to hurt people. Sometimes the truth hurts, but is that a reason to hold it back? Even if Carly got upset, I'd bet a hundred lemon tarts it would be short term and she'd move on. At some point, you need to consider the long term, and consider your own happiness, too, and what this could mean for your future. It's impossible to keep everyone happy all the time, as much as I know that bothers you."

He drained the rest of his beer and put the bottle on the coffee table. Hank shifted and draped his head across Jamie's thigh.

"I don't want to be like Dad," he finally whispered. "Always chasing a new feeling. Never settling or being content with what I've got." What he felt around Elliott was like nothing he'd ever experienced before, it was true. It wasn't something he'd constantly been chasing. On the contrary, she'd come out of nowhere like a heat wave in December.

He hadn't been looking for her and never saw her coming.

Now, though, he could hardly think of anything else. He wanted to talk to her, be in her presence. He wanted to know more about her and let his gaze roam over her freckles and study the colors in her eyes.

He wanted to touch her and find out if it still felt like fireworks.

Would this feeling always be unique to him and Elliott? Or was it possible he could feel it again with someone else? If this was the feeling his dad and brother were after, he could hardly blame them for wanting it, even if their methods of going about it were pure shit.

"You're not, Jamie. You. Aren't. Dad," she repeated pointedly. "Hear me?"

He cleared his throat. "Yeah."

A loud noise sounded in the background, and Blythe groaned. "I gotta go check on Jake and Holden before they tear up my living room. Just do me a favor, okay?"

"Maybe."

"Something tells me this won't just go away. Consider the consequences—both of them. Worst-case scenario, both women hate you and neither end up in your life."

"Is this supposed to be helping?"

"You didn't let me get to the best-case scenario."

It didn't seem possible anything was worth the risk of what she'd just said. "What's that?"

She paused for a beat, probably for dramatic effect.

"You end up with everything you've ever wanted."

130

Jamie laid low over the next two and a half weeks, avoiding thinking about his conversation with his sister. Blythe and his buddy Ian texted him a couple of times, but he'd declined their offers to hang out. He'd been looped into a barhop Tara organized, and while he was pretty confident he and Carly would be fine around each other, he didn't want anyone else to feel awkward. It was too soon.

He'd never minded being alone and kind of enjoyed the peace and quiet, truth be told. He spent his days at the nursery or on jobsites, headphones in and content to be outside. He'd long ago decided trees made damn good colleagues—living, breathing, selfless companions that offered beauty, shade, and life without expectation or judgment.

Other than spending a day with his nephew and regular Tuesday dinners with his mom, he spent his evenings at home, reading and running. The latter had become a necessary outlet, and Hank wasn't complaining. In fact, he'd become a complete nuisance on the two days Jamie'd taken a break, constantly barking at his leash and pawing at the door.

Which brought him to his current situation: beseeching his beloved dog with an apologetic gaze.

"I can't do it, bud," Jamie said from his sprawled position on the couch. "I spent the day with Holden to give Blythe and Jake some time to themselves, and that kid ran me ragged. Four-year-olds are no joke."

Hank sat by the door and barked.

"No."

Another bark.

"Hank, no."

A sad, high-pitched whine.

Jamie made the mistake of catching Hank's eye and groaned. He couldn't resist that pathetic face. "*Fine*, we can go outside, but only to the park, okay? No run today. My calves are toast."

Jamie rose from the couch, and Hank leaped up, circling his legs and nearly knocking him over. "Easy." He slipped the leash on, and Hank fairly yanked him through the door.

He took a deep breath as they stepped into the evening air. Sunset was Jamie's second-favorite time of day, just after sunrise. There was just something about those moments of transition when his part of the world went from night to day and back again. The stillness, the colors, the opportunity for something new . . . It never failed to give him a sense of calm and the urge to just stand still and breathe. Just for a second.

Resisting Hank's intent to pick up the pace, Jamie strolled through the buildings and to the grassy knoll leading up to the dog park. He wasn't prepared for Hank to suddenly veer right, and he cursed as he barely caught himself from falling on his ass.

"What the—"

"Hank!"

Elliott materialized to his right, sitting in the grass with her legs extended straight in front of her.

In the fading daylight he hadn't even noticed her.

A grin split across her face as she welcomed Hank into her arms. "You're energetic today, aren't you?"

"Always," Jamie muttered, followed by a "Hey."

She glanced up at him. "Hi."

It was the first time they'd spoken since deciding to give friendship a try.

Hank planted one paw beside her and another on her thigh, licking her face. She smiled again and laughed, her face significantly brighter than when she'd looked at Jamie. He glanced away, irritated.

He was jealous of his damn dog.

"How are you?" Her voice floated up, soft and tentative.

"Fine. You?"

"I'm good."

He slid his gaze back to her. Was she really? Her eyes looked tired, and she absently brushed her hand across her upper collarbone, something he'd noticed she did often, almost a nervous gesture. It was impossible to tell with the way she kept her expression cool—placid, almost.

Then he noticed her clothes. Shorts, T-shirt, running shoes. Phone and earbuds on the grass beside her. "Are you going running?"

"Yeah. I took a lap around the building to warm up and stopped to stretch."

He frowned. "It's almost dark."

She angled her head, eyebrows lifting. "I see that."

Part of his brain tried to interject—this wasn't his business. "You shouldn't run out here by yourself at night."

"There are lights everywhere."

Yeah, but just outside the path dark corners and bushes lurked everywhere. Countless places for someone with nefarious intentions to hide. And if she had earbuds in, unaware of her surroundings? He didn't like it one bit.

Basic facts pointed to a woman in that kind of situation being less safe than a man. It sucked, but that was how things were. He'd have felt the same if it were any woman in this scenario.

Probably.

Hank leaped at her side and crouched on his front paws, tail wagging with ferocity.

"Would you take Hank with you?" Jamie asked.

She glanced at his dog, then back at him. Her eyes narrowed. "Because you think I can't take care of myself?"

Jamie swallowed. "I'd be lying if I said it wouldn't make me feel better, knowing he was with you, but mostly because he's dying to go. I've taken him running more than usual lately, and he's gotten used to it. I babysat my nephew today, and I'm exhausted, but he's been driving me crazy ever since I got home. You'd actually be doing me a huge favor. Otherwise he'll be bouncing off the walls all night, and I won't get any sleep."

She eyed him, considering. Hank shifted back on his haunches, a sudden picture of perfect manners, as if he knew something important was at stake.

Jamie tried one last time. "He'd love you for it." Not to mention Jamie's peace of mind. "I'm in 26A; you could just bring him by when you're done."

Hank whined, and Elliott's face went soft. Jamie could have hugged him.

"You're sure?" she asked.

He dropped the leash by her feet before she could change her mind. "Completely."

She stood, brushed off her shorts, and picked up the leash. Hank sniffed her shoes and pranced back and forth, aware of what was coming.

"You ready?" she asked him, and Jamie's heart squeezed. Hank barked.

She slid her gaze back to Jamie and shrugged, smiling.

"I guess we'll see you in a bit."

CHAPTER SIXTEEN

Elliott

Elliott lasted three miles before she quit, and it wasn't because of the usual reasons, like burning lungs or a muscle cramp.

It was her brain.

Every runner knew the sport was mental as well as physical. More so, even. That was one reason she loved it so much—it was a place she'd found she could stop worrying and stop thinking about anything *but* the run. She could plug in her earbuds, listen to something with a strong beat, and focus on the pound of her feet across the pavement.

Not today. Instead of thinking about appropriate things like the perfect weather or the date she'd had with Stephen the night before, only one subject occupied her focus.

A tall ex-baseball player in gray sweatpants and a fitted white T-shirt, with mussed, dirty-blond hair, like he'd just run his fingers through it. She always looked for the dimple, because who wouldn't want to see that man smile? But today was the first time she'd noticed the thick vein descending each bicep, intersecting the crease of his elbow and leading to the most deliciously sculpted forearms she'd ever seen.

Climbing trees did that body good.

She groaned and walked to the nearest curb, taking a seat and dropping her head into her hands.

She hated herself for being so attracted to Jamie. It was half of the reason she'd agreed to go out with Stephen last night—in the hope that spending time with another man might broaden her perspective and show her what else was out there. Stephen had given her an easy out when he'd texted with a Hey, if you never reconnected with that Jeremy guy, still want to hang sometime?, but she'd wanted to go.

Jamie had been front and center in her brain for so long, she figured maybe she just needed a do-over in the man department. With someone different.

Stephen took her bowling, and she'd had a good time. He was an interesting guy, and their conversation flowed easily. He mostly talked about himself, though, spending a good chunk describing his tattoos in extreme detail, and he seemed uncomfortable if the topic took a turn toward anything related to her illness. She didn't try to bring it up, but it had been such a big part of her twenties, it was hard to leave it out completely.

As she ran, Hank keeping stride easily beside her, she'd quickly realized her efforts were futile. Because while she could imagine Jamie's jawline with disturbing accuracy, she couldn't recall even one of Stephen's tattoos. Instead of wondering what Stephen thought of their brief kiss goodnight, she wondered if Jamie ever said her name when she wasn't around.

The telltale burn of impending tears pricked beneath her eyelids, and she rubbed the back of her hand across them.

"Dammit," she muttered. She scratched Hank on the head and stood, making her way to Jamie's building.

They arrived at his apartment and she knocked. A few seconds later the door opened to reveal a shirtless Jamie.

He stood there, one thick arm braced against the doorframe, with all that dark-blond hair, expressive hazel eyes, and those stupid hot glasses on his face, and miles upon miles of smooth skin stretched across taut muscles. Oh God, were those freckles on his shoulders?

Her jaw drifted downward and she caught herself, snapping it shut.

"Oh, sorry. Hang on just a sec . . ." He released the door and stepped away, catching it again just as it was about to click shut. A white T-shirt hung around his neck, and he threaded his arms through it.

Elliott simultaneously wanted to thank him and weep with disappointment.

Hank nosed his way into the apartment, and she held out the leash.

Jamie took it, seemingly careful not to touch her fingers, and leaned down to unclip the other end from Hank's collar. "How'd it go?"

"Great. You were right—he's the perfect partner."

Jamie grinned and her heart stuttered. "Told you."

"Thanks for letting me borrow him."

Hank took a few steps behind Jamie and collapsed onto the carpet, panting happily. "No, thank you," Jamie said, laughing. "Look at him."

Elliott smiled. "He's such a good dog."

"I'm lucky to have him."

Their eyes met and held, and Elliott realized just how close they stood. If she took one step forward, her chest would brush his. Something flickered in his gaze, thick and warm, and the air surrounding them turned still and expectant, as if the very universe was poised for their next move.

"Want some water before you go?" he asked.

Despite only running half her planned route, she *was* thirsty. It would only take her a few minutes to get to her place for literally the exact same thing, but . . . "Sure."

He held the door open wider, and she stepped inside, resisting the impulse to smell him as she passed. She perched on the edge of the couch near the door. She wouldn't stay long.

Jamie filled a glass with ice water and brought it to her, lowering himself to the armchair furthest from her. His legs extended so far one knee brushed the coffee table.

It was then she noticed the flowers.

"Are those peonies?"

He smiled. "Yeah, they're my favorite. My mom had so many she didn't know what to do with them, so she gave some to me." An adorable flush crept up his neck. "I, uh . . . Having plants around makes me happy."

She remembered.

His apartment was full of life, with several other potted plants dispersed around the living room and kitchen. She didn't have a single thing at her place. "Peonies are my favorite, too."

His gaze locked on hers, another tangible connection arcing between them. It was really inconvenient, how perfect they seemed to be for each other.

He swallowed and adjusted his glasses. "So how far'd you end up going?"

"Not as far as I wanted," she admitted.

His brows came together. "Was it Hank?"

"No," she said quickly. "He was great." She scrambled to find a reason to give him other than his too-handsome face and took a drink to buy some time. Finally, she offered a different truth. "I think I'm just tired. I haven't been sleeping well."

Concern etched heavier on his face. He leaned forward a little, bracing his forearms across his knees. "Why not?"

She rotated the cold glass between her fingers. "I've, um, had some trouble with anxiety since the transplant. Actually," she clarified with a humorless laugh, "that's a lie. It started after my first diagnosis when I was seventeen. Even when I'm considered cancer-free like I am now, I'm constantly terrified the leukemia will come back. I went into remission once, but it came back. The transplant is supposed to work better, but it's not a guarantee."

Something in his eyes when she said that last part flickered in . . . distress? It was hard to tell, and he quickly dropped his gaze. "Would you know if it was back? Based on how you feel?"

She shrugged. "My first symptoms were vague. Like fatigue and headaches. Lots of other things can cause that stuff, too. I had some bruising, which I now know was because my platelets were low. Every time I see something on my skin, I desperately try to remember if I bumped into something recently, just so I have an explanation."

Jamie's head slowly moved back and forth as he processed. "That's . . . rough. I'm really sorry you have to deal with that. I can't imagine having that kind of thing weighing on me."

Hank rose from where he'd landed on the floor and approached her, shouldering his way to sit on the floor between her legs. She couldn't help but grin at him, the goofy dog. Something about his presence— and Jamie's—made the words spill out. "It wasn't so bad when I was in the hospital or living at home. At least there, I had people around me. In the hospital I was attached to so many machines, if anything went wrong the nurses knew it before I did. It was annoying as hell but comforting at the same time, to know someone else was keeping an eye on me. And even though it wasn't that intense at my parents' house, at least I knew someone else was there. If I thought something was wrong, I could just call out and someone could help me."

She should have stopped there, but she kept going, her voice nearly a whisper. She hadn't realized just how badly she'd wanted to talk about this with someone. "I wanted to live alone because I feel like I should. And I *want* to, I really do. I'm twenty-eight and have never done it. I'm an adult, for crying out loud. But when I'm in that apartment, alone, all I can think about is the fact that if something happened to me while I was in there, no one would know. I have no one to call out to. No one to help me." Those fears had led to her short-term lease agreement in the first place, and she'd almost cancelled twice since arriving to Omaha, ready to throw in the towel and head back home. Hank laid his head on her knee, and she found comfort in the weight of it. "It just gets to me sometimes. At night, mostly."

Elliott closed her eyes and took a deep breath. She'd never admitted any of that out loud before.

When she opened them again, she found Jamie sitting very still, just watching her, his expression somehow compassionate and troubled at the same time.

"I'm sorry," Elliott said, embarrassment creeping in. Why had she said all that? "I didn't mean to unload that on you. I just . . . That's why I can't sleep."

Jamie said nothing. He gripped the back of his neck, his gaze dropping beside her to the floor. With this profile view, a muscle flexing in his cheek became visible, as if he were clenching his jaw.

Well. She'd freaked him out. She took a huge gulp of water, forcing the ice-cold liquid down. She'd finish it and get the hell out of here.

"I wish . . . ," he started, his voice so low and throaty something warm slid across her skin. He pressed his lips closed for a second, met her eyes, and tried again. "I wish there was something I could do. To help."

That was the thing, though. No one could. "Thank you," she said anyway, because she appreciated people's concern for her. Pity, she didn't care for, but genuine hope for her well-being was always welcome.

"I started a terrible book the other day. It was so boring I was asleep in under five minutes. We're talking really, really bad. Wanna borrow it?"

She laughed, and it felt really, really good. "What was it?"

"Some pretentious memoir that hit the *NYT* bestseller list last week. I've had more time to read lately, so I figured why not? It was a mistake."

It wasn't lost on her his "time to read" was likely due to his breakup. "I mean, I'll give it a shot. I'm pretty desperate at this point."

He dipped his chin in a small nod, looking pleased with himself, and stood. She drained the glass while he went to another room and was on her feet when he returned.

He noticed and opened his door as he held the book out to her. "I hope you hate it as much as I did."

She tucked it in her arm. "Thanks. For . . . everything. Hank, the water, the book."

The conversation.

She'd never admit it to him—barely even acknowledged it to herself—but she felt just a touch lighter as she walked through his door.

"Would you want to do that again?" he blurted from behind her.

She glanced over her shoulder.

He shifted so his hip held the door open but made no move to follow her. "Run with Hank, I mean. I meant what I said a while back, that you'd be welcome to take him anytime you want. He loves it, and it would help me out on days I'm too busy to take him myself. I, um, I could give you my number. You could just text me if you wanted to come grab him."

That was probably a bad idea. And yet, some foolish part of her thrilled at the idea. "Oh. Sure."

She swallowed and faced him again, unlocking and holding out her phone. With a small smile he took it and programmed in his number, then handed it back.

"I hope this is okay, but I want you to know you can use it anytime. If you need anything, even just a reminder someone's close by. I know it's not the same as your family or friends, and I'm definitely no doctor. But I'm a few minutes away, and if you ever needed help . . ." He paused for a beat and slid his hands into his pockets. "Or even just a friend. I'm . . . I'm here."

Tender emotion flooded her, and she kept her eyes down, refusing to look at the man who made her feel things she didn't want to. She almost deleted his number right then and there.

"I'm sorry," came his quiet voice. "You don't have to use it, obviously. I—"

She shook her head quickly, swiping at her cheeks. "No, it's not that. I appreciate the gesture, really. It's just . . ." She paused to collect herself. "You're a really nice guy. That's all."

His forehead creased as if he were in pain. "I'm not."

"You are. Not everyone would offer to do that."

"It's nothing, Elliott. If it would help you sleep better and feel safe, I'd . . ." He stopped suddenly and clenched his jaw, as if trying to determine if he should keep going. The words he finally spoke were quiet but fierce.

"I think I'd do just about anything."

CHAPTER SEVENTEEN

Elliott

The book actually worked. Whether it was the dull, never-ending descriptions or the sheer physical and emotional exhaustion of the day, she'd never know, but either way, she was asleep ten minutes after climbing into bed.

It backfired, though, in spectacular fashion. Because even though she drifted into blessed slumber, she also dreamed about Jamie.

It was inevitable, really, that she'd fall asleep to the mental image of his shirtless torso composed of muscles stacked in perfect rows. As she drifted off, her memory took her back to the night they met, the meddling bitch.

Of course, things went very differently this time. Better, as dreams usually went, and she went straight to the moment when he'd rasped those desperate, desire-tinged words into her mouth.

"Come home with me."

She sucked in a breath at the feel of his tongue tracing her bottom lip.
"Okay."

He stilled. Lifted his head a few inches.

Their gazes collided. "Okay?"

She nodded, and in the next second was being pulled along the sidewalk behind a huge, sexy man, power walking as if he were in some sort of competition. His hand was warm and large, his fingers threaded between each of hers.

He led her to a black truck in a nearby parking lot. The lights flickered when he unlocked it. She thought he might open the door for her, but instead he grabbed her face between his palms and pressed an open-mouthed kiss to her lips.

Elliott fell back against the door with a moan, wrapping her arms around his shoulders. He pressed into her and gripped her thigh just above her knee, pulling her leg up and around his waist. Fire exploded in her belly, and she tangled shaky hands in his hair, pulling and tugging like a crazed, horny teenager.

"I need—" he started, but she captured his lips again, swallowing the words.

"I know," she murmured, shifting her pelvis.

He groaned and lowered his head to her neck. His facial hair grazed the tender skin of her neck. "I need to get you out of here."

Somehow he slid their single, entangled unit of bodies far enough to the side to get the door open. She fell into the seat and cupped her hand around his neck, pulling him halfway into the truck. They were nothing but tongues and lips and teeth.

And hands. Good God, his hands.

"I can't drive like this," he choked out. He pulled away, his eyes twinkling when she let out a squeak of protest.

He was in the driver's seat so fast he must have jogged around the truck. He took one look at her, and at the fire burning in his hazel eyes, Elliott snapped.

She jumped on him. Literally. Twisted around, hurdled over the console, and straddled him.

"Fuck," he said in the best way. His hands went straight to her hips, pulling her as close as they could get in this position, and sucked her lower lip into his warm mouth.

Her hands slid under his shirt, tickling up his ridged abs and to his chest. He shuddered, kissing her harder for a beat before dropping his head back. "Elliott."

She traced his earlobe with her teeth. "Hmm?"

"Let me get you home first. Please."

"No. Figure something else out." She glanced in the back seat. "Looks roomy enough."

"I'm six-three."

She straightened and rolled her eyes. "Show off."

He laughed, his bright eyes taking in every inch of her flushed face. "You're so damn beautiful."

Her chest ached. "Yeah, this needs to happen now." She tried to pull her legs out to climb into the second row, and her back hit the steering wheel, sending the blare of his horn into the parking lot. They both froze.

"Oops."

Jamie's eyes darted through the windows. When he seemed convinced no one was around, he gripped her hips in his palms. "I can't have sex with you in the back seat of my truck."

"Why not?"

"It doesn't feel right."

"I want you to."

He closed his eyes and inhaled a shaky breath. "If someone saw us . . . we could get arrested."

"Why, are you loud?"

"Shit," he muttered, a sexy smile tilting his lips. "What am I going to do with you?"

"Take me in your back seat, I hope."

His fingers flexed, his thumbs pressing against her hip bone just shy of the point of pain. He studied her, as if trying to read her face.

She'd already said it out loud. Twice. It was his call now.

He nodded quickly. "Okay. Just let me . . ." He reached around her to turn on the ignition. With Elliott still straddling his lap, he leaned to the right and slowly moved to the back of the lot to a darkened corner, away from other cars.

When he flipped the engine off, she grinned and traded his lap for the bench seat in the back. He reached into his console and held up a condom with a cock of his eyebrow and somehow maneuvered his large body to join her.

His fingers slid through her hair, sending tiny shivers of sensation down her spine. He pressed his forehead against hers. "Sure about this?"

"Yes," she whispered, and sealed her lips to his.

Today wasn't a good day.

She'd had good days and bad days since moving to Omaha. On good ones, Elliott felt confident, fulfilled, and energetic. Usually, those were days she met with a client (which, thankfully, had become a more frequent occurrence), worked at Starbucks, or when she holed up at a local café or coffee shop to work on a design project she was excited about.

On bad days, loneliness crept in. She missed her parents, missed Yuka, and got inside her head. She questioned if coming here had been the right choice, stressed over the next lab draw and oncologist visit, and wondered if the cancer would come back and she'd just die of leukemia anyway.

What if all this progress was pointless in the end?

She'd promised herself she wouldn't run back home to Lincoln all the time, because that defeated the purpose of trying to do life without the constant support system she'd depended on for so long. Even if they vehemently denied it, they needed a break from constantly watching over her, too.

But for some reason, the absence of those she loved the most hit hard today. She wasn't sure why, but the fact she'd had dreams of Jamie almost nightly the entire week since she first went running with Hank probably didn't help matters.

Reminders of how things could have been if she'd made a different choice that night had been relentless.

Stephen had texted her a few times, too, which probably should have made her feel better. A nice, attractive guy who'd taken her out wanted to keep talking and see her again. But instead of agreeing to a second date, she'd stalled with an excuse about a deadline for a new client.

She spent the morning texting with Yuka over breakfast, then decided to finally go look for art for her apartment. Her parents' house was full of paintings they'd collected from all over, and one in particular hung in her old bedroom. She'd spent countless days in bed, too tired and sick to get up for anything except to pee, and the bright colors in that painting had always been a source of comfort. Maybe having some color on her walls here was what she needed to feel more at home.

She got dressed and drove to Dundee, the historic neighborhood Jamie had told her about. Her budget was limited, and she figured she was more likely to find something she could afford there than at the fancy galleries in Old Market.

The artist co-op opened at ten, and she must have been one of the first people in the door because the large room she entered was completely empty. Paintings hung on every wall, with even more propped on tables or along the floor. A few sculptures dotted the space, and the middle of the room was filled with tables of jewelry, soaps, and other handmade goods. Elliott slowly made her way around the room, reading the little cards next to the paintings to learn about the artist and their piece, and to take note of the price. Some were completely out of her range, while others seemed to be priced well below what they were probably worth.

She kept going back to one of a mountain range, hanging next to the window. At least, she was 99 percent sure that's what it was. The shapes were fairly distinguishable with a flat foreground and triangular, jagged structures jutting into the sky, but the use of color stood out in its nonconformity. Instead of green, brown, and blue, the canvas was awash with pinks, oranges, purples, as if the pine trees were peach and the rock faces a bright magenta. Occasional golds and charcoal-gray imitated shadows, with a few strokes of emerald green and white here and there, but not where you'd expect.

Nothing about the images were typical, yet she knew exactly what she was looking at.

"What do you think?"

Elliott jumped at the voice and spun around. A woman sat in a dark-green chair near the back, smiling and waving.

Elliott pressed her hand to her racing heart. She crossed the space. "I'm so sorry. I didn't see you when I came in."

"Don't worry about it. I kind of blend in back here." The woman, who wore a long, colorful skirt and her salt-and-pepper hair in a braid down her back, gestured to her wrapped foot. "I had a little accident and can't get around well right now, so I'm sort of stuck."

"Oh, I'm sorry."

"I'm fine. Even if my husband disagrees. He made me stay home the first week, but I told him I'd divorce him if he tried to stop me today. He's already called me twice." She rolled her eyes. "Men."

Elliott laughed, liking this woman already.

"But I can still tell you anything you want to know about the art or the artists who show here. Did you have any questions?"

"Actually, I'm interested in that mountain painting at the front. Do you know if the artist has any more like that? I was hoping to buy a few."

The woman smiled. "As a matter of fact, that one's mine. I have more, but they're at my studio. I'm here most of the day, but if you had time tomorrow I'd be happy to meet you there and show you what I have."

"Really?"

"Of course." She handed Elliott a business card that said, MAUREEN MILLER, PAINTER WITH HEART. "The address is on there. How's two?"

Elliott grinned, her mood lifting. "Two would be perfect."

CHAPTER EIGHTEEN

Jamie

Unknown: Do you have a hammer?

Jamie was about to respond with *Wrong number* when a second message came through.

Unknown: It's Elliott.

The way his breath caught wasn't normal.

It was just . . . He'd sort of given up on hearing from her. It had been two weeks since he'd put his number in her phone and . . . nothing. Not even a text to share her number, and no requests to take his dog out.

He was a little offended on Hank's behalf.

He'd told himself it was probably for the best, though, because when she'd told him about her anxiety and planted the image of her being sick or afraid and alone in her apartment, he'd been stunned by the force of his reaction. He'd damn near asked her to move in with him, which wouldn't have come off weird at all.

Jamie: Sure, what's it for? Need me to bring it over?

Elliott: Hanging some stuff, and that would be awesome

Elliott: Bring Hank if you want. I miss him.

Jamie glared at his phone, then eyed his dog, looking all adorable curled up in his favorite bed by the coffee table. "You have no idea how lucky you are, do you?"

Hank sprung to his feet with interest when Jamie grabbed his baseball cap and rose, then followed him to the hall closet. Jamie rummaged through his toolbox and grabbed the hammer, and soon the pair were trekking across the complex.

Elliott answered the door right away with a grin and her eyes lit with excitement. Her hair was pulled up in a ponytail, but several pieces had slipped out and fallen around her face.

"Find the art you were looking for?" he asked, trying not to notice how adorable she was like this. He liked every version of her, even the subdued Elliott he'd seen most often this time around. But this energized version, brimming with happiness, was an Elliott he hadn't seen since . . . well, since the night they met.

Thinking about that was . . . a mistake. A visceral memory slammed into him of their teasing, suggestive comments while beating egg whites and the urge to kiss the hell out of her right there in the middle of the crowded room.

And the searing kiss they'd shared later.

"Yes, and I'm obsessed with them." She held open the door, and as soon as they were inside, she crouched down to cuddle Hank's neck. Jamie inhaled deeply through his nose and tried to stay cool. Ignoring her excitement was one thing—not swooning at the way she adored his dog was a different story.

Hank licked all over her face and she laughed, the sound like a balm to his soul. "I missed you, too," she murmured.

"I'm surprised you haven't borrowed him yet." He regretted the words immediately. How pathetic did that sound?

She stood. "I know. I thought about it a couple times." She scrunched her nose. "But I talked myself out of it because I didn't want to bother you."

Bothering him was exactly what he wanted her to do.

He pointedly glanced at the hammer in his hand and said lightly, "You don't seem to have a problem bothering me for tools?"

She laughed. "I was desperate. I can't wait to get these up."

She pointed to three paintings lined up along the living room wall. Her lips curved into a smile, and she pressed clasped fists to her chin, rocking back on her heels. "Aren't they great?"

He unclipped Hank's leash and stepped to the side to get a better look. He knelt down, balancing on the balls of his feet. They were large—probably three by four feet—and outdoor scenes. "Oh yeah, these are definitely cool. I like the colors."

"Me too." She sounded almost breathless. "It feels like every time I look at them, I notice something new. A different blend of color or a texture I didn't see before."

"Where'd you find them?"

"I went to Dundee, like you suggested." She pointed to the one in the middle. "That was the only one on display, but I met the artist and asked if she had more like it."

"That's awesome." He regarded them for another moment, then stood and checked out the rest of the room. His eye caught on a bouquet of aging flowers in the middle of the coffee table, and an ugly sensation settled low in his belly. Jealousy wasn't an emotion he was familiar with, and certainly wasn't welcome when it came to Elliott.

She's not yours.

But . . . where had they come from? A man? A friend? Had she picked them up for herself, just because?

He'd go with the last one, because if he spent too long considering another man vying for her attention, he'd be tempted to create his own bouquet for her, all with fresh blooms from the nursery. He'd arrange something a hell of a lot better than that one.

She caught him eyeing the vase, and her lips twitched. "I couldn't find peonies anywhere."

God, was he that obvious? He kept his face carefully neutral and cleared his throat, hoping to move on before he did something idiotic like offer to bring her some. "So what's the plan? Have you measured and marked where you want them?"

She chewed on the inside of her cheek. "No. I just know where I want them."

"They don't look too heavy. Do they have wires in the back?" He reached to the side to tip one piece forward.

"I don't know."

"Got a level?"

"No."

He dropped his chin to his chest. "Elliott."

"What?"

He lifted his eyes to hers, trying not to smile. "Were you just going to hammer nails in the wall and hope it worked out?"

"Maybe?"

He released a dramatic sigh. "Okay. First, I need to go back to my apartment and get more stuff. The paintings are already wired, but we need a tape measure, level, and picture hangers. Then we need to measure the spot and mark it—"

"Jamie?"

He stopped.

"Can you stop mansplaining and just do it?"

Laughing, he went for the door. "Yeah. I can do that."

"Hank can stay with me."

Jamie noted where his dog had already made himself at home on her couch. "He seems good with that."

He went back to his place, gathered the supplies in his toolbox, and returned. She told him where she wanted them and he got to work, determining where the nails should go, marking the spot with a pencil.

"So is this all the art you wanted?"

"It's all I'm going to buy. I like photography, and thought maybe one weekend I'd find some cool places to take pictures around town. If I get any good shots, I can print them and hang them in my room."

"I'm not sure what subjects you're looking for, but there are some cool old barns outside the city. Some are close enough to the road you could get shots from just off the highway. They'd look great in black and white."

"You have an idea for everything, don't you?" she said.

Jamie nodded and picked up a picture hanger and the hammer for the first one. He lifted his arm. "You sure this is where you want it? No going back after I start."

"I'm sure."

He hammered the small nails into the wall, and she grabbed the painting and brought it over.

"So how'd that book work for you?" he asked as he took it.

She laughed. "Really well, actually. I had a great night's sleep after you gave it to me."

He glanced over at her and found her face strangely flushed. She seemed almost embarrassed for some reason, so he didn't call attention to it. "I'm glad. This look even?"

"Perfect."

They repeated the process with the other two, and he tossed the hammer to the carpet before positioning the final painting on the wall.

As he worked, she told him about her recent clients and the project she was finalizing for his sister's bakery. He told her about a book he'd recently read that threw him for a loop in the best way, and she asked for suggestions for the best Mexican restaurants around town—which wasn't difficult, because he hadn't met a salsa he didn't like.

"Good?" he asked before stepping away from the final painting.

Her eyes were bright. "Yes, I love it. Thank you so much."

"Anytime."

Seriously, he'd do anything for her, anytime.

A heavy silence descended, though Hank didn't seem to notice, completely passed out and snoring on the edge of her couch.

"We'd better get out of your hair. Hank, come."

"Oh, okay. Sure." She took a step forward and her toe caught the lid of the toolbox he'd left open, pitching her forward. Jamie immediately reached out to steady her, his hands closing around her waist, and hers blindly reaching out and landing on his forearms. She regained her balance in his arms, her hip brushing his and her hair near his face.

Her breath hitched.

His heart stopped.

They both froze and he closed his eyes, fighting the urge to pull her closer, body flush against his. Energy pulsed through him, charged and thick.

She tipped her chin up and regarded him, eyes wide and cheeks flushed. Her pupils widened at the same time one of her thumbs shifted across his skin.

Had—had she just *caressed* him? That was on purpose, right?

In that moment, everything but her flew straight out of his mind: Carly, his dad, his worries about mass deforestation and global warming. All forgotten.

His gaze dropped to her mouth. Her lips parted and her grip tightened on his forearms. He wouldn't make a move—would leave it up to her—but he sure as hell wasn't going to be the one to pull away.

Hank chose that moment to obey Jamie's command and jumped down, coming over to shove his nose between their thighs.

She blinked as if coming back to herself and edged sideways, dropping her arms.

"Sorry," he muttered.

"No, um . . . thanks." Her cheeks were still pink. She knelt to close the toolbox and latch it, then rose again to hand it to him. "This would have taken a lot longer without your help."

He took it from her, careful not to touch her skin. Her apartment suddenly felt warm, and he needed to keep her at arm's length if they were going to continue whatever avoidance ritual they were doing.

Elliott ruffled Hank's ears in goodbye, and they left, Jamie struggling to make sense of everything that had just happened.

She'd come to him for help: good.

They'd talked and, as far as he was concerned, enjoyed each other's company: really good.

When she'd fallen into his arms, she'd looked at him like she wanted him: fucking awesome.

Then she had pulled away and hadn't looked at him again: possibly the worst thing that had ever happened to him.

Back at his apartment, he crashed onto the couch with a frustrated growl. He just enjoyed being with her so damn much. He loved her kindness, her sense of humor, her determination and strength. He loved that she was sweet to his dog and the way he felt her eyes on him when she thought he wasn't looking. He wanted to sit beside her and learn about her, and he wanted to kiss her until he could hardly breathe.

There were times it felt like she wanted those things, too. But then she'd pull away, and he was back at square one.

It took a while, but he finally fell asleep and, the following morning, found a surprise waiting for him. When he opened the door, about to step into the hallway on his way to work, something on the ground caught his eye. He looked down and barked out a laugh.

It was a *National Geographic* encyclopedia on ocean animals with the section about narwhals marked with a scrap of notebook paper. He slid the book onto his coffee table and went to the door a second time, a huge smile now on his face.

His phone buzzed in his pocket and his heart lurched.

Was it Elliott? Maybe she wanted to make sure he'd gotten the gift or was interested in taking Hank out again. Even better, maybe she just wanted to talk to him for no reason at all.

But when he pulled the device out and regarded the screen, his smile disappeared.

Carly: **Can we talk?**

CHAPTER NINETEEN

Elliott

ChantalPlans Instagram Post

Friends, get ready for a new and improved website from your favorite Event Planner—coming soon from @EHBranding. I met Elliott through our dear friend @ Carly.P—and you won't believe this woman's talent. Can't wait for you to see the new site—stay tuned! Oh, and if you're a fellow business owner in the Omaha area, go check out Elliott's work and give her a follow. You won't regret it! #eventplanning #party #partyplanner #smallbusiness #localbusiness #oma-habusiness #omahaparties #chantalplans

Elliott smiled when the post notification popped up on her phone. She shared it to her Stories and immediately switched over to a text message.

Elliott: Hey! I just wanted to thank you again for connecting me with Chantal. I can't tell you how much I love her and what a great opportunity this is for me.

Carly: Girl of course. You deserve it

Carly: What are you up to? It's been a minute and I'd love to catch up

It had been more than a minute—Elliott hadn't seen Carly once since that night at the raw-food bar when Tiffany had opened her big mouth. Elliott had kept pretty close tabs on Carly's social media, though, trying to glean how she was doing after the breakup. Everything seemed perfect as always, but social media never told the whole story.

One reason she'd kept her distance was the fact that she'd just met Carly, and if she was upset about everything with Jamie, surely she'd want to spend time with friends she was close to. Elliott didn't want to impose.

Also, though, Elliott was a coward, plain and simple. Even if Yuka insisted the end of Carly and Jamie's relationship wasn't her fault, she still felt guilty, as if she was solely responsible for what had happened.

Plus, what would she do if Carly brought up "Jeremy"? Disappearing probably wouldn't work a second time, and she wasn't sure how she'd handle it. She'd never been a good liar, which she usually figured was a pretty good trait to have, but in this situation it meant she wouldn't think well on her feet.

Hopefully by now Carly would have forgotten all about it. Or had been too drunk that night to even remember it the next day. Either way, Elliott wanted to visit with her regardless, especially after everything Carly had done for her and her business.

Elliott: I'm at Green Tree working on Chantal's website, actually.

Carly: I'll be there in ten

Elliott ordered a new cup of coffee while she waited, unable to focus on client work as butterflies filled her belly. She hoped she and Carly could continue their friendship, but she couldn't help thinking about all the ways she'd deceived her, even if it was (mostly) with good intentions. She could come clean and tell the truth today—what better opportunity would she have?

But doing that affected Jamie, too, and while he'd admitted the initial lie-by-omission was a mistake, he'd also said things would only get worse if they brought it up now. Hurting Carly more than she probably already was (Who could lose Jamie and be okay with it?) was the last thing Elliott wanted to do.

Carly walked in right on time, her eyes searching the café. Elliott raised a shaky hand and smiled.

"Hiii!" Carly held out her arms, and Elliott rose to hug her. "Long time no see. How are you?"

"I'm really good. Busy, thanks to you." They sat across from each other.

Carly did a little fist pump. "I was happy to do it. It's been fun to help some of my favorite people around town. Hell, Blythe offered me free cupcakes for life for connecting you two. What's better than that?" She laughed, face bright and happy.

Elliott searched for any visual indication Carly was depressed, lonely, or suffering and found none. No dark circles under her eyes, no slouched posture, no wrinkled clothes. Carly looked perfectly put together and sublimely happy.

Not like someone who'd just lost the love of their life.

Carly leaned forward, her eyes lighting up. "I actually came here to thank *you* for everything you've done for me."

Elliott thought for a moment but couldn't come up with anything she'd done to help Carly. "What do you mean?"

"That's one reason I wanted to meet with you, besides just catching up. I'm going to post it on my socials soon but wanted to tell my friends in person. And you, because you played a big part in this decision." She clasped her hands together under her chin, dark hair spilling over her shoulders. "I'm moving back to Oklahoma."

"Really?" Elliott had never been to Oklahoma and didn't know much about Carly's childhood there, but Carly's smile was bigger than Elliott had ever seen it.

"Ever since I was a kid, I've always loved style and fashion. But it never seemed like something I could make a career out of, so I went the safe route and picked accounting. I figured I could always express myself through what I wore, no matter what my job was."

Clothes weren't something Elliott paid a lot of attention to, but now that she thought about it, Carly was the best-dressed person she knew. "That explains all the fashion boutiques you're always posting about." Elliott had checked one out once and felt so out of place she'd made an awkward loop around the store and gotten the hell out of there.

"Yes! Leaving Silvia's behind might be harder than all the free cupcakes I won't get from Blythe, but she promised to ship me stuff whenever I want. Anyway, I have this friend back in Oklahoma City, Mai, who's a personal stylist. She's tried to get me to come work with her before, but I never had the nerve to actually do it. I didn't have a lot of money growing up, and doing something like that just seemed too risky. Working on commission? No way. So I stayed here with my safe accounting job, watching Mai's business flourish and wishing I could be part of it but never doing anything about it.

"Then I met you. The way you didn't let your past stop you from getting what you want out of life was so inspiring. And when I heard you talk about how much you love what you do and why you want to do it? It reminded me why I love fashion and why I want to share that with others, so I called Mai to see if the offer was still on the table. You're such a badass, moving and starting a new business from scratch, and I guess . . . I guess I want to go after what I want with that same intensity, you know?"

Elliott couldn't help but match Carly's enthusiasm with a wide grin. "I had no idea you were interested in that, but personal styling suits you. I'm so happy for you."

"Me too. I can't wait, honestly. I mean, I'm so glad I came here for school, and I've loved living here. I really needed to get away from Oklahoma City for a while after high school, and I'll never regret coming here. But it never really felt like home. And then, when Jamie and I broke up, I kept asking myself what was keeping me here. When Mai said she had a spot for me, it felt like a sign."

It never really felt like home. Would that have played into the staying power of her relationship with Jamie if they'd stayed together? What if a long-term future with him had never been Carly's plan?

Elliott shoved the thoughts away, ashamed for grasping at excuses to justify pining for Carly's ex. "So it's, like, official, right? You're doing it?"

"Yup. The styling gig is part-time for now, but I work for a regional accounting firm, and they have an office in Oklahoma City. I'm going to do both for a while until I build up a client base."

Elliott laughed. "Just like me."

"You, me, Stephen . . . We're all out here hustling to pay rent and do what we love, too. I feel like I'm finally doing something for myself for the first time in forever."

Elliott was a little envious of how certain Carly was about her decision—must be nice not second-guessing yourself all the time. "I love that for you."

"We'll keep in touch, right?"

"Of course, are you kidding? I'll be living vicariously through your new fancy fashion life." Elliott shot her wide eyes. "Especially if you pick up any famous clients. Who's famous in Oklahoma?"

Carly frowned, thinking. "Carrie Underwood?"

"I think James Marsden is from there, isn't he? I want to say Brad Pitt was born there, too."

Carly's jaw dropped. "Oh my God, I'll move tomorrow."

Elliott laughed. "None of those people still live there."

"Hey, you never know where a good fashion connection will take you."

"In that case, if you happen to meet Nick Jonas, maybe casually mention you've got a friend in Nebraska who makes a damn-good vanilla latte and gives excellent back rubs."

"Nick Jonas? Really?"

"Don't judge me."

Carly laughed. "Consider it done." She arched a brow. "Back rubs, huh? What does Stephen think about those?"

Elliott's surprise must have shown on her face, because Carly added, "I heard you two have been talking."

She had? Who else had he told? "Yeah, we went out before he left on that photography trip." He'd left shortly after she'd put off a second date with the excuse she needed to work, and had only returned yesterday with a promise he'd stop into Starbucks to show her his best shots. "It was fun, but not quite to the back-rub stage," Elliott said noncommittally.

She didn't have the balls to turn the question back on Carly, but she couldn't help but wonder: Was she excited to meet new men back in Oklahoma City? Maybe someone from her previous life she was interested in reconnecting with?

And if she was, would it change anything? Elliott had told Jamie she wouldn't date him, but that was before she saw how content Carly was. Elliott had been worse off after only one night with him, for goodness' sake.

Which was either hopelessly romantic or incredibly pathetic.

But even if Carly wasn't pining after Jamie, that didn't mean she'd be okay with Elliott making a move on her ex. Ex-boyfriends were iffy—usually considered off-limits to friends and family. Their history made things extra complicated, and Elliott still didn't want to risk hurting Carly's feelings.

Carly left soon after, promising to let Elliott know if she had any sort of going away party. Unable to focus on work, Elliott only stayed another ten minutes and called Yuka once she reached her car.

"Carly's leaving town?" Yuka shrieked. Sometimes, Yuka was the calm and collected one in their friendship. This was not one of those times. "I hope you're on your way to Jamie's place as we speak to jump that man."

There was an irresponsible, wanton part of Elliott that wanted to do just that.

And how. But . . . "I'm not."

"Goddammit, Elliott. This is why we can't have nice things."

"Don't you think something about it still feels wrong?"

"No. I don't."

"Not even a little?"

"I'll allow you to wait until she's actually relocated, but after that, you're out of excuses."

"What about the woman version of Bro Code? You don't date your friend's exes? Or in my situation, you don't date your stem cell donor's ex?"

"Something tells me there's not a formal rule for that one. You're in uncharted territory here, Ellie."

She groaned. "That makes it worse."

Yuka paused for a moment; then her voice took on a more serious tone. "Answer me this: What if Carly finds someone else back home? What if she gets married and has a family? Would that change things?"

Elliott's heart screamed the affirmative.

Yuka kept going. "Would you finally put yourself and Jamie out of your misery and give it a chance? Or does Carly get to claim him forever, even after she's moved on? You still gonna give her dominion over Jamie and your love life one, five, ten years down the road?"

Elliott frowned, shrinking in her seat. "Jeez, Yuka."

A heavy sigh escaped the speaker. "I'm not trying to be hard on you, but I really want you to see this for the opportunity it could be. There's something to be said for honor and thinking of other people, and I think you've gone above and beyond to tread lightly in this twisted situation you were put in. And you've repeatedly considered Carly before yourself. But there's also a point where self-sacrifice goes too far. They broke up. She's moving away. This could be the second-best thing that ever happened to you. You deserve happiness, too, you know?"

"I'm happy," Elliott said weakly.

"Sounds fake, but okay."

"I am!"

"Who the hell do you think you're talking to, here? You can't lie to me. I know you only offer short-term services for clients and still haven't signed a long-term lease there. You're scared to put down roots with anyone or anything. I understand, because your life has been interrupted so many times, but I'm just afraid if you keep that up, you're never going to connect anywhere. Or with anyone."

Elliott pressed her lips together and inhaled deeply through her nose, processing Yuka's words. She just wanted to find her own life and a steady pace here. Find a rhythm that would prove she could be here and make something of herself.

And she could do it alone. She didn't *need* Jamie to be happy. Need and want were two different things, and wanting him was a question she hadn't examined until recently.

"Your happiness is what matters most to me," Yuka began. "But since you seem to be so obsessed with taking responsibility for that of others, I'll ask this: Do you want Jamie to be happy?"

More than anything, but Yuka'd use that against her for sure. She settled on a less intense response: "Sure, I do."

"What if being with you is what he wants?"

"I—I don't know. I'm not sure that's true."

"Why not?"

"He hasn't said so." But the way he looked at her sometimes . . .

It was the same way she looked at him when he wasn't paying attention.

"What if he did? Would that change things?"

"I don't know."

"Honey, you'd better figure it out and soon. Because something tells me when Carly's gone, that man's coming for you."

One week later, Stephen stopped by Starbucks when Elliott was about to go on break. He brought his laptop, and she spent several minutes reviewing his gorgeous photos of the Louisiana wetlands.

Her mouth dropped open when she came across a close-up of an alligator. "Oh my God. How close were you to that thing?"

Stephen laughed. "I kept a respectful distance. I was in a kayak, and most of them were along the shore, lying in the sun. I felt safer on the water than I would have walking by one of them."

She kept going and paused at a shot of a blue heron taking flight. "I think this one's my favorite."

He grinned. "Mine too."

"These are really incredible. You have a gift, Stephen."

He shrugged, though his cheeks turned pink. "Thanks. You're the first person I've shown them to."

That felt . . . special, and not like something she deserved. Especially when she'd concluded she and Stephen were better off friends.

"When do you get out of here today?" he continued.

"Seven." She was pretty sure she knew where this was going and scrambled to find the right words to let him know where she stood.

Stephen closed his laptop and slid it in his bag, tossing out a casual, "Would you want to grab dinner tonight?"

It was strange, really, how one part of her recognized what a catch he was—creative, friendly, attractive—while another had zero interest in him beyond friendship. Even if she wanted it to, her heart just couldn't be bothered with the great guy sitting beside her. It was better for both of them if he moved his sights elsewhere.

She swallowed, trying to come up with something honest but that wouldn't hurt his feelings. Letting guys down wasn't something she'd done often. Or ever, really. "Stephen, I had a great time hanging out with you, and you're such a great guy. I just . . . there's a lot of change in my life right now, and I think I need to focus on getting my business going. You know?" All true statements. Virtually everything in her life was different from how it was this time last year, and she *did* need to focus on her clients. "I've got a lot going on, and I'm not sure I'm ready to add dating into the mix."

Other than a brief drop in eye contact, Stephen didn't seem too bothered by her rejection. "Definitely, no worries." He looked at her again with a seemingly genuine smile. "If anyone understands what it takes to hustle a side business hoping it becomes a career, it's me."

She nodded, grateful for his easygoing nature. "Thank you. I hope we can still hang out as friends, though?"

He stood and slung his backpack across one shoulder. "This is still my favorite Starbucks, and sometimes friends slip friends unsold pastries from the day before, right?"

"They do," she said with a laugh. She turned and eyed Suzie, who pretended not to watch them from behind the counter. "Suzie would love to hook a friend up, too, you know. Which one do you like best?"

He raised his brow in interest when she mentioned Suzie, then shot her a wide grin as he headed for the door. "All of them."

She went back to work after he left, informed Suzie she and Stephen were most definitely not an item and that Suzie had full permission to make a move, and then went home a couple of hours later. She arrived at her apartment to find a large hardcover book propped outside her door. The cover was designed with bright colors and metallic-gold lettering.

The Book of Mythical Beasts and Magical Creatures.

The section about unicorns was marked with a bookmark that said READING IS MAGICAL. He'd added a slip of paper that said, "I think maybe you haven't tried the right kind of chocolate."

His dark, bold handwriting sent a bright warmth fizzing through her chest, suffusing her limbs with pleasant heat.

That man's coming for you.

The meaning behind Yuka's words sent a flare several inches lower, sending complicated sensations of guilt and want searing through her. She'd just told Stephen she couldn't handle dating right now, but clearly her heart found that irrelevant when it came to Jamie.

She put down the book and her things and settled on the couch with her phone.

Elliott: Love the book, still hate chocolate. All kinds.

Jamie: But you're missing out on so much

Elliott: Yuka tells me so every day

Jamie: I'd like to meet this Yuka. I think I'd like her

Elliott: You would. Everyone does

Jamie: Hey, I have a favor to ask

Elliott: Okay

Jamie: I wanted to see if you'd be interested in watching Hank this weekend

Elliott: Sure. Are you going somewhere?

Jamie: Wichita for a tree-climbing competition

Elliott: A what?

Jamie: Arborist thing. We compete to do movement in trees and learn about new techniques and equipment and stuff

Her lips quirked. How adorable was that?

Elliott: Wow. That's . . . interesting.

Jamie: It's all very tough and manly, if you must know

Elliott: You say that, but all I can picture is a bunch of kids fighting over who has the best tree house

Jamie: Mine was for sure

Elliott: Yeah? Build it with your dad?

Jamie: No

It had taken nearly a minute for him to respond. That single unpunctuated word seemed to pack a lot of weight, and Elliott got the feeling maybe she'd said something wrong. She scrambled to think of something else to say, but another message came through.

Jamie: I leave pretty early Friday morning, could I bring him over Thursday?

Elliott: Sure, I'll be home after five.

Jamie: You're sure you don't mind?

Elliott: Are you kidding? I'd love to have him. I'm honored you trust me with him.

Jamie: Honestly I'm worried he won't want to come home

Elliott: That's a risk you'll have to take

Jamie: lol. See you Thursday.

CHAPTER TWENTY

Jamie

Jamie: 🐾 Checking in on my dog. Is he behaving himself?

A photo appeared almost immediately, and Jamie laughed and leaned his head back on the couch. Ian and some of the guys had gone out for drinks, so he was enjoying the peace and quiet in his hotel room after being in the hot sun all day.

Jamie: Is that a bone? It's the size of his head

Elliott: We ran seven miles this morning. He deserved it

Jamie: Wow, yeah. That's awesome.

Elliott: He's been perfect. We're having a blast.

It wasn't the first time Jamie'd been jealous of his dog, and it probably wouldn't be the last.

Elliott: How's the tree climbing?

Jamie: Good. I'm exhausted

Jamie: And before you make fun of me, it's harder than it looks

Elliott: I'd never make fun of a grown man climbing trees

Jamie: Glad we're clear on that

He paused for a moment, resting his phone on his thigh. He stared at a dull water spot on the ceiling and wondered if he should say good night. He'd had no qualms about using his dog as an excuse to text her. And it had definitely been nothing but an excuse, because there was no doubt in his mind she was pulling out all the stops to take good care of Hank. He wanted to *keep* talking to her. Ask how her day was and if she had plans later. Maybe somehow they'd come upon the topic of Stephen, because he'd heard they'd gone out and was dying to know if anything was happening there. Maybe she'd say something like *We're just friends* or *I had a terrible time*. Bonus points for *Stephen's kind of an asshole*.

Uncharitable of him? Probably.

Did he care? Nope.

He opted for something less invasive.

Jamie: What are you up to tonight?

Elliott: Thought it was pretty obvious

She sent a second photo of Hank.

Jamie: Get yourself a big bone, too?

The literal second he hit "Send," he groaned aloud.

Jamie: I didn't mean that the way it sounded

Jamie: Can we forget I said that

Elliott: Hahahaha

Elliott: Not a chance, but I meant I thought it was obvious I'm hanging with your dog

Jamie: No big Saturday night plans?

Elliott: Nah, I wasn't feeling all that great this afternoon so I figured I should stay in.

Not feeling great? What did that mean?

Jamie: Is everything okay?

He waited several minutes for a reply, a nervous energy filling him when she didn't. Not even three dots to indicate she was typing something.

Jamie: You still there?

Five more minutes passed with no response. He stood, phone in hand, unsure what he was planning to do from Wichita but antsy all the same. She said she wasn't feeling well and dropped off the conversation.

Had something happened? Sure, she could have set her phone down and gotten distracted, or maybe she took Hank out to pee. But they'd been in the middle of texting back and forth and suddenly . . . nothing.

When I'm in that apartment all alone, all I can think about is the fact that if something happened to me while I was in there, no one would know.

What if she wasn't okay?

He gripped the back of his neck and without another thought, called her.

She answered on the third ring. "Jamie?"

She sounded confused, but fine.

He sank back down into the cushions, blowing a breath through his lips. "Are you okay? I just . . . Sorry. I, um, you said you weren't feeling well and then stopped responding." He suddenly felt like an idiot. "I just . . . wanted to make sure everything was fine . . . ?"

"Yeah, I'm good. I'm sorry. My mom called, so I was talking to her."

"Oh." Well. "That's good."

"That was nice of you," she said, and it sounded genuine. Not the tone of someone weirded out by his overprotective reaction. "I . . . didn't mean to worry you."

He desperately searched for something to say. *It's okay* didn't feel right because he probably shouldn't have worried about her. She wasn't his to worry over, and he was trying not to come off like an obsessive creeper. *I wasn't worried* wasn't it, either, because obviously in those few minutes he had been.

They were friends, though, right? Sort of? It was an acceptable reaction . . . ?

Before he landed on a response, she spoke again, probably wondering why he was just sitting there breathing into the phone. "I don't think I'm sick or anything; it's probably just stress-induced. It happens sometimes when I'm close to my next oncologist checkup. I start over-analyzing every little thing."

He leaned forward and propped one elbow on his knee. That had to be hard as hell, always wondering. "I'd do the same thing. How often do you have to go in like that?"

"Just once a month. My appointment's on Tuesday."

"I'll think boring thoughts for you."

"Thanks?"

He grinned. "During physicals for baseball, that's what our coach always said. When it comes to doctor visits, boring's always best."

She laughed lightly, and a silly pride filled him at having made her laugh. "Good point, and I hope you're right. I'm sure everything's fine, and having Hank here was helpful, actually. He helped distract me."

"By demanding belly rubs every hour on the hour?"

"Plus two laps around the dog park and the dinosaur leg he's chewing on."

"Sounds like he's got you wrapped around his little finger."

"He's so freaking cute it's hard not to. How do you resist those big brown eyes?"

He laughed. "I don't. He's spoiled as hell."

"I'm not helping matters."

"That's okay. He deserves all of it and more." Jamie had adopted Hank shortly after moving back to Omaha, and he'd been a steady, comforting presence during his injury recovery. There'd been nothing better than coming home from a grueling day of physical therapy to his happy, loving dog, who looked at him every single time he walked through that door like he'd invented the chew toy.

Hank had also been there in the months following Elliott's disappearance when Jamie'd gone out of his mind for a little while, unable to find her and wondering if he'd just missed out on the love of his life forever. If he'd only ever have one day with her.

Yet here he was, one year and a few months later, sitting in a hotel room and talking to her on the phone while she spooned with his dog on her couch.

A strange, sudden emotion swelled in his chest—something like gratitude, or maybe ill-advised ambition—and he swallowed. "Hey, can I ask you something?"

"Sure."

"The night we first met, when I asked you for a secret, you said sometimes if feels like no one understands you. I remember because I've felt the same way for a long time, and I've always wondered what it meant for you. Would you tell me?"

She hummed, like a soft sound of contemplation, and he settled deeper into the cushions, propping his feet on the coffee table.

"I guess I just meant I've experienced a lot of things few people do. I got cancer as a teenager, and I've had a stem cell transplant. People say one of the best ways to get through hardship is to talk about it, but most of the time when I try that, it just makes people uncomfortable. They can't relate and don't know what to say.

"Yuka and my parents are the only ones I feel like I can be brutally honest with. They'll let me rage and cry and vent anytime I need to, and always find something to do or say that makes me feel better. But even they don't understand completely. No one can."

He wished he was with her right now. Sitting across from or beside her, taking in the expressions on her face while she spoke. "You've dealt with more shit before the age of thirty than some people do in a lifetime."

"Some have had it worse," she said quietly. "I remember one girl I met at the infusion center whose family had a genetic condition that put them at higher risk for cancer. By the time the gene was detected, she'd already lost her dad, uncle, and two brothers to various cancers. She and her mom were the only ones left, and she'd just been diagnosed with colon cancer."

"Oh my God, that's terrible. I can't even imagine." His stomach dropped to his toes even thinking about it. "But you've been through a lot, too. And still, you're so . . ." He trailed off, again struggling to put words to what he saw in her.

"I'm so . . . what?"

Jamie rubbed a hand across his sternum. "You're just . . . incredible." Incredible, beautiful, strong. "I hope that's okay for me to say."

It was silent for a few seconds, then she spoke. "It's okay to say." The smile in her voice brought a similar expression to his own face. "It's nice to hear someone thinks that of me." Before he could scoff and inform her everyone she met probably thought the same, she kept going. "Your turn. Why do you feel like no one understands you?"

"Nah, you don't need to hear about my shitty family right now."

"It's okay if you don't want to talk about it. But I'd like to know."

Jamie ran a hand through his hair and vacantly gazed at the television he'd muted earlier. Being one of the millions of kids who struggled through a parents' divorce seemed like nothing compared with having cancer, but after her honesty, he owed her the same. And while he'd rather hear more about her, he liked that she wanted to get to know him. "I guess I've just always felt a little split between my family. There are three of us kids—Greg's the oldest, then Blythe, then me. We were pretty close when we were kids, but then my parents got divorced. My sister picked my mom, and my brother picked my dad. I was too young to understand much and didn't really side with anybody. I spent more time with Greg and my dad at first, because I figured they were guys like me and that's where I should be. But the older I got, the more I realized how little I related to them. Now I spend much more time with my mom and sister than with them."

When he paused, she said, "I don't know what it's like to be a kid watching your parents get a divorce, but I watched Yuka go through it. It wasn't easy."

"No, it's not. My brother has followed in my dad's footsteps in every way, and I know they expected the same from me. But I just couldn't. My dad runs a loan consolidation business. He started it from the ground up, turning a three-employee start-up into a multi-million-dollar company. He likes to go big and take risks, even though some of them have led to layoffs and lost jobs for his employees. Oddly enough, he always emerges from those bad decisions unscathed."

She made a sound of disapproval, and he liked her even more because of it.

"I know, believe me. And now my brother works for him and is quickly climbing the ranks in the company. Long story short, they think my career choice is a joke. It's too soft, I guess, to work with plants. Apparently, they don't care trees turn something harmful into the one thing we need to breathe."

He probably sounded ridiculous, defending trees as if they were his protected employees. But in a way, they sort of were. "The only time I felt like they were proud of me was when I was drafted. What's more impressive than being a baseball star?"

"I can think of several things," Elliott said.

"So can I." He smiled, absurdly pleased she didn't seem all that impressed by the baseball thing. She wasn't fawning over it being a major loss to have missed the opportunity to be a pro athlete. "I wasn't much of a partyer in high school or college. Was kind of a geek, actually, because I'd rather be outside with a book than at a party. But after I got word from the scout that I was as good as drafted and likely to be an early-round pick, my brother suddenly started paying attention to me. He always wanted to take me out with his buddies, and my dad never missed an opportunity to tell me how proud he was of me. It's funny how quickly that all stopped when I got injured and was released."

"That's bullshit," she burst out, then paused. She took a breath, and her voice gentled. "I'm so sorry, Jamie."

"Don't be. My dad and brother were crushed, but I was relieved. I liked playing baseball, but I never wanted to make a career out of it. I wouldn't have chosen to go out the way I did, but it worked out all the same." He absently rubbed one socked heel across his shin. "They've never treated me the same, and I guess that's what I meant that night. My mom and Blythe accept me for who I am, and I should be happy with that. But it still feels like I'm only part of half of my family."

"Sounds to me like you're with the best half."

He grinned. "I think so, too."

They kept talking for another two hours, but it didn't even feel like they scratched the surface of everything they could have talked about. He told her about adopting Hank and how he'd named him after Hank Aaron, his favorite baseball player, and that he'd never been to a concert, which she insisted they remedy. He was all in with anything that involved her. Them, together.

She told him about her love for art and photography, and how working on her high school yearbook committee had led to her interest in website and graphic design. He learned more about her parents and the bookstore they owned, and he regaled her with stories of the trouble he and Blythe often got into when they were kids.

He only ended the call when Ian came in, loud and a little tipsy, and Jamie wasn't ready to answer questions about Elliott yet. He avoided Ian's inquiry into who he was talking to, and thankfully, his friend moved on, forgetting about it moments later.

It wasn't so easy for Jamie, and when he climbed into bed to get some sleep, Elliott Holland wasn't far from his mind.

CHAPTER TWENTY-ONE

Elliott

After spending the weekend with Hank, Elliott desperately wanted a dog.

But not just any dog. She wanted Hank. He'd been the best running buddy, cuddle buddy, and meal buddy.

She loved him.

Her heart broke a little at the knock on her door Sunday evening. Hank let out a bark and she laughed.

"That's just your dad."

She opened the door and there he was, a duffel bag slung over his shoulder. His wavy blond hair was messy and perfect, the dark frames of his glasses the tiniest bit crooked across his nose. His hazel eyes looked tired and happy as they scanned her face.

He was so handsome.

She swallowed, ignoring her body's plea to step forward and into his personal space. "How was it?"

"Good. Fun."

"Win anything?"

His cheeks flushed, from pride or embarrassment she wasn't sure, and he unzipped the side compartment of his bag to pull out a tiny trophy.

She giggled and clapped her palm across her mouth. "I'm sorry."

He glared at her even as a smile tipped his lips. "It's fine. You can be jealous."

"Oh, I am. A participation trophy?"

"Excuse you. This is second place in the Work Climb category."

She squinted and leaned forward. "Ah. So it is."

"That's enough," he growled, stuffing the trophy back into his bag. "Where's my dog?"

Choking back another laugh, she opened the door wider and stepped aside. Hank hadn't moved from his spot on the couch.

"Seriously?" Jamie asked him. "First my dog sitter makes fun of my trophy, and now my dog doesn't even care I'm home."

Hank lifted his head to regard Jamie, his tail wagging.

Jamie dropped his bag and crouched down, slapping his thigh. "Come on, boy. I missed you."

That was all it took. A blur of yellow fur launched off the couch and darted into Jamie's arms, slathering kisses all over his face.

Elliott couldn't blame him, honestly. If Jamie were hers, she'd greet him that way, too.

"He's already had a run today," she said, gathering a few toys scattered around the couch. If she stood there watching how adorable they were together, she might do something stupid, like tell Jamie she'd missed him. "And I fed him dinner."

"How many treats did he weasel out of you?" Jamie gave Hank a final scratch and stood, a grin on his face and one eyebrow raised.

"I don't know what you're talking about."

"I sent him with a full bag. Am I getting any to take back with me?"

She just stared at him for a moment, blinking. Her shoulders fell. "No."

He laughed, a warm, rich sound, and her eyes immediately zeroed in on the dimple just beside his smile. That damn dimple, plus those sparkling eyes . . . This man could ruin her if she wasn't careful.

That was if he hadn't already. She stubbornly refused to even consider how deep her feelings went, preferring to pretend they weren't there, like any other mature, emotionally stable adult.

Jamie stuffed the chew toys in his bag and stepped sideways, probably to grab the dog bed next to the armchair, but he stopped and just stood there for a minute. His back was to her, so she wasn't sure what he was looking at. Was he noticing that the dog bed had obviously remained unused? When he brought it, he'd said she didn't have to let Hank on her furniture, and if she told him no, he'd know to use the bed on the floor instead. But she'd liked having Hank's warm body next to her, despite the hair he left behind.

Or was it the dessert book on her coffee table, the one she'd shown him but hadn't given to him because at the time he'd been in a relationship?

The Nebraska Medicine appointment reminder beside it?

"Jamie . . . ?" she began.

He turned, lifting one hand to drift it across his chest, the movement seemingly absent-minded, like something he did when he was uncertain. "Do you want him to stay?"

"What?"

"Hank. You said your appointment's on Tuesday . . . Want to hang on to him until after you see your oncologist and get the results?" Behind his glasses, his eyes held a mixture of sincerity and worry, as if he thought maybe offering this to her was an overstep. "He's obviously happy to be here, and maybe he could distract you for a few more days. If you want."

Elliott stood rooted to the floor, unable to move despite the warmth radiating from the center of her body. Her heart seemed to slow even as her pulse fluttered, a lump forming in her throat.

When was the last time someone considered her like that? The last time someone other than her family thought about her with kindness and care and offered something for no reason other than to make her feel safe?

Jamie cleared his throat and gave her an uncertain smile. He leaned down to grip the bed in one hand and straightened. "Or you might want him out of your hair. Have your apartment to yourself again?" He lowered his voice conspiratorially. "I won't tell him, I promise."

She lurched forward and threw her arms around him. Didn't let herself think too much about it and wonder how he might respond or what it meant. All she knew was he was being thoughtful and kind and saying *Thank you* just didn't feel like enough.

She'd obviously surprised him, because he didn't react at first. Just stood there like a statue, unmoving and rigid.

Then the dog bed hit the carpet with a thump and his arms came up, curving around her waist and back. He was so much bigger than her, and the arm at her waist wrapped all the way around, his palm fanning out across her side, thumb reaching her rib cage. The other shifted up her back with a slight pressure, pulling her in. She closed her eyes and inhaled deeply.

God, he smelled good.

She should have loosened her grip and stepped back but couldn't seem to make her feet move. She stood there, flush against his body, waiting for who knows what. Her skin felt tight and hot, and her racing pulse had nothing to do with obscure worries about her health. This time, it was all Jamie.

As if someone else controlled her body, she shifted her head so her forehead pressed against his chest, and she just stood there, breathing him in, exhaling into the soft cotton stretched across his skin. Her fingers curled around his shoulders, gripping him tighter.

A shudder went through him, and his chest moved up and down as if he forced each drag of air into his lungs. He made no effort to move either, and by all accounts, it seemed they could stay here, entangled in the entryway of her apartment, forever.

Ever so slowly, his upper arm shifted, and his fingers slowly moved up, up, into her hair. An involuntary shiver shot down her spine as he delved his hand between the strands. Blood rushed in her ears, roaring in the silence, and her lungs seized on what very well could have been her last breath.

His head dipped low, warm breath brushing her earlobe.

She couldn't—wouldn't—move. Everything around her shifted and swirled, the ground dropping out from beneath her, threatening to take her down if it weren't for his arms around her.

"I looked for you."

His voice was a deep, low rasp. Her eyelids burned as the words settled beneath her skin and gathered in a chamber of her heart, the same place she'd stored every memory of him. His nose brushed the skin just at her hairline as he breathed out a sigh. "I'm so pissed at you," he murmured into her neck, the first press of his lips there like a shock to her system. "If you'd given me your full name, your number, a fucking email . . . *something*. Anything."

A whimper left her throat, and she didn't even have it in her to be embarrassed. Nothing mattered but his warm, hard body and the trail of his lips down the curve of her shoulder.

She'd dreaded hearing words like this, and yet . . . they were like a balm to her soul. Like coming across the one thing she'd been searching her apartment for all month.

"I looked for you for weeks. *Months.* I couldn't stop thinking about you. But you just disappeared and left me with nothing." That final word came out on a harsh breath.

"I'm sorry," she whispered, throat tight and full. "I didn't know . . ." What? That she'd fall for him after one night? That she'd make it through and see him again? That they'd be so irrevocably connected for the rest of their lives? ". . . I'm sorry."

She could hardly grasp one emotion before another took its place. Comfort, relief, regret, shame. Grateful that she could be here again, with his heartbeat mere inches from hers, his face buried in her neck and his hands memorizing her body.

It was short-lived.

"If I'd known you'd come back, I wouldn't have—"

"No." She sucked in a breath and yanked back, shaking her head. "No. Don't."

What was she doing?

He released her right away, but his arms were slow to fall back to his side. A muscle flexed in his cheek as he clamped his full lips together, silencing the rest of the sentence. His nostrils flared as he stared at her, the green flecks in his eyes somehow brighter.

She pressed both fists to her forehead and took several breaths, willing her heart to calm and her brain to clear. Her gaze dropped several inches to his collarbone because yes, she was a coward.

"Don't say you wouldn't have gotten back together with . . . her." Her throat was a parched desert as she tried to piece together her reaction and explain it to him.

"Okay." Jamie's eyes seemed to drink in her features, his gaze slowly sliding across her face. He held very still. "Is what Tiffany said that night true? You talked about me . . . dreamed about me? When you were in the hospital?"

She tucked her lips between her teeth and nodded. She wasn't afraid to say it—not like she'd been before—but she was trying not to cry.

"When you came back, did you want to see me again?"

She nodded again and took a steadying breath. "But when I did—"

"I was with Carly."

"Yes," she confirmed. "I can't pretend that didn't change anything. I owe her everything."

It changed everything that day, without question. But so much had happened since then, and she wasn't sure where to go from here.

"I meant what I said. I didn't break up with her with expectations from you." He ran a hand through his hair, muscles in his forearm rippling. "It needed to end no matter what, and just days from now she's leaving for a job she's always wanted. Believe me when I say it's better this way for both of us."

If Elliott hadn't seen and heard it from Carly herself, she might not have believed it. But she had, and she did.

"I'll respect your choice about us. Always." The way he said the word *us* nearly buckled her knees with wanting. *Us . . .* If only. "If you can't get past the fact Carly and I were together once, I'll figure out how to live with that. But that might mean I have to stay away from you, because I'm starting to think I can't just be your friend. Not now, not yet. I've tried and I'm failing miserably." His gaze locked on hers, eyes blazing. "I still want you, Elliott. I want to be with you, spend time with you, and learn everything about you. I want to touch and hold you, and I want to kiss you more than I've ever wanted anything. I've tried to stop. I've tried so fucking hard to stop, and it's like deciding to live without air. I don't . . . I don't know how to do that. I don't know if I can."

Elliott would never know how she held herself back in that moment. It took literally every cell of strength to resist what her heart was screaming at her to do: take that step forward and seal her lips across his.

She'd never wanted anything more than the man standing before her, and she'd had reason to make some pretty serious wishes in her lifetime.

But if there was one thing Elliott had learned in her screwed-up life, it was this: some decisions couldn't be made lightly. She'd made informed consent an art form, signing lines to state she had, in fact, read every single page she'd been given about the risks and benefits of procedures, chemotherapy, transplantation, and more. She hadn't just flipped to the last page and signed, either—she'd actually read every. Single. Word. She was a person who had to know what she was getting into and whether the benefit was worth the risks.

She never signed unless she was sure, because then if something went wrong, she knew she'd considered all angles and was going in with her eyes wide open. She'd hope for the good while being prepared for the bad.

"I . . ." *I want you, too.* ". . . I think I just need some time."

She'd been in Omaha almost three months now, and Jamie had been single for two. Carly was moving to Oklahoma this week. How much time would she need before she let herself say yes? Would it ever be enough to give herself grace?

For both their sakes, she hoped she could get there. Soon, maybe. She just wasn't there today.

"I get that. I probably need some time, too." He reached up and rubbed both hands down his face. "I don't know why everything had to happen the way it did, but you have to know I'm just happy I found you again. Because I've never, *never* felt like I did the night I met you. Not before and not after."

"I know." Her voice was so quiet she barely heard it, herself. "It's the same for me. Even if I didn't want it to be."

Something softened in his eyes, and he swayed toward her, sending his rugged, masculine scent into her space. "If you decide it's too much, I'll figure out how to live with that. But hear me when I say: if you decide to give this a try, I'll be here. Waiting for you."

Was she out of her damn mind not to jump him right this second? To just go for it, everything and everyone else be damned?

Yes. Yuka would kill her.

Was she going to drag this out to sift through her nerves because this was a big deal with serious possible ramifications, and maybe to assuage her guilt a little?

Also yes.

Was she an incredibly lucky woman to have a man like him willing to wait while she figured her shit out?

So much so she was starting to think she didn't deserve him.

She traced her toe along the carpet. "Would you really let me hang on to Hank for a few more days?"

"I'd feel better if you did. Honestly that's half the reason I asked you to watch him. I knew he'd love being here, but he's just as spoiled when he goes to my mom's place, and I thought maybe you'd like the company."

The words rushed forward without thought, as if her brain knew if she considered them first they'd stay unspoken forever. "You're making it really hard not to kiss you right now."

His lips parted on a forceful exhale, like she'd punched him in the stomach. He dropped his head back and closed his eyes. "Don't say things like that."

Her skin warmed at his husky tone, and she swallowed. "Sorry."

"I should go."

Yeah, he should. "I'll bring him back Wednesday?"

He turned away from her and quickly went for the door as if he didn't trust himself if he stayed. "Sounds good."

With one last look that burned her from the inside out, he left, Elliott and Hank staring silently after him.

CHAPTER
TWENTY-TWO

Wednesday, August 14

Elliott: Are you serious with this?

    Jamie: Good morning to you, too

    Elliott: Tarts: 70 Recipes for Your Everyday Kitchen?

    Jamie: The cheesecake on page 37 looked pretty great, don't you think?

    Elliott: It looks delicious. It's unfortunate the author is misinformed.

    Jamie: Let's call a truce

    Jamie: (it's a tart)

    Elliott: I don't do truces

    Jamie: Have you asked Blythe her opinion yet?

    Elliott: No, I'm too scared.

    Jamie: Fair

Friday, August 16

Jamie: Got any good books? I need something new.

    Elliott: Lots, what are you looking for?

    Jamie: Just pick a couple favorites. I'm up for anything.

    Elliott: Okay. Trade for the best book you've read recently?

Jamie: Done.

Jamie: I was gonna take Hank for a walk in a few, we'll stop by after.

Elliott: See you soon

Sunday, August 25

Elliott: I'm running on fumes today thanks to you and that thriller you gave me. It's a good thing I work at a coffee shop

Jamie: Did you see that twist at the end coming?

Elliott: WHAT TWIST IM NOT THERE YET

Jamie: Wow, I won't ruin it, calm down

Elliott: I've had six cups of coffee there will be no calming

Elliott: Now all I want to do is get home to finish it!

Jamie: I'm not doing any better over here, got any more of those Lisa Kleypas books? I finished both of them.

Elliott: Like 30 more

Jamie: This Winterborne guy. I can't tell if I think he's an asshole, if I want to be him, or if I have a thing for him

Jamie: "not five fucking minutes"

Jamie: I could never get away with saying something like that

Elliott: I wouldn't be so sure

Jamie: •• Noted

Tuesday, August 27

Elliott: Can I grab Hank for a run tonight?

Jamie: Definitely

Thursday, August 29

Elliott: [image]

Elliott: Know anything about these?

Jamie: They're wild coneflowers. I found them when I was out on a job today and thought you might like them

Jamie: I hope that's okay

Elliott: They're beautiful. Thank you

Sunday, September 1

Jamie: There's a documentary on the history of graphic design on Netflix, seems up your alley

Elliott: Ooh, thanks

Elliott: Perfect timing, I just finished that biography you gave me

Jamie: Did it make you rethink all your life choices

Elliott: Basically

Jamie: Me too

Elliott: So should we quit our jobs and travel the world with nothing but a fanny pack?

Jamie: God, no

Elliott: Hahaha

Jamie: To be clear, it's not because I'm not adventurous, I just can't leave Hank behind

Elliott: Right

Jamie: I'm also not afraid of flying

Elliott: Now I definitely think you are

Jamie: It's a perfectly rational fear being that far off the ground

Elliott: You climb trees every day. I've seen the trophy

Jamie: Yeah 30 feet . . . 30,000 feet—those are the same

Elliott: Touché

Jamie: Road trips are better, anyway

Elliott: I love road trips. Haven't been on many but there's something so exciting about hitting the gas station right before you leave, loading up on snacks and drinks, and plugging in that perfect playlist

Jamie: Best road trip band: Go

Elliott: Beach Boys

Jamie: What
Elliott: I panicked
Elliott: Can I change my answer
Jamie: Please
Elliott: Hozier
Jamie: Much better

Monday, September 2

Jamie: Hey remember that time you said the Beach Boys were your favorite band ever
Elliott: Did you need something?
Jamie: Was just trying to think if I have any embarrassing idols like that
Jamie: Turns out I don't
Elliott: The word idol was never used
Jamie: Might as well have
Elliott: Shouldn't you be working?
Jamie: Probably

Tuesday, September 3

Elliott: Hey remember that time you didn't know narwhals were real?
Jamie: You're trying to make up for the Beach Boys thing and it's not working
Jamie: Also I was never fully convinced until you gave me that book
Jamie: Did you know the females don't have tusks?
Elliott: No way.
Elliott: The dudes are probably insufferable flaunting their extra appendage
Jamie: Horn length contests all day long
Elliott: Such fragile egos, all of you
Jamie: Hey

Wednesday, September 4

Elliott: If you won the lottery, what would you do with the money?

Jamie: That's random

Elliott: I've got a headache, which I'm sure is nothing, but I wanted a distraction while the meds kick in. Otherwise in ten minutes I'll have convinced myself it's a brain tumor or stroke.

Jamie: You okay? Want me to come over?

Elliott: No, I'm fine. Just wanted to talk to someone for a little bit and Yuka's busy.

Jamie: I'm second string?

Elliott: Yes

Jamie: Okay I'll take it

Jamie: I gotta think about that for a second though

Jamie: How much we talking?

Elliott: 100 million

Jamie: Damn

Jamie: Okay—I'd plant a million trees

Elliott: [Tree hugger Jamie has entered the chat]

Jamie: Ha, What about you?

Elliott: Pay off my parents' mortgage and donate the rest to cure cancer

Jamie: I can't think of anything better.

Jamie: (but could you maybe plant just one tree)

Elliott: Okay but I'm not climbing it

Jamie: deal

Thursday, September 5

Jamie: Up for a run tonight with me and Hank?

Elliott: Sure

Jamie: Come by at 7?

Elliott: See you then

Friday, September 6

Elliott: Thank you for the flowers. What are these?

    Jamie: Black-eyed Susans. This is the best time of year for them

    Jamie: If you want me to stop giving them to you, I will

    Elliott: I don't want you to stop.

CHAPTER TWENTY-THREE

Elliott

Mondays were Elliott's favorite day of the week.

She always thought Mondays got a bad rap, but then again, days of the week had never meant to her what they did for other people. Cancer didn't care what day of the week it was. Chemo didn't care about weekend parties or social calendars. From the age of seventeen, she'd been in and out of hospitals, doctor's offices, and infusion centers. She'd taken most of her college classes online and didn't follow a standard Monday-through-Friday course schedule. Even now, she worked for herself and at a coffee shop that opened hellishly early, so no day of the week was off-limits.

Still, she'd always looked forward to Mondays. Maybe it was because in the early days of her parents' bookstore, it was the only day they closed. Owning a small business was hard, and they worked all the time. But when Monday rolled around, she had them all to herself.

When she'd hit middle school, they started hosting Monday-night poker, and the house would fill with laughter and a smorgasbord of finger foods Elliott pilfered when no one was looking. As she got older, she joined the game when she felt well enough and had become a pretty decent card player.

She hadn't been back home for a Monday, or a poker night, since the move nearly four months ago, but apparently Mondays still stuck with her because she woke up that morning in a great mood. Miraculously, she'd slept pretty well and felt fresh and energized.

The good vibes didn't last long.

She had a meeting with Blythe that evening—the printed menus with custom hand lettering (no *Melt My Fart* typos to be seen) had finally arrived, and she couldn't wait to show her. Everything was in her bag and ready to go, but with several hours to kill, Elliott had just sat down at her computer to check her email when her phone rang.

Her eyebrows shot up when she saw who was calling. Tristan Underwood was a friend from Elliott's days as a leukemia patient basically living in the oncology ward of the hospital. Tristan had been a year younger than Elliott and diagnosed with leukemia around the same time. They'd gone through virtually identical treatments, and at the time, she'd been one of Elliott's closest friends. Yuka was there, too, at the beginning, but with a different type of cancer and drastically different treatments. Tristan had known exactly what Elliott was going through.

Tristan lived in a tiny town several hours away, so once the inpatient portion of her treatment ended, Elliott hardly ever saw her. They'd kept in touch, even if communication had become less frequent over the years. Tristan had been one of the first people Elliott called when her cancer relapsed, and again after they were pretty sure the stem cell transplant had been successful. They hadn't spoken since then, though . . . so it had been close to a year.

When was the last time Elliott had spoken to Tristan's mom, whose name flashed across her screen? It had to have been at least three times that long.

"Hi, Mrs. Underwood," Elliott greeted her. "What a pleasant surprise."

"Good morning, Elliott. How are you?"

Something about her tone sent an unpleasant shiver down Elliott's spine. "I'm good. Is everything okay? How's Tristan?"

The shaky breath on the other end of the line told Elliott she didn't want to hear what came next. "I'm sorry to call so early, and under these circumstances. But I didn't want you to hear it from anyone else. Tristan passed away over the weekend."

Elliott's hand covered her mouth. Almost immediately her eyes burned with tears. "Oh my gosh, what happened? Did the leukemia come back?"

Mrs. Underwood sniffled. "We'd just confirmed the diagnosis last week. She hadn't been feeling well, but we hoped . . . after all this time that it was something else. It was aggressive and quick, and by the time we got an answer and made a plan, she was gone. We didn't even get a chance to start treatment."

Hot tears slid down Elliott's cheeks. "I'm so, so sorry."

"We are, too. I really thought we were past this, you know? She's been in remission so long, and . . ." She trailed off, openly crying now. "It just doesn't seem real."

Elliott swiped her hand under her chin where tears dripped onto her shirt. No matter how intimately involved she was in the cancer community, nothing would ever prepare her for news like this. "She was such an incredible person and meant so much to me. Is there anything I can do for your family?"

"No. Tristan's the only thing I want, and you can't give me that. No one can. I just wanted you to know what happened, and to tell you Tristan loved you so much. You were like her big sister that year she was in the hospital, and I know it would have been a dark time for her without you. I can never thank you enough."

"She was the same for me. She never let cancer stop her." She'd been a bright light no matter how low the circumstances, even earning the nickname Sunshine from the nurses. It suited her then and she'd lived up to it ever since.

Mrs. Underwood laughed softly through her tears. "That was true until the end. She went after every single dream she had. Held nothing back. If there's anything that makes this any more bearable, and I don't say that lightly because no parent should witness their child leaving this earth, it's that I know she lived every second of this life to the fullest. She experienced love, happiness, and joy, and I'm so grateful for it."

"Me too." Elliott swallowed past the lump in her throat. "Please let me know if you think of something—anything—I can do. I mean it."

"I will. Just . . . take care of yourself, okay?"

"I will," Elliott said, suddenly wondering if she was really doing all that good a job. "I promise."

Several hours and a good, healthy cry later, Elliott pulled herself together and made her way to Melt My Tart. The updated website had been live for several weeks, and the menus were the last piece of the business agreement with Blythe. Elliott was a little bummed she wouldn't have an excuse to spend time with her anymore.

She entered the bakery, which was busier than Elliott had ever seen it. Customers occupied most of the tables, and five people stood in line, waiting. A harried Blythe rushed around behind the counter, and her eyes went wide when she spotted Elliott. Blythe frantically waved her closer, and the second Elliott was near the pastry case she said, "Thank God. Could you pop back here for a second?"

"What?"

"My closer had car trouble and couldn't get here. I just need someone to help pour coffee and box things up. Do you mind? Just until this line dies down?"

Elliott glanced around. Why not? "Sure, I can do that." She rounded the corner and put her purse down. "Just tell me what to do."

"Wash your hands. Sink's back there."

Elliott did as she was told and spent the next hour helping Blythe with her customers. The setup here was pretty different from Starbucks, but she could follow directions. The pies, tarts, and cakes were already pre-sliced, so all she had to do was put things on plates or into pre-sectioned boxes. There was a minor snafu with a chocolate mousse brownie that ended up on the floor, and Elliott was just glad Yuka hadn't been there to witness it. She might have cried or eaten it straight off the floor.

When they'd cleared out the line, Blythe handed Elliott a bottle of water. "Thank you so much. You saved my ass."

Elliott leaned her hip against the back counter and took a long drink. "That was crazy. Is it always like that on Monday nights?"

"Didn't used to be, but it has been getting steadily busier, which is why I started scheduling two of us here in the evenings. Being on my own tonight confirmed how necessary that is."

"Agreed."

Blythe pushed hair back from her face. "You get to take some credit for that, you know."

That was taking it a little too far, but Elliott grinned despite herself. This was exactly why she loved this job. "Not true. Your food is that good."

"Obviously," Blythe allowed. "But most of the new business has been driven by online orders. Which you set up for me."

"Okay, okay." Elliott laughed. "I'll own that. But really, I can't tell you how happy it makes me. This place is the best in town, and soon you'll be voted Best Bakery in *Enjoy Omaha* magazine."

"From your mouth to God's ears."

"Ready to see the menus? Or do you wanna wait until you close?" They had five minutes to go, and Elliott was in no hurry.

Blythe did a visual sweep of the store and settled her gaze back on Elliott. "Now, please."

Her enthusiasm bolstered Elliott's excitement to show her, and she handed them over. Blythe squealed loud enough that the older couple near the counter twisted around to look at them.

Elliott winced. "Sorry. Excuse us."

"These are so freaking perfect," Blythe gushed, holding the bright-pink menus in front of her face. "You're a genius, Elliott. Seriously."

"They turned out really great. I know the custom lettering took longer, but it was totally worth it."

"You were so right. I *love* them." Blythe put the menus down and hugged her. "I'm telling everyone I know about you. You'll be able to quit working at Starbucks in no time."

Elliott laughed. She probably could right now, truth be told, but she didn't mind her shifts at the coffee shop, and even as a part-time employee, she was eligible for health insurance. Unless she started turning away design jobs, she didn't see herself leaving anytime soon.

"How about coffee after I close up?" Blythe asked.

"Sure, thanks."

Elliott made herself useful and boxed up the remaining pastries. She stuck them in the double-door fridge in the back while Blythe walked out the final customers and locked the door behind her, flipping off the OPEN sign. Elliott returned to the counter and rested her elbows across the top as Blythe poured her a cup and slid it across.

Elliott took a deep breath, savoring the aroma. "Mmm. Thanks."

"So," Blythe said, clearing her throat. "How are you?"

Something felt strange in Blythe's tone, though Elliott couldn't put her finger on why. "Fine?"

"Yeah?"

She nodded and took a small sip of the hot beverage. "Yes. Why do you ask?"

"No reason."

Elliott narrowed her eyes. She didn't know Blythe all that well, but they'd spent a decent amount of time together. "I . . . don't believe you?"

Blythe sawed her teeth across her bottom lip and shifted on her feet. "You shouldn't. But I promised Jamie I wouldn't get involved."

"Wouldn't get involved in what?" Elliott cocked a brow when Blythe didn't immediately respond. "We've established something's up, so there's no point in hiding it now. That's not cool."

She sighed audibly. "Fine. Just . . . I only want what's best for him, okay?"

"Sure." *So do I, I think.*

"I promised I wouldn't say anything, but . . . whatever." She scratched at the side of her nose and looked at the ceiling for a moment. "I know who you are, okay? I know about the night you and Jamie met and went to that baking class."

Elliott blinked. "You do?"

Blythe nodded, looking a little guilty.

"For how long? Did you know it was me from the beginning?"

"No. It wasn't until that day we looked at the website mock-ups. You said you didn't like chocolate, and it jogged my memory. Jamie'd told me about you back then, and after the shock of seeing my brother so animated over a woman, I couldn't get past the fact he said he'd met someone who didn't like chocolate. I'd never heard of such a thing, and I didn't connect the two until later that night, but . . . I finally did."

"Oh." Elliott wasn't really sure where to go from here. "I'm sorry I didn't mention it. It was such a brief meeting I didn't expect you to know who I was, and—"

"I don't care about that at all. I wouldn't expect you to tell me anything about it—you didn't know me."

"Oh," Elliott said again. "Okay."

"Jamie and I are close, okay? I know what he's been dealing with these last few months since you've been back. It hasn't been easy for him, so I was just thinking maybe it hasn't been easy for you, either. So . . . are you okay?"

Shit, was she about to cry for the second time that day?

Blythe kept going. "I can't imagine you have many people you can talk about . . . *this* . . . with." She waved a hand around. "Because of everything with Carly and all that."

Elliott took a sip of coffee to buy some time while she thought. From the limited interactions she'd had with Blythe, she seemed genuine and trustworthy. Jamie obviously felt the same, to have been open about this with his sister, and that only added more points in her favor. Yuka was the only person Elliott had talked to about Jamie, and while Blythe certainly wasn't an impartial party, it could be nice to have a fresh perspective.

"Carly's the only reason I'm alive right now."

Blythe's expression remained neutral. "Yes."

"Isn't—" Elliott reached across to rub her arm. "Doesn't it seem horrible when you think about it? I kissed her boyfriend, she saved my life, I move to town a year later and make said boyfriend break up with her. And now he wants to be with me for real, and I think I want that, too, but how? How can I do that to her?"

The kindness and empathy in Blythe's eyes made Elliott think this wasn't the first time Blythe had heard something along these lines. What had her conversations with Jamie been like?

Blythe tipped her head toward the empty café. "Want to sit down?"

Elliott followed her and they sat at the same table where she had first met Blythe to discuss working together.

"You may not want my advice—and actually, I wouldn't even call it advice. That's what I give Jamie, but he's my brother and sometimes he's an idiot so I basically have to tell him what to do every once in a while. I'm in no place to tell you to do anything, but I'd love to share some observations with you, if that's okay."

God, to be a fly on the wall sometime when Blythe lectured Jamie. That was probably entertaining as hell. "I have no idea what I'm doing, so by all means. I'm open to anything you've got."

"First things first. He wasn't Carly's boyfriend when you two first met. Neither of you did anything wrong that night, so let's get that out of the way now."

Elliott gave a little nod. "Yeah." She knew deep down it was true, and Yuka'd told her the same thing, but it was nice to hear someone who hadn't sworn best-friend fealty to Elliott say it.

"Second. She saved your life, yes. You moved to town. But you didn't make Jamie do anything. He did what he thought was right, and I'm one thousand percent certain it would have happened eventually anyway. He and Carly's relationship has always been strange to me, in that it always just seemed like a convenience thing. Even so, he's tried hard not to be an asshole like our father, and to take commitment seriously. So when you came back to town, it didn't take him long to realize being with Carly wasn't the best thing for either of them. He knows you're different, Elliott. That what happened between you two was something extraordinary."

Elliott's voice cracked. "It was."

It still is.

A quiet moment passed before Blythe spoke again, her tone gentle. "You don't have to answer this, but . . . does part of you want to try with him? See what happens?"

"Part of me?" Elliott almost laughed. "More like *every* part of me. Everything except this voice in my head telling me I shouldn't because of his history with Carly. But with every day that passes, that voice gets quieter and quieter, and I don't know how much longer I'll listen to it."

Blythe offered her a small smile. "I'd be lying if I said that didn't make me happy, but only because I want Jamie to be happy. If the expression on your face is any indication, you seem to really like him."

More than was healthy, probably. "I do."

"He's extremely into you, too, if you didn't know. Like, embarrassingly so."

Elliott's smile couldn't be stopped. Hadn't she felt this exact thing, less than a mile away, sixteen months ago? A bubbly sort of giddy excitement filling her chest at the mere thought of spending more time with the handsome blond man with the sexiest dimple she'd ever seen?

"I'm gonna say one more thing, and then I should probably head out so my four-year-old doesn't completely annihilate my husband before dinner." Blythe retrieved her phone and pulled up Instagram. "But I just wish you'd both stop looking at the past and consider what could happen next, because it looks like Carly has. Did you know she's already seeing someone?"

Elliott blinked at the screen. How had she missed that?

Carly had posted the selfie yesterday, her arm extended to capture herself and the handsome, dark-haired man standing behind her, his head next to hers as he pressed a kiss to her cheek.

"But . . . she's only been gone a month."

Blythe shrugged and took her phone back. "Sometimes that's all it takes." She arched a brow. "Sometimes it only takes one night."

Touché.

"Look, I'm not saying you have to do anything because of that. If you have other reservations, that's between you and Jamie. But if Carly's the only thing holding you back, it just seems like that's maybe not something you need to worry about anymore, you know? Love can be messy and inconvenient. It doesn't always show up at the most opportune time, or even with the person we always thought. But that's what makes it so magical. She's moved on and living her life. Why can't Jamie do that, too? Why can't you?"

"I—" Elliott started, then stopped. She honestly didn't have an answer for that.

"If what you and Jamie have is the real thing—even if it *could* be the real thing—I just worry you'll never forgive yourselves if you let it pass you by."

Mrs. Underwood's sentiment about Tristan felt timely. *She lived every second of this life to the fullest. She experienced love, happiness, and joy.*

Something shifted. Something deep and irrevocable and meaningful, and Elliott had the urge to jump out of this chair and run to Jamie's apartment right this second.

She wanted to.

She *needed* to.

Standing, she grabbed her bag and circled the table, bending to give Blythe a hug. "Thanks for the coffee," she whispered, and headed straight for the door.

Blythe's words scrolled through her brain as she drove straight to her apartment complex.

Love is messy and inconvenient, and you'll never forgive yourself if you let it pass you by.

And Jamie's from several weeks ago, sending a shiver through her, even now.

I want you, Elliott. If you decide you want to give this a try, I'll be waiting for you.

Of course she wanted to give it a try. She'd pined after this man for over a year, and her feelings had only deepened since he'd come back into her life. Jamie was everything she never knew she wanted in a man.

Kind, thoughtful, intelligent. Observant, reserved, and a good listener. A dog lover and a tree hugger. A beer-drinking, salsa-eating runner, who brought flowers and left books on her doorstep.

After the shock of losing Tristan, it was clear no one knew the time they had left on this earth, and Elliott didn't want to waste any more time.

She didn't even go home first and headed straight for his building. Unable to wait for the elevator, she took the stairs to his floor and knocked, forcing her feet to stay flat on the ground as anticipation built in her chest.

Jamie opened the door. Her breath hitched at the sight of him, barefoot in jeans and a gray T-shirt, his glasses slightly crooked on his ridiculously handsome face.

He regarded her with lonely eyes and ran a hand through his thick hair. "Hey."

"Hi," she said, and stepped forward until her lips met his.

CHAPTER
TWENTY-FOUR

Jamie

Jamie died the second Elliott kissed him.

He came back to life when she didn't stop.

He wrapped his arms around her waist, lifting her against his body to carry her inside as the door swung shut.

Her arms clamped around his shoulders in a viselike grip, as if she was worried he'd disappear. She kissed him with urgency and impatience and without finesse, and it was utterly perfect.

Vaguely he wondered what had changed. What had happened to bring her here and kiss him like this?

He didn't care enough to ask.

Disoriented, he took another step back as he lifted his head to figure out which way he needed to go to get her somewhere—a couch, a bed, a fucking table—and he tripped over his overly excited dog.

Jamie went down with a crash, his hip hitting the coffee table and his flailing arm pushing the remotes to the floor. His glasses went flying. He landed on his back with a grunt, and Elliott ended up on top of him in a tangle of limbs.

They looked at each other and burst out laughing. Hank shoved his wet nose between them and went back and forth, licking their faces.

"Um," Jamie said.

Her eyes dropped to his lips, and she came at him again. He elbowed Hank out of the way and dropped his head to the carpet, burying his fingers in her hair and inhaling her scent as he tasted her. Her tongue entered his mouth as she straddled him, and he'd never cared less that he was on his back on the floor. They could be rolling around in the dirt as long as Elliott's lips were on his.

He angled his head to kiss her deeper, his hand spanning the back of her head, tracing her ear with his thumb. She shivered as her fingers moved all over his chest and abs, leaving trails of fire everywhere she touched.

The pressure had been building for sixteen months. Now that it was finally happening, he didn't know how to be gentle. He was too far gone. Had denied himself too long.

He shifted her hips to where he wanted her, and she let out the sexiest little sound he'd ever heard.

"Oh my . . . Jamie," she panted, sitting up a little, which put more pressure there, and his eyes almost rolled to the back of his head. "We're on the floor. I didn't mean to, um . . ."

"Do I look like I care?" He lifted his hips a little. He pulled her back down and growled against her lips. "Does it feel like I care?"

Her already flushed cheeks went a deeper shade of red. She kissed him for a long moment before she pulled back again. "Still. I didn't mean to come over and attack you like that." She slid off him and stood, holding out her hand.

He lumbered off the ground on his own, knowing if he touched her he'd just pull her back on top of him. "Again, I'm not complaining. Do that every day. Please."

Hank wormed his way between them and sat in front of Elliott, his tail sweeping the floor. Jamie didn't have to see his face to know he was giving her his best puppy-dog eyes.

She laughed and knelt down to hug him. "Hey, bud. I didn't mean to ignore you, but I was on a mission." She nuzzled his neck and rubbed his ears, and as he watched them, Jamie's heart filled to the brim.

Also: a mission?

Was that her way of saying this was a go? She wanted to be with him for real?

He was too afraid to ask. Was that pathetic? That even if she walked out the door right now, he'd take these last several minutes over the alternative?

They'd spent a lot of time together the last couple of weeks. Running, talking, trading books. Once she spotted him at the dog park with Hank and came out to sit with him while Hank spent an hour running himself ragged. He'd learned a lot about her, and she him.

They'd become friends, and it had been incredible.

But it wasn't enough. Not for him.

After she'd finished loving on Hank, she straightened. He hadn't even gotten a good look at her when he first opened the door. She was perfect in jeans and a relaxed V-neck shirt showing off that sexy collarbone that drove him crazy. The tiniest hint of her port was visible on the left side before disappearing underneath her shirt. Her face was devoid of makeup, and her soft hair hung straight to her shoulders, where just seconds ago he'd pressed his nose to inhale her citrusy scent.

She was so very Elliott, and he could hardly breathe.

Her gray eyes searched his face, and she stepped forward to slide her hands around his waist. She laid her cheek against his heart, breathing deeply and humming with satisfaction when he returned the embrace.

"So," he finally said.

"So."

"We gonna talk, or should we just head to my room?"

She smacked his chest and he laughed.

"Seriously, though . . ." He wanted her with a ferocity that quite frankly scared him.

She looked up at him with a smile. "I vote for both, but we should probably talk first."

"Yeah, probably. But you have to sit over there." He sat in the armchair and pointed to the couch. "I need to keep my distance if you don't want me to touch you."

"Same," she agreed, though she looked just as unhappy being several feet away. "Thanks for giving me some time."

"I'd never want this if you weren't sure. It might have killed me if you didn't decide to give me a chance, but it was a risk I was willing to take." He passed a hand across his jaw. "I might regret asking this, but what changed?"

"Everything and nothing at all."

"I see."

She laughed. "Nothing changed about the way I feel about you. It's been the one constant ever since we met, a lingering awareness that never faded. At first it was warm and good and gave me hope. But even when it became something sort of dark and that I felt guilty about, it was still there. No matter what I did or how hard I tried to pretend it wasn't."

"Add to that a few months of pathetic pining, and I've had the same experience." He'd been a real stage-five clinger to her memory.

"I'm sorry," she said again. "I'll always wish I handled that night differently."

He shook his head. "Don't be." He wasn't trying to make her feel bad. He'd do it all over again as long as they ended up here, tonight. "What matters is now and what happens next."

"Your sister said the same thing," she said with a wry grin.

"Did she?" He wasn't sure how he felt about his sister meddling, but Elliott was here, so who the fuck cared?

"Yeah. I stopped by there tonight, and we talked it out. She made a lot of good points."

"She usually does."

"After talking to her, and based on what Yuka's been saying for weeks now, it seems . . . different somehow," she said. "Now that more time has passed and Carly has left town. I know it's stupid, and it's probably just in my head. But no matter how much I like you and how badly I want to be with you, it doesn't change the fact that I owe Carly everything."

"What did change, then?"

"Since the moment I found out you and Carly were together, I've lied. To you, Carly, myself. I've tried to convince myself we could just be friends and that would be okay. It wasn't until Blythe said Carly started making plans that didn't involve you, and I saw her laughing with someone else, that I let myself admit what an outrageous lie that was."

She seemed to study his face when she said the part about Carly with someone else. He hadn't known Carly was dating again, but the news didn't upset him. On the contrary, he was relieved. His hands shook with anticipation of where she might take this. "What's the truth?"

"The truth is, I've thought about you every single day since the night we met. The memory of you carried me through months of solitude in a hospital bed. There was one week when things got kind of scary and my body wasn't doing well, and I honestly wasn't sure I'd come out of it. I'd picture your face and think of the things we talked about and the sweet things you said to me and told myself if I could just be strong enough to get through it, I'd let myself come find you someday." She swiped at her cheeks, smiling through her tears. "I really did move to Omaha for a job and to start fresh. But I could have done that anywhere. There's a reason I wanted to do it here, in this town. That reason was you."

In one fluid motion he was up and at her side, his palms framing her face.

She covered his hands with hers. "I can't even begin to tell you how crushed I was when I saw you and Carly together. But I forced myself to accept you were with someone else and that my chance with you was gone. If I really have a second chance, this time I won't let you walk away without telling you how incredible I think you are, and how badly I want you to be mine."

He pressed his forehead to hers. "I'm not going anywhere. You fit me like no one else ever has." He tilted his lips forward and kissed her softly.

"I think you might be everything I've ever wanted," she whispered.

They kissed for several minutes, thorough and unhurried. Instead of hiding behind mutual self-denial, they were stepping forward to explore what was there all along, and God, it felt good.

Somewhere in the back of his mind he wondered how this kiss compared to their first one at the hotel and quickly decided this one was better. This time he *knew* her. He knew more than just her middle name and a few random facts about her personality. Now he knew who she was and who she wanted to be. He knew what she'd gone through to get here, and that he wanted to walk beside her as she continued on the road to achieve her dreams.

"Jamie," she murmured.

"Hmm?"

"I . . . want you. But do you think we should wait?"

"Why?" Maybe in this moment it felt like zero to sixty, but in reality this was more than a year in the making.

"I don't know." She glanced up at him from beneath long, dark lashes. "Can we, then?"

He smiled against her mouth then stood and reached for her hand, leading her farther into his apartment than she'd ever gone. He paused at the door and ushered her in, then turned to Hank, who had followed them. "Sorry, bud. No dogs allowed for this part."

He closed the bedroom door, leaving Hank in the living room. When he turned back to Elliott, her hand covered her heart. "Did you see his face?"

Jamie chuckled at her distress. He loved his dog, but . . .

He stepped closer and smoothed her hair back. "The first thing he'd do is jump in the bed with us. I'd be distracted and that's unacceptable." He dipped his head and pressed a kiss to her neck. "I want to focus on you, and only you."

She tilted her head to the side to give him better access. Her audible sigh was thick with desire, but when she slid her fingers into his hair, her hands were shaking. Jamie reached up to take her hands and wove their fingers together, lifting his head to look at her.

"You okay?"

She nodded, her gray eyes wide and focused on his face. "I'm good," she reassured him. "Nervous and excited, but in a good way. It's just been a while. A couple of years."

Years? It made sense when he thought about it, with everything she'd gone through. That meant she hadn't slept with Stephen, and all he could think about that was, *Thank fuck.*

He kissed the back of her hand. "We don't have to do this tonight."

Smiling, she walked backward until her legs hit the bed, pulling him with her. "I want to. Do you?"

He snorted at the ridiculous question. "Clearly."

Her smile widened and his heart stopped beating. She released his hands and pulled her shirt over her head before scooting back to lie down. Immediately he put his hands on her, sliding his palms up her smooth stomach. He pressed a kiss to her belly button, eliciting a giggle from her.

"I love your laugh," he said to her ribs. "Making you smile puts me on top of the world."

"You must be there now," she said, sounding a little breathless. "I can't stop smiling."

He grinned and delivered another kiss between her breasts. "Me either."

She tugged at his shirt, and he yanked it off, watching her devour his body with her gaze.

"Your body is incredible," she sighed. "I can't stop looking at you."

He slid one hand up her side while the other burrowed under her back to press her up and against him, bringing their hearts as close as they could get. "And I can't stop touching you."

Leaning up, she captured his lips, and they kissed long and slow and deep. She wrapped her legs around his waist, the fabric of her jeans brushing the bare skin of his back, and he arched into her. She moaned at the same time he let out a groan.

She hadn't been with a man in years, and he could take that two ways. One, she probably wouldn't notice if he was a fumbling idiot as he lost his mind over her. It took a little pressure off, but he also considered the second point, which was this: she'd gone a long time without, and she deserved the very best he could give her. She deserved fireworks.

Jamie smiled as he slid down her body.

He was up to the task.

CHAPTER
TWENTY-FIVE

Elliott

Elliott woke up with a dog at her feet and a large, naked man at her back.

Hank sensed she was awake and immediately thumped his tail on the mattress. Smiling, Elliott held her index finger up to her lips.

"Shh," she whispered. "You'll wake your dad."

Jamie shifted behind her and tightened his grip around her waist. "Too late."

Her stomach dipped at his low, sexy, sleep-tinged voice. One of his knees slid between hers and he brushed her hair back, nuzzling at her neck.

Her body came alive immediately, warming her from the inside out. She rolled over to face him, and they both stopped moving for a few seconds, heads on fluffy pillows, just looking at each other.

"Good morning," she said, a huge smile spreading across her face.

"Good morning, beautiful." His large hand came to rest on her cheek, and there wasn't even a trace of awkwardness this morning after.

A tightness clenched inside her chest as her heart throbbed, permeated with emotion. Mostly extreme happiness, some disbelief she was actually here in his arms, and a small measure of apprehension.

It felt too good to be true.

He slid closer and kissed her softly. "I can't believe I'm waking up next to you."

She closed her eyes and ran her hand up and down the smooth, hard muscles of his back. "Me either."

Their lips came together again, and her stomach filled with the fluttering of a thousand butterflies. She thought back to last night and how perfect it had been. Jamie was attentive and considerate, constantly asking what felt good and if she wanted something different.

She couldn't think of a single thing that hadn't felt wonderful. They'd smiled and laughed, and been serious and focused. Her cheeks heated at the memory of his body stretched taut over hers, his face twisted with pleasure and determination as he moved.

It had been just like her dream, but better.

He grinned at her. "Whatcha thinking about?"

Her eyelids fluttered. "What? Nothing."

"You're blushing."

"Am not."

"Are too."

"Fine. I was just comparing last night to the time I dreamed about us doing . . . that."

His smile widened. "Your dreams were like that, huh?"

Her face flamed hotter. "The best one was. We were, um . . . in the back seat of your truck."

His eyebrows shot up. "Really? That sounds cramped."

"You were pretty resourceful and made it work just fine."

"Sounds like me." He pressed a kiss to her jaw. "But please tell me the real thing was better. I can't let Dream Jamie win this one."

"Dream Jamie did some good work, but you won fair and square." She trailed her hands down his chest and abs, and his muscles contracted as she passed over the ridges. "Honestly, how are you this sexy?"

"I should ask you the same thing." He rolled on top of her, caging her in between his forearms and thighs. He met her gaze. "I'm crazy about you."

Jamie kissed her lips, then worked his way down her throat. He trailed his tongue along her collarbone, then stopped at her upper chest. Shifting to one side, he brought his hand up and traced the pads of his fingers over her port.

"Will you have this forever?"

"No. I hope not, anyway," she said, glancing down at his fingers brushing the device buried under her skin. "I probably should have had it taken out by now. I've just been scared to."

His hazel eyes grew concerned. "Because you're worried you might need it again?"

She nodded. "I got it out after my first remission, and the cancer came back, and I had to get a new one anyway. I guess I'm just waiting until I feel confident I beat it this time."

"What do you think that will take? For you to feel good about it?"

"I'm not sure. The hundred-day mark after a transplant is a big milestone. So is a year, and I passed both of those. But I still don't feel ready. I was cancer-free for several years the first time before it came back."

"Didn't you say a transplant is supposed to work better than what you had before?"

"Yeah." She didn't know what else to say. Had no explanation for why she let fear rule her, or why she still had this underlying feeling something would go wrong eventually.

Jamie didn't seem to mind. He didn't push her for more information or try to convince her everything would be fine. He couldn't promise that, and she appreciated the fact he wouldn't say the empty words when he had no control over the outcome. He simply brushed his lips over her skin, right there, where needles had pierced through so many times she'd lost count.

"Whatever happens, I'll be here."

She shifted upward and kissed him hard, and as they moved around the bed, lost in each other, Hank whined and jumped off.

Jamie laughed and Elliott glanced at him worriedly. "Do we need to let him out?"

He shook his head and buried his face in her neck. "Nope. I snuck him out around three in the morning, after you woke me up for round two."

Elliott bit her lip. "Oh."

"Now, where were we?"

Jamie made love to her once more before they got out of bed. Elliott's legs were a little wobbly, and he chuckled when she slowly made her way to the kitchen.

He handed her a cup of coffee with a smug grin.

She arched a brow. "Proud of yourself?"

"That I'm a little dehydrated, my back hurts, and you're having trouble walking? Hell, yes."

She pursed her lips and sat at the kitchen table. Hank was by her side right away and lay his head on her thigh.

Jamie sat across from her and frowned. Hank looked up and flicked his brown eyes between them for a few seconds, as if trying to decide who he should sit by.

"I know, bud. I don't like this, either."

Jamie stood and scooted his chair next to her. He took the coffee mug from her hands and set it on the table before grabbing her by the waist and hoisting her onto his lap, then dragging the cup to sit before her again. "Better."

Elliott spun around so her legs dangled to the side and sipped her coffee, admiring his disheveled sex hair over the rim of her cup. His glasses perched on his straight nose, and she couldn't decide how she liked him best. He was sexy as hell with them, but when they'd been in bed last night and he'd looked at her with those hazel eyes so close and unobstructed . . . that had been pretty wonderful, too.

He appeared to be studying her, too, and the curve of his lips and spark in his gaze made her feel warm and beautiful. Resting a large hand on her hip, he took a drink.

She tried not to worry about crushing his legs. "What time do you have to be at work?"

"As luck would have it, I'm off today."

"I have you all to myself?"

He hummed into her hair. "Do you work at Starbucks today?"

"No." She had other stuff she could work on, but . . . it could wait.

"Can I take you out tonight?"

She bit her lip. "Like, *out* out?" There was nothing she wanted more, but there were a lot of people around town who knew him. Knew Carly. She didn't regret coming here last night, or everything that happened after . . . but she wasn't quite ready for the world to know.

He studied her for a few seconds, understanding dawning. "Thinking we should lie low for a while?"

She lifted one shoulder, glad he didn't seem offended. "Maybe?"

"You're probably right. I wish I could take you out, though. On a real date."

She leaned into his chest. "I don't need that." His body was warm and solid, and she could have stayed there all day.

"Why don't we do it here? Get dressed up and have dinner and drinks. Pretend we're out in Old Market doing the same thing."

She tipped her head back to look at him, grinning. "I love that idea."

"I can't cook, though." He sounded so disappointed in himself, she laughed.

"We can order takeout. That Indian place down the street."

"They have the best tandoori." His thumb slipped beneath her shirt to sweep back and forth over her skin. "I can't wait to see what else we have in common. And how we'll handle things we don't."

"Like the cheesecake thing?"

"Exactly." He looked over at the coffee table, and she followed his gaze to the bright-blue cover of the book about ocean animals. "Can I have that book of pies now? I might find something in there I want Blythe to make."

"I'll think about it."

He laughed, kissed her hair, and then inhaled deeply. "Damn, you always smell so good. Let's have our coffee, eat, and make out on the couch, and then I want to take you to my trees."

"Your trees?"

"Yep. Every arborist has a favorite tree. It's a rule. I have two and I want you to see them."

Jamie drove her forty-five minutes south of Omaha to a small farm. After passing a yellow farmhouse, he turned onto a bumpy, single-lane dirt road and continued on for about ten minutes before pulling off into the grass.

"This was my grandparents' place," he explained as he opened the door. "But I know the people who bought it. They hardly ever come out to this part of the land. They don't care if I visit every once in a while."

Elliott was glad she wore jeans as Jamie helped her over the wooden, three-rail fence and took her hand as they crossed a field of tall grass. At the top of a small hill sat two massive trees casting shadows on a single park bench.

"They're white oaks. Probably a hundred and fifty years old, at least. The leaves turn the most stunning red in the fall."

The trees stood alone in the field, and the solidarity only added to their majesty. "They're beautiful."

"I used to come out here in the summers after a long day of working the farm with my grandpa. He got onto me a few times for disappearing before the work was done, but I didn't want to miss all the daylight," he said with a laugh. "He died a few years ago, and my grandmother followed him pretty quick. He was a great man. I have no idea how my dad turned out the way he did."

"I wish I could have met him."

"Me too." He squeezed her hand and started forward again, settling onto the bench and pulling her against his side. "One year on my birthday, they had this bench put in for me. The best time to come is at dawn, when the sun has just come over the horizon and the mist is rising from the field."

"We'll have to come back, then."

"I'd like that. I haven't been out here in months." He leaned his head back against the bench and closed his eyes, breathing deeply.

Elliott lay her head against his chest, content to feel the rise and fall of his body and listen to the rustle of the leaves in the breeze. Her heart was like a sponge in water, soaking up the joy of being with him in this perfect moment. She wished she'd brought her camera.

She was so comfortable and warm against him, she startled when he spoke.

"This is a good place to share secrets," he said softly.

"Is it? Bring a lot of girls here?"

"You're the first. But I told myself a lot of secrets under these trees. Sometimes I came out here and said them out loud to no one and let the wind carry them away. There are some secrets I've never told anyone, and some I've only told you."

She shifted to gaze up at his face.

"I've never told anyone else how relieved I was when they released me from the team. I'm never admitting to anyone else that I didn't know narwhals really existed. And you're the only soul on earth who knows I've read a Lisa Kleypas novel."

"Not only that you read it, but you read it in *one sitting*."

"I've never laughed so hard, rooted so hard for a shy girl who doesn't dance—"

"A wallflower."

"Right, a wallflower—all while being sort of turned on half the time. It was a, uh . . . unique experience."

He grinned and shook his head as Elliott laughed. How she was lucky enough to be with this man, right here and in this moment, she'd never know.

His fingers drifted up and down her arm. "So. What do you have to add to this perfect spot for secret telling?"

She twisted her lips to the side while she thought. "I used to love chocolate. I would have given Yuka's obsession a run for her money."

"Really? What happened?"

"Chemo. It changes the way things taste. Sometimes they come back, sometimes they don't. And while it's sort of a blessing in disguise because I know it's not healthy, I sort of miss having that experience. I see the look on people's faces when they take that first bite of their favorite dessert, and I wonder if they know how lucky they are. To be able to enjoy that."

"The look on your face the first time I saw you taste our soufflé gave me a semi, so I'd say you have that to fall back on when you want to enjoy something."

She burst out laughing and smacked his rock-hard stomach.

"It's true."

"I guess you're right," she said, still giggling.

"What else?"

She was tempted to sit up and face him when she spoke her next secret but thought it might be easier to stay where she was, head down and pressed against his chest. Her version of speaking the words into the wind.

"This one makes me sound like a terrible person," she said.

"Some of mine do, too."

She swallowed and clamped her eyes shut. "From the second I ran into you at that bar, even knowing you were with Carly, if you'd have kissed me I wouldn't have stopped you."

He stilled beneath her, and for a split second she regretted saying it. But it was the truth, and it was better he knew what kind of person she could be. The selfishness she was capable of.

Jamie's fingers tipped her chin up, angling her face as he gazed down at her. His hazel eyes swam with some unidentifiable emotion.

His voice was thick and weighted. "I wouldn't have been able to stop, either."

"I'm glad we didn't. If we'd crossed that line before, I don't know if I could have lived with myself."

He nodded, just barely. "I know."

He leaned down and brushed his lips against hers. Once, twice, then again. Her heart took off like a bird in a cage, trying to break free and follow their words as they floated away in the breeze.

After a few minutes she flipped over on her back, propped up her knees, and rested her head in his lap. She admired his handsome face as he slid his fingers through her hair, sending currents of sensation down her body.

She reached up and wiggled his glasses. "How badly do you need these?"

He shrugged. "I mean I could make do without them, but I have trouble reading street signs and stuff."

"Yeah. That's not important."

He laughed. "I have contacts but they drive me crazy."

"I love these. You're so hot in them."

He cocked his head to the side. "Really?"

"*Yes.*"

A few beats of silence passed, and Jamie smiled at her, an ornery glint flashing in his eyes. "Maybe when we get back to my truck we can take care of your fantasy to get laid in the back seat."

"That might revoke your open invitation to come out here."

He shrugged. "It would be one hundred percent worth it."

They got back to the apartment complex midafternoon, and Jamie had shoved her in the direction of her apartment, saying he had to get ready for their date and order her a damn fine curry.

Two hours later, she'd showered, shaved, and lotioned and was back at his doorstep in one of only two dresses she owned. It was sleeveless, robin's-egg blue, and fell to midthigh. The best part was the design showed off her cleavage but still covered up her port, which wasn't easy to find. It wasn't the most practical for a cool September evening in Nebraska, but she felt pretty and was only outside walking between buildings.

Jamie opened the door and her mouth went dry. He wore tailored gray slacks, a black belt cinched around his trim waist, and a crisp white dress shirt with the top two buttons open. His hair was perfectly tousled, and a dark-blond layer of scruff covered his jaw.

His chin dropped to his chest as he looked her up and down, and his mouth went slack. "Elliott. Fuck."

"I mean, if you think you're up for it again," she teased, her cheeks heating at his obvious appreciation.

He wrapped his hands around her wrists and pulled her in. His body was solid and warm and smelled as if he'd just stepped straight from the shower. "I'm up for it, all right." He bent low and kissed her thoroughly.

Staying in for a private dinner had been a very, very good idea.

A muffled bark came from somewhere, and she pulled back, breathless. "Where's Hank?"

Jamie scrunched his nose. "I put him in my room. I just thought you might not want his hair all over you tonight. I wasn't sure what you'd be wearing, and . . ." He trailed off, passing a hand across his jaw.

"That's thoughtful," she said. "But I love him, hair and slobber and all. You never have to put him away when I'm coming over."

His face lightened. "Are you sure? You don't mind?"

In response, she walked to his bedroom door and opened it. Hank came barreling out, nearly knocking her down.

"Did that mean old man lock you away?" she crooned, kneeling down to kiss his head. "I'll never let him do that again. I promise."

She glanced at Jamie and found him watching them with a fond expression, but one of his eyes was twitching. "Is it weird that sometimes I'm jealous of my dog?"

Laughing, she stood and kissed his cheek. "Don't worry. I've got enough to go around."

He'd set up his kitchen table with candles, and he pulled out her chair to wait while he dished out their food. The rich scents of cumin and turmeric filled the kitchen. He paused after pulling the containers out of the bags and unbuttoned his shirt cuffs. Elliott watched, her eyes growing wide, as he rolled up his sleeves as if he were moving in slow motion. Each movement of his long, thick fingers and every flex and pull of the muscles in his forearms was like her very own private striptease.

When he paused long enough for her to notice he'd stopped, her gaze snapped to his face. His eyes were on her, his expression hot. When he spoke, his voice was like warm honey poured over her skin. "Never stop looking at me like that."

She exhaled a shaky breath. "I won't."

He finished what he was doing and set the plates on the table, kissing her hard before he sat across from her. They talked about her business for much of the meal, and what she'd been working on for Chantal. She told him about a food-truck doughnut shop that was looking to start a brick-and-mortar store in Benson, and who'd called her after getting her card from Blythe.

Jamie listened attentively and got excited with her, and she realized she seldom felt so acknowledged—so *known*—by another person.

"So I have a question," she asked at the end of the meal, suddenly nervous.

He looked at her curiously. "Okay."

"I was planning to go to Lincoln next weekend. To visit my parents." She gripped her hands together in her lap. "Would . . . um. Would you maybe want to come with me?"

A wide grin spread across his face. "Really?"

"Yes. I'd like for them to meet you, if you want to."

"I'd love to."

CHAPTER
TWENTY-SIX

Jamie

"Ready for this?" Elliott asked, her eyes lit with excitement.

"I don't think any man is ever ready to meet the parents of the woman he's dating," Jamie said. He'd worried about this day all week and peppered Elliott with questions about her parents day and night to be better prepared.

Okay, mostly during the day. At night they were . . . otherwise occupied.

"But if they're as great as you say they are, I think we'll get along just fine."

"Just remember what I told you."

"If they ask me to play poker, I'm in."

She nodded with a grin, and they exited the car. He opened the back door for Hank, who jumped out and immediately took off to sniff a nearby tree.

"Hank, get over here." His dog did as asked, and Jamie clipped a leash to his collar. "We need to make a good first impression, bud."

"He's gonna love Dodger," Elliott said. "They'll run each other out in the first hour, I bet."

"I can't wait," Jamie said. He'd been thrilled when Elliott suggested they bring Hank along to play with her parents' German shepherd.

They crossed the grass and Jamie kept his free hand loose by his side. Should he hold her hand? Were public displays of affection frowned upon during the first meeting?

Man, he hadn't done this in forever.

Thankfully, Elliott made the choice for him and grabbed his hand as they approached the modest, two-story house. Purely out of habit, he glanced around the yard, which was simple but well maintained. He couldn't fault her parents' choice of potted plants on the porch, where several varieties of chrysanthemums bloomed, thriving in the cool September air.

Elliott rapped on the door just before she opened it, immediately setting off a string of loud barks from within.

Hank puffed up and perked his ears, his tail trembling, as if he wasn't sure if this was a threat or a friend to be excited about. Elliott patted his head. "He's a sweet boy, just like you. You'll see," she said. Then she called out, "We're here."

A tall woman with long, dark-brown hair came around a corner as they stepped inside, and for several minutes everyone was distracted by the commotion of introducing the dogs. Jamie kept Hank leashed for the first few minutes while the massive dogs sniffed and circled each other.

When Dodger went down on his front legs in a playful crouch and Hank rolled onto his back, Jamie grinned. "I think they're good."

He unclipped Hank's leash, and the canines were off like a shot. Elliott's dad appeared, average height with salt-and-pepper hair and an easy smile, and opened the back door. "Get outside, both of you. I won't have you knocking anything over."

The dogs disappeared, he closed the door, and everyone sort of paused, looking at each other in the sudden silence.

"Mom, Dad, this is Jamie. Jamie, these are my parents."

Jamie stepped forward with his hand extended. "It's nice to meet you, Mr. and Mrs. Holland."

"It's Mary and I'm a hugger," her mom warned, brushing his hand away and pulling him in for a tight hug.

"Even better," he wheezed.

"Call me Jim," Elliott's dad said with a laugh.

Jamie made a point of meeting the man's gaze as he gave a firm handshake.

Elliott squeaked and he glanced over to see her mom hugging the shit out of her, too.

"We've missed you," she said. "Tell me you've decided you hate Omaha and you're moving back?"

"Tomorrow," her dad added.

Jamie held up a hand. "Whoa, she just got there. There's still so much to see and do, I couldn't possibly let her leave yet. Not until she experiences everything."

Mary gave him the side-eye. "How long will that take?"

Jamie's gaze rested on Elliott's happy, beautiful face. "Just might take forever."

Elliott's cheeks turned pink—he was becoming dangerously addicted to making her blush—and she smiled. "I've missed you both so much. But you know Omaha is a better town for what I'm working on."

"Fine." Jim gestured into the house. "Let's get out of the entryway. Either of you want anything to drink? What time is it?" He checked his watch. "Two thirty. That's acceptable to have a beer on a Saturday, right?"

Jamie liked this guy already. "Definitely."

"What can I get you?"

"What have you got?"

Mary just shook her head. "Here we go."

Jim nodded sagely. "Come on. You're about to see something really special."

"Any surprise involving beer has gotta be a good one."

"Grab me a seltzer, will you?" Mary called out as Jim led him through the kitchen.

"You got it," Jamie called back. "An IPA for you, Elliott?"

She answered the affirmative as Jim eyed him. "You already know what she likes, huh?"

Jamie cleared his throat, trying to read the man's expression.

"Mm-hmm," Jim muttered. He opened the door and they stepped into the garage.

A double fridge stood just to the left, filled to the brim with every selection of beer Jamie could possibly imagine. Stouts, pilsners, pale ales, ciders.

He stood stock-still. "Have I died?"

"I know." Jim went to work, grabbing various bottles and cans and handing them to Jamie. He fished four glasses from the freezer, and they went back inside, only to find Mary and Elliott had gone outside to the back porch.

Dodger and Hank were running around the sizable backyard, chasing each other and stopping occasionally to roll around on the ground, nipping at each other's tails and ears.

"I haven't seen him play like that since he was a puppy," Mary said.

Jamie passed out the drinks he'd carried and settled onto the loveseat next to Elliott. "How old is he?"

"Ten."

"Wow. He looks great."

"Jim walks him several miles every day."

"It's how I keep both of us young and fit," Jim said.

Mary popped open her seltzer. "—ish."

Jim regarded his wife. "Was that about my being young or being fit?"

"Both."

"I'm not the one who went gray at fifty."

Mary narrowed her eyes. "You said you liked my natural color."

"I do. Until you think you can call me old and get away with it."

Mary laughed and the two shared an affectionate smile.

Jamie grinned and took a sip of his beer, putting his other arm around Elliott's shoulders.

"How long have you had Hank?" Jim asked.

"A couple of years. Found him at a shelter, believe it or not. One look at those brown eyes and I was a goner."

He was partial to gray eyes, too.

"We adopted Dodger from a shepherd rescue foundation when he was just a puppy. It was right after our sheltie passed away, and I didn't think I'd be ready for another dog so soon," Mary said. "But the house was too quiet. Bringing him home really helped us with the grief of losing a pet."

Jamie nodded. "I remember when the chocolate Lab I grew up with died. I swore I'd never get another dog, but now that I have Hank, I can't imagine anything different. I'm not sure I know how to live without a dog."

"I'm not sure I want to," she said with a grin.

"Okay, less about dogs and more about Elliott's new boyfriend," Jim said. "Tell us a little about yourself."

Elliott had told them as much about Jamie as she could without getting into details about how they met or either of their connections with Carly. Her parents just knew Elliott had met him more than a year ago and they began officially dating recently after reconnecting in Omaha.

"Sure." He'd expected a question like that. "I was born and raised in Omaha. Youngest of three. I went to Creighton, where I played college baseball—"

"Wait."

His attention swiveled to Jim.

"You played baseball at Creighton?"

"Yup. From '08 to 2012."

The older man narrowed his eyes. "Jamie . . . Jamie . . . what's your last name, again?"

"Sullivan." He tilted his head in confusion as Jim tapped his fingers against his knee, regarding him thoughtfully.

"Jim loves baseball," Mary supplied. "Where do you think Dodger got his name?"

Jamie grinned and gave Jim an appreciative nod. "Hank's named after Hank Aaron."

Jim held out his drink and Jamie took his arm from Elliott's shoulders to tap their glasses together. Then Jim set his down and slapped his knee. "Wait. I remember you!"

Jamie's eyebrows went up.

"Second baseman, right?"

No way. "That was me. Did you watch?"

"I don't follow college ball much until the College World Series starts. You're a great ball player. You were part of the winning team one year."

"My junior year."

"They spotlighted you all the time during the games. Talked about how likely you were to go pro. But I don't remember hearing much after that. Did you not . . . ?" He trailed off, as if realizing a little too late it might be a touchy subject.

"It didn't work out."

Jim's shoulders fell. "Oh. I'm sorry."

"Don't be," he said, and grabbed Elliott's hand. She squeezed gently. "I'm not."

Something in his face must have shown his sincerity. "Oh. Well, I'm glad, then."

"Seems things worked out for the best anyway," Mary said, glancing between Jamie and Elliott.

He looked over at Elliott. "What do you think? Did things work out like they were supposed to?"

A thousand emotions passed across her face as she looked at him. Everything from sadness to tenderness and so many in between. Everything except regret.

Their road to this place hadn't been ideal. But he couldn't find it in himself to regret it, either.

"Yes," she said. "I think they did."

The four of them continued talking for another hour before Mary stood and said she'd better get started on dinner. The dogs had crashed at their feet, and she stepped over their panting bodies with a laugh.

Jim brought out a round of ice-cold water for everyone and regarded Jamie with a twinkle in his eye.

"Oh no," Elliott muttered.

"Jamie," Jim started.

"Yes, sir?"

"After dinner, what do you say we play a hand of poker?"

Hours later, Jamie sat propped on the bed in Elliott's room, legs extended and arms folded behind his head.

"You didn't tell me they'd completely clean me out," he said dejectedly.

Elliott's laugh floated from the open bathroom doorway. "I told you they were ruthless. It's not my fault you didn't believe me."

"After spending time with your dad this afternoon, I had my eye on him. Your mom, though? She seemed so sweet."

"And now she has all your money."

"Damn." He shook his head, staring at the ceiling. "Who woulda thought?"

Elliott stepped out from the bathroom in tiny black shorts and a tank top, and he surveyed her body from head to toe.

Then back up, slowly.

He swallowed hard when she approached him with a sultry smile, flipping the light off as she went. His breath hitched, body tight with anticipation, when she climbed on top of him, settling onto his lap. He moved to put his hands on her, but she shook her head.

"Leave your arms like that." Her voice was low as she ran her hands up and down his biceps, bunched up in the position they were in.

His heart pounded and threatened to punch right out of his chest. From the very beginning it was as if it had been trying to get out of his body and into hers, where it belonged. The sensation only became more intense when they were near like this.

She kissed him softly. "They loved you."

"I adored them," he said.

"Good." She brushed a kiss along his jaw.

He couldn't handle this much longer. He needed his hands on her skin.

"I've never had a guy in this room."

He cleared his throat. "I bet your dad sleeps with one eye open."

"No," she laughed softly. "Mom's the one they were all scared of."

"I seriously underestimated that woman."

Elliott's tongue traced his bottom lip, and he forgot all about her parents. His hands were shaking.

"I'm glad I brought you here, though," she said. "You make me feel so . . ."

He swallowed hard when she moved up to sit right on his groin. "So what?"

She tugged at his hands and put them on her body. "Desperate for you to touch me."

"God, yes." His hands roamed all over, everywhere he could possibly reach, and he lurched forward, kissing her hard.

She rocked against him, and his stomach bottomed out.

"You have to be quiet," she said on a moan.

He'd have snorted if he wasn't so turned on. Instead, he tangled one hand in her hair and traced his other thumb just below her ear, a spot he knew drove her crazy.

They'd been intimate for only a week, and already he knew her body so well. As he knew she would, she let out a low moan.

"Shhh," he teased. "Quiet."

CHAPTER TWENTY-SEVEN

Elliott

Elliott woke up before Jamie. She considered tucking herself under his arm and going back to sleep, but the aroma of freshly brewed coffee pulled her from the warmth of the bed. She cast a quick look at the man sleeping there before she opened the door.

Jamie was on his stomach, his arms forward and hands buried under the pillow, feet hanging off the edge. The comforter was perfectly positioned to expose most of his toned legs and muscled back, and when her eyes traveled back up to his messy, dark-blond hair, the temptation to curl back up with him was dangerously strong. But she hadn't seen her parents in a while, and it might be nice to have a little alone time with them.

She crept downstairs and found her mom at the kitchen table with a cup of coffee. Hank, who had slept downstairs next to Dodger, immediately greeted her, his tail going crazy.

"Morning," Elliott greeted her.

"Good morning. Coffee's fresh."

Elliott was already reaching for a ceramic mug. "Smells divine."

"Got it at this new coffee shop down the street. They roast it in-house."

After pouring liquid gold to the brim, Elliott joined her at the table and took a sip. "So good."

"I think so, too." Her mom eyed her over the rim of her own cup. "How'd you sleep?"

She kept her eyes on the table. "Great, thanks."

"Mm-hmm."

Elliott scrunched her nose and scratched her temple. "Anyway, what do you think of Jamie?"

"I like him."

"Yeah?" Elliott grinned. "You didn't like any of the other guys you met. All two of them."

"They weren't good enough for you."

"Jamie is, though?"

"He's as close as a man could get, I think."

"What about women?"

"Same answer."

Elliott ducked her head, her smile widening. "I think so, too."

"He looks at you like you invented beer and baseball."

Elliott looked up at that, a laugh of pure joy slipping out. "He does?"

Her mom nodded. "I don't think I'll accept anything less on your behalf ever again. It's like you're everything he's ever wanted."

That's how Elliott felt about Jamie, no question. What did others see on her face when she looked at him? She'd never been good at hiding her emotions, and she wondered how she'd gotten by those first few weeks in Omaha without every single person knowing how hung up on him she was.

Elliott wrapped her hands around the warm drink. "It hasn't been easy for us. At the beginning, anyway."

"Relationships are rarely easy," her mom said, unconcerned. Never one to push Elliott to talk when she wasn't ready, she didn't ask for details. It was one thing she loved about her mom, and one of the biggest differences between her and her dad. "There are good days and bad days, and the best thing to hope for is to find someone who loves you on both."

"What a load of bull," Elliott's dad said, striding into the kitchen. "I definitely only love you on the good days."

Her mom grabbed an orange and chucked it across the kitchen. Her dad ducked and Jamie caught it the second he appeared in the doorway.

"Whoa," he said, eyes wide.

Her dad straightened and gave him an impressed nod. "Nice reflexes."

Jamie winked at Elliott and set the orange on the counter, then bent low to love on Hank.

"Coffee?" her dad asked Jamie as he poured himself a cup.

"Please."

"Cream or sugar?"

"Hell, no." He stood up and paused. "Uh. I mean, no, thank you."

Her dad just laughed. "I like you more and more."

Elliott's mom shook her head, and Elliott just sat there with a ridiculous grin. Cup in hand, Jamie kissed Elliott's hair as he passed and took the chair beside her.

"So what's on the agenda for you two today?" her dad asked. "Up for another round of poker?"

Jamie groaned. "Even if I wanted to, I'm broke."

Her mom drank her coffee, a serene expression on her face.

"We're having lunch with Yuka," Elliott said. "We'll head back after that."

"Well, okay. But you'd better come back soon. Both of you."

"Before we head out, there's a pine tree out back I noticed last night with a few dead branches on the bottom," Jamie said. "I could take care of those, if you don't mind."

"That would be great," her dad said. "But I'm not sure we have the right tools."

"I've got stuff in my truck," he said. "Maybe I can earn some of my money back?"

Elliott's mom stood. "Nope."

Jamie chuckled and shook his head at Elliott. "Ruthless," he mouthed.

They met Yuka at a Mexican restaurant with a dog-friendly outdoor patio. Jamie and Elliott arrived first and found a table, which Hank immediately stretched out under. He'd run around with Dodger all morning, and Elliott wouldn't be surprised if he slept the rest of the day.

"Well, if it isn't my best friend and the man who stole her from me," Yuka said from behind them.

Elliott grinned as Yuka hugged her around the neck.

Jamie held up his hand, and Yuka slapped her hand against his before taking a seat. Elliott and Yuka had FaceTimed enough while Jamie was around last week that it was like they were old friends now, too. "I'd argue she moved to Omaha without knowing she'd run into me, but I prefer to believe she came looking for me."

"You're not far off," Elliott admitted, and the smile on Jamie's face melted her from the inside out.

"Oh, I almost forgot." Jamie jumped up and grabbed his keys from the tabletop. "Be right back."

Yuka gave Elliott a curious glance, and Elliott shrugged.

"So how was meeting the parents?"

"It was perfect."

"Mary take all his money?"

"Of course."

Yuka shook her head. "That woman, I swear."

"You should come play next time."

Yuka snorted. "Yeah, right. I'm saving up to buy a house, remember?"

"You're good at poker, though. Haven't you beaten my mom before?"

"Once, and it was after her eye surgery and she was having trouble reading the cards."

Elliott laughed. "I forgot about that."

"Even then it was close."

Jamie came back and slid a paper bag across the table.

"What's this?" Yuka asked.

"Just a little something."

Yuka opened the bag and stood to peer inside. Her eyes bugged out, and her hands went to her cheeks. "Cookies!"

"And one chocolate mousse brownie. Better eat that one soon, though—it's been out of the fridge for two days."

She clapped her hands and ran around the table to hug him. "Thank you thank you thank you!"

"You're welcome."

The second she got back to her chair, she dug around for the brownie.

Elliott grabbed Jamie's sleeve and pulled him close for a kiss, her heart full at the gesture for her best friend. Then she laughed at Yuka. "You're not gonna at least wait until after lunch?"

"You heard the man," Yuka said, taking a bite. "Gotta eat it now."

A server came to take their drink orders, and Jamie and Elliott watched in amusement as Yuka devoured the brownie.

"You gotta tell your sister to open a store in Lincoln," Yuka said. "Put it right next to campus, and she'd be rolling in cash."

"Only if she never meets Mary," Jamie muttered, adjusting his glasses.

Elliott snorted and nudged him with her shoulder. "You ever gonna get over that?"

"Probably not."

"Anyhoo," Yuka said, wiping her hands off. "How's it going with you two? I mean, I know it's *good* because Elliott tells me stuff. But how's it going, like, with Carly and stuff?"

Jamie leaned close, his eyes twinkling. "It's good, huh?"

Elliott rolled her eyes. "You know it is."

He rolled his shoulders back in a show of confidence before his expression took on an air of gravity. "Carly doesn't know about us. She told me she was moving, but other than that we've barely spoken since we broke up. No one else knows."

"Aren't you worried she'll find out at some point?"

Jamie raised a brow at Elliott. Yuka's directness wasn't new for her, but she supposed it could take some getting used to.

"We haven't really gone anywhere anyone might see us. We've been staying in a lot."

"Nice."

Elliott rolled her eyes. "Not like that."

Jamie gave her the side-eye. "It's a little like that."

Yuka laughed and Elliott punched him in the arm.

"Well, either way," Yuka said. "I'm glad you two figured it out. I like you for her, Jamie."

Jamie reached over to squeeze Elliott's hand and tipped his head at her best friend. "I like me for her, too."

After spending two hours talking and laughing over chips and salsa, Jamie and Elliott headed back to Omaha.

When Jamie parked, Hank bounded out to sniff a nearby tree. Jamie headed in the direction of his building, stopping short when Elliott didn't follow.

"What are you doing?"

She gave him her best beseeching look. "I need to get some work done."

"Work? What work?"

"I told you the owners of that doughnut shop called me. I really need to get a few ideas down for their website."

"Bring your laptop over."

She shook her head. "I can't focus when you're around."

He looked as if he might argue, but he knew she was right. The chemistry between them was off the charts. Take what had been there all along and subtract a long list of reservations, and suddenly one plus one equaled five hundred.

"Now kiss me goodnight and I'll see you in the morning."

His eyes went wide. "I thought we were talking, like, two hours. You're not coming over *at all?*"

She let out a sad laugh. "I know. I just . . . I need to get this done. I'll make it up to you tomorrow, I promise."

He stepped forward and backed her against the truck. She smiled up at him, loving the happiness emanating from his hazel eyes. "Just come sleep with me, at least. I've gotten used to you being beside me. I won't even touch you"—She shot him a skeptical look.—"much. Just a little."

She dropped her forehead to his chest and huffed out a breath. Gripping his shirt in her fists, she pulled him flush against her body.

"Jamie," she whispered.

He dipped his head to bury his nose in her neck, inhaling deeply. "Hmm?"

Her voice trembled as the words tumbled out. "I—I think I'm in love with you."

He jerked his head up and stared at her, his expression unreadable. His eyes darted back and forth between hers. When he didn't respond right away, unease started creeping in.

She frowned.

"I love you," he blurted out. "I do. I love you so much, Elliott."

Thank God.

He kissed her just within the bounds of propriety for the public space they were in. Somehow she extricated herself and went the opposite direction, the burning weight of Jamie's eyes on her back the entire time.

She ended up right back on his doorstep two hours later.

CHAPTER TWENTY-EIGHT

Elliott

"Evening, everyone. Welcome to our support group. Looks like we have a few new faces here tonight, so why don't we go around the room and introduce ourselves?"

Elliott sat stiff as a board in the uncomfortable folding chair, scraping at her thumbnail. Averting her gaze, she hoped someone else would start them off. She didn't know what to say about herself. Just her name? How old she was? Her job?

This was a cancer survivor support group . . . Should she tell everyone what cancer she had and how long she'd been cancer-free? Or would they avoid the subject completely and pretend they were just regular people getting to know each other?

The woman sitting to her left raised her hand with a joyful chuckle. "I'm not new, so I'll go first. I'm Keri and I'm a six-year survivor of breast cancer."

Elliott peeked over at Keri while she spoke. She had short black hair and looked to be in her midthirties. Massive gold hoops dangled from her ears, swinging as she spoke animatedly. "I'm from Miami but have been here in Omaha for the last three years. Husband's job moved me from the beach to this flyover state, but I gotta say, it's grown on me. Except in the winter."

A chorus of laughs went around the room. Elliott smiled.

"I'm a physical therapist and mom to two little boys. And I've been coming to this group for . . . What is it, Joe?" She peered at the man who had greeted everyone and introduced himself as the group organizer. "Year and a half?"

"Sounds about right," Joe said. "Who's next?"

Might as well get it over with.

"I'll go. I'm Elliott and I'm from Lincoln. I just moved to Omaha a few months ago. I'm a graphic designer for small businesses. I was first diagnosed with leukemia when I was seventeen, and after a stem cell transplant last year, I've been cancer-free for almost a year and a half."

"Welcome," Joe said with a smile.

The remaining twelve attendees introduced themselves, and Joe took the floor again. Elliott mostly listened during the remainder of the meeting, thankful the rest of the questions to the group were sort of a free-for-all and answer-if-you-feel-comfortable type. She wanted to get a feel for how things went before she put herself out there, but she had to admit it was nice to hear others speak aloud some of the things she'd dealt with in the last year.

When the meeting was over, Keri approached her.

"Nice to see another young woman," she said with an awkward laugh. "I was beginning to think I was the only one my age around here who'd had cancer."

Elliott grinned. The rest of the group had primarily been older women and men, with one younger man in his twenties. He'd disappeared as soon as the meeting was over.

"It's nice to meet you," she said. "My, um . . . boyfriend found this group for me. I've struggled a little with anxiety since the transplant but never looked into a support group like my doctor suggested. I think it took another voice suggesting it to get me moving."

"I get that. We go through so much during treatment, seems like we should be able to handle the aftermath no problem, doesn't it?"

Elliott nodded. "Exactly. It doesn't feel right that I can go through everything a stem cell transplant entails, but I can barely sleep in an apartment by myself."

Keri's dark eyes softened with compassion. "I know exactly what you mean." She reached into her purse and pulled out a vibrating phone. "I'm so sorry, but it's my husband. He's got the kids . . ." She scrunched her nose and her eyes went wide.

Elliott laughed.

Keri reached in her purse again and pulled out a business card. "I'd love to chat some more. Have another friend in the city who's been where I have. Text me sometime if you want to meet up."

"That sounds great. Thank you."

Keri smiled and waved as she turned and answered the call. Elliott slid the card into her back pocket and left shortly thereafter.

She drove back to the apartment complex feeling lighter, something she hadn't even known she needed. She'd been so happy with Jamie these last few weeks, but having someone else to talk to who'd been through cancer treatment was a huge relief.

"You can talk to me about anything," Jamie had said when he told her about the group. "But there are some things I'll probably never understand. Here's the information if you ever want to give it a try."

So she had, and she was glad she did.

The next month was one of the best of Elliott's life. She and Jamie fell into a routine, rotating whose apartment they stayed at (Hank was welcome at both) and having takeout from the Indian food place at least once a week.

In mid-October they went back to his favorite trees, and she brought her camera. As Jamie promised, the leaves had turned a bright orange-red, standing out in stunning contrast against the green grass and blue sky. She printed and framed two copies of her favorite shot, hanging one on the wall of her room and giving the other to Jamie.

She shared several meals with his family—some with his mom, and some with Blythe and her husband and son. She had yet to meet his dad or brother, but knowing how Jamie felt about them, didn't mind him taking his time on that front. Getting to know the people who were important to him meant more to her, anyway.

She'd also gone to the cancer survivor group again, had a coffee date with Keri, and hadn't struggled quite as much with anxiety, even on the weekend Jamie had traveled to visit an old college buddy. She'd signed a six-month lease on her apartment and started looking for one of those coworking office spaces to start using when working with clients.

Elliott knew what it was to have family who took care of her, but she'd never known the dedication and attention of a lover. A passionate one, at that. Nights spent in his arms were her favorite part of the day, followed closely by getting ready beside him in the morning.

"What do you say we have a date night tonight?" Jamie asked one such morning. His toothbrush hung out of the side of his mouth, and Elliott leaned close to the mirror, applying mascara.

"Sounds like a lot of work," she said, only half joking.

He laughed. "Counter proposal: How about we roam around a bookstore for a while? Then get takeout and come back for . . . other stuff?" He waggled his brows.

"Where did I find you? I literally can't think of a better way to spend the evening."

"Are we nerds?"

She grinned at his adorable, unconcerned face. "If we are, I don't care."

Her happiness was reflected in his return smile. "Me either."

Eight hours later, they were on their second lap around a local bookstore, Jamie hefting around a basket growing alarmingly full of books.

"I might need a new bookcase," Elliott observed.

"Excellent investment if you ask me." He put down the basket at the end of a row and slid his hands into his pockets as he regarded the shelf. After a moment he reached up and grabbed one. "What about this one?"

She glanced over. "*Questions for Couples: Get to Know Each Other*? Do we need help in that area?"

"No. But it might be fun to talk through some of this stuff." He flipped it open. "For example, I'd probably never think to ask what fruit and vegetable you'd combine to create a fruitable."

"Yeah, because that's a super weird question."

He consulted the book again, then glanced up with a gleam in his eye. "How soon did you have erotic thoughts about your current partner?"

Sooner than she wanted to admit. "When you ate our soufflé and made all those sexy noises."

His throat bobbed on a heavy swallow. "You started it."

"Is that your answer, too?"

He shook his head. "Before that."

She felt the tingle that shot through her from the top of her head to the backs of her knees. How many feet separated them across this aisle? Two? Three? "When?"

"When you argued with me about pies at the bar."

The urge rose up to ask him to describe those erotic thoughts in detail, but she tabled it for later. "You still like arguing about that."

He grinned. "I do."

They stared at each other for a prolonged beat, and she huffed out a breath. "What else you got?"

"What's your most treasured possession?"

"A vintage nineteenth-century copy of *Pride and Prejudice*." She'd been so scared it would get lost or damaged in the move that it was still at her parents' house. "I bet I can guess yours."

"Oh yeah?"

"Hank."

He laughed. "He'd like to think so."

She cocked a brow. "Am I wrong?"

"No." He flipped a few more pages. "What did you think was stupid until you tried it?"

"Wordle."

He laughed. "Blythe was so into that for a while. Mine's La Croix."

"The drink?" Now that she thought about it, he did have several flavors in his fridge at all times.

"Yeah. For so long I was like, 'It's fancy water; what's the big deal?'" He pursed his lips in disappointment. "Then I tried it. The Passionfruit is fucking delicious."

"You're adorable, you know that?"

He seemed to fight a smile, trying to keep up whatever annoyance he wanted to have about his addiction to carbonated beverages. "Okay, last one's the best one. If you could pick the perfect location for a first kiss, where would it be?"

"Outside, against the brick wall of a hotel in downtown Omaha."

His lips tipped up in a soft smile, his gaze warming, the silliness from a few seconds ago gone. "Best first kiss of my life."

"Same." Still, butterflies filled her belly when she thought about it. "But if you'd asked me that question before that night, I'd have said the library."

"Really?"

"Yeah. You know, like those scenes in the movies where a couple finds some stack in the back and makes out against the shelves? I always wanted to disappear with a guy like that in a place where everyone's supposed to behave and follow the rules. I guess the thought of a mean librarian catching us made it seem super exciting."

One brow notched up, and he slid his fingers across his jaw. "Wanna hit the library after this?"

She gave him a saucy smile. "I don't know . . . Doesn't seem all that different from a bookstore."

He dropped the book in the basket and slowly approached her, checking the aisle to make sure they were alone. Her eyes remained locked on his, playful and welcoming. She wasn't much for PDA, but this back corner of the store was empty, and she'd never not want to kiss this man.

He stopped with his feet bracketing hers, their chests brushing as her back pressed against the wood. An audible sigh left his throat when he dipped his head to whisper in her ear, "I think I love you more than books."

"You *think?*"

"I do. I definitely do."

"That's a lot of love."

"Mm-hmm." He gently nudged her nose with his. "What would you pick? Books or me?"

Her arms roamed up his back. "What kind of books?"

"Wow." His voice held a trace of humor. "Um, mystery?"

"You."

"Sci-fi."

"You, for sure."

"Self-help."

"Definitely you."

"Romance."

She sucked in a breath. "Oh. Um . . ."

He cupped the back of her head and covered her mouth with his.

She pulled back a moment later, breathless. "Fine. You convinced me."

Voices suddenly sounded to their left, and two people appeared at the end of the row. Jamie stepped back, but not quickly enough to hide what they'd been doing.

"Oops, sor—Jamie? *Elliott?*"

It took Elliott a long second to process the familiarity of the face who looked back at her in surprise.

The ground seemed to drop from beneath her. Her first instinct was to grab for Jamie's hand, but she quickly pulled back when Stephen's eyes followed her movement.

"Hey, Stephen," Jamie said smoothly. "Tara."

Stephen just looked at them, impassive. "Are you two . . . ?"

She and Jamie hadn't talked about how they might handle someone they knew finding out about their relationship. It was bound to happen, but she'd figured the more time that passed, the less of an ordeal it might be. Fewer side-eyes, less questions, minimal judgment.

Content in their bubble of romantic bliss, she'd pretended this exact scenario was unlikely and not something she needed to worry about. She and Jamie mostly kept to themselves, partly because they were both introverts who preferred staying in, but also because no matter how much they told themselves what they were doing was completely appropriate and consensual, it would raise eyebrows in front of a certain crowd.

This one, in particular.

Jamie's voice startled her. "Yeah." He sounded so calm, so sure. "We are."

Elliott had seen Stephen only once at Starbucks since she'd told him she just wanted to be friends. He'd seemed completely fine—not bothered at all—but she'd also used the excuse that she was too busy with her business to date. Now here she was, obviously doing exactly that. She didn't want to hurt Stephen, of course, but that was actually low on the list of concerns rapidly building in her mind. At the top of the list was—

"Does Carly know?" Tara asked.

No one spoke for a beat.

"It's . . . new," Elliott managed. Her feelings for Jamie were anything but, but they didn't know that. She and Jamie hadn't acted on anything until after Carly moved, and she'd cling to that for all it was worth.

It also didn't answer the question, but it seemed to be enough.

Stephen shrugged as if the shock had already worn off and he was totally fine with it. "Well. Cool."

Tara was harder to read. She'd never seemed to like Elliott much, and a glint of disapproval shone in the gaze she swung back and forth between Elliott and Jamie, almost as if gauging the distance between them.

"Well, we'll see you around," Stephen continued, nudging Tara's shoulder with his.

Jamie stepped forward. "Hey, wait." Tara and Stephen paused. He glanced back at Elliott before turning to them again, a flash of guilt in those hazel depths. "I, um, haven't talked to Carly since she left town, and like Elliott said, we just started seeing each other recently." That part was true, at least. "I assume she'll hear about it now, though, and I think it's best if it comes from me. So please don't say anything to her. Let me be the one to do it."

Stephen lifted a shoulder again, as if he hadn't planned to get up in anyone's business in the first place. Definitely a *you do you* kind of guy.

Tara, on the other hand, pursed her lips together. She'd probably planned to have her phone in hand, dialing Carly's number as soon as they hit the Travel and Leisure aisle.

"Please," Jamie said again.

Thankfully, Tara finally nodded, and Stephen stepped in to usher Tara back the way they came.

Alone again, Elliott faced Jamie, whose usually confident stature now slumped in defeat. He just looked at her, a heavy sigh escaping his chest.

"Guess I have a phone call to make."

CHAPTER TWENTY-NINE

Jamie

The following afternoon, Elliott went back to her own apartment to give Jamie privacy to make the call.

He hadn't even had to ask—she'd offered—and he was grateful because he had no idea how this conversation would go. He had no idea how Carly would react, and he didn't want an audience for this. Except Hank, who was a welcome presence at Jamie's side as he lowered himself to the couch, phone in hand. He took two deep breaths, willed his heart to slow down, and dialed Carly's number.

She answered on the third ring. "Hello?"

A tiny part of him braced for any lingering affection at the sound of her voice, but none came. He felt nothing but nerves and a genuine hope their friendship would remain after this. "Hey, Carly." Hank nudged his thigh, and Jamie rested a palm on his fur. "How are you?"

"Great. Just leaving the gym." The voices in the background suddenly quieted, like she'd walked out of a building. "It's good to hear from you."

"Yeah, it's been a while. Kinda weird, not seeing you around, but I've been pretty busy, and you're . . ."

"Not there anymore?" she said with a laugh.

"Yeah." He swallowed. "How's Oklahoma? Everything going good down there?"

A few muffled sounds came through the phone, then the close of a car door. "It's really great, Jamie. I know it's only been three months, but I'm so happy here. I get to see my mom and my old friend Sasha all the time. I love the new job so much I can't believe I didn't take Mai up on it before now."

"You're glad you did it, then?"

"Yeah. I am." She paused. "How are you?"

"I'm good. Really good."

"Yeah?"

"Yeah."

"I'm glad to hear that." She sounded like she meant it. After a beat, she asked, "So were you just calling to say hi, or . . . ?"

He leaned forward over his knees and pressed a fist to his forehead. He'd sat on it all day and still didn't know how to start. What was the best way to say it?

"I did want to say hi. I've been wondering how you were doing," he started. "But there's also something I wanted to talk to you about. I, uh, wanted to tell you I've started seeing Elliott."

"What do you mean?"

"I'm . . . dating her. We're together. Romantically." He closed his eyes and shook his head. That was one way to do it.

She said nothing for a moment, and he forced himself not to fill in the silence. Let her hear it. Process it. "Oh."

"I just didn't want you to hear about it from someone else, and . . . I don't know." Suddenly restless, he stood and walked to the window. "I wasn't sure if it would upset you. I guess I wanted to tell you myself. In case you wanted to talk about it?"

"It's definitely . . ." She trailed off. "Surprising. When did that happen?"

"Um, a couple months ago?"

"A couple *months*?"

Hadn't it been? Maybe not—God, why hadn't he been prepared for that question? "Not quite. I mean, I don't know exactly. It was after you left, and we'd been broken up for a while by that point anyway—"

"How soon after I left?"

"A month?" Why did it sound like a question?

"Wow."

He was tempted to bring up the guy he'd heard she was with in Oklahoma, but it would be a defense mechanism. Deflection from why he'd called in the first place, which wouldn't do any good. He needed to face this head-on.

She deserved that much.

"I . . . wasn't expecting this. Her." He ran a hand through his hair, staring aimlessly through his blinds. "Is it okay?" He winced. *Don't ask her permission.* "I mean, are you okay? Does it bother you?"

"I don't know. I don't think so, but I'm still processing. I mean you're free to do what you want, obviously. You were never one to move on that quick after a breakup, so I wasn't expecting it. Especially not with her."

The words came without thought. "I wasn't, either, but sometimes love catches you off guard."

Carly sucked in a sharp breath, and he dropped his head back, mouthing, *Fuck.*

"Love?" Her voice was quiet but in a way that made the hairs on his neck stand on end. "You just met her. I introduced you two." She paused. "Right?"

Why, why had he said that?

This was supposed to be a courtesy call to tell her about his current situation, not tell her the truth about when he met Elliott for the first time. The *real* first time. Yeah, it was more to save them all useless heartache than anything else, because he was certain no matter when he'd met her, they'd have ended up here. Elliott was perfect for him in every way that mattered, and the circumstances of their meeting would eventually fade into the background of their lives together. Still, he'd meant to stick only to recent details.

It was the only part of this conversation he'd planned for. But now that she'd asked him point-blank about it, his plan suddenly felt shortsighted. Being selective about what he shared was different from straight-up lying, and he faltered.

"Right?" Carly pushed.

Would this follow him around forever if he kept on this trajectory? Constantly worrying about what he said and if it made sense, along with the timing of supposedly not knowing Elliott beforehand? He didn't want to hurt Carly, but he didn't want to hide, either. He wanted to be able to talk about the night he and Elliott met without fear someone might overhear, make the connection, and feed it back to Carly. Enough people had been there the night Tiffany rambled on about the man Elliott was in love with, it would cause a stir within their circle of friends, especially if it came out incidentally.

There was nothing that group loved more than secrets and gossip, and what might be a minor argument now could be a disaster down the road.

With a heaviness in his heart, he sat and rested his head against the wall. He should come clean now. Tell Carly everything, get it out in the open, and let the chips fall where they may.

"Not exactly."

"What are you talking about?"

Jamie scrubbed a trembling hand down his face. "I'd met Elliott before. Before her transplant."

Part of him wished he could see her face. Was her silence from anger or confusion? "I don't understand."

"It was last year, in May. We weren't together then, and I was meeting someone from a dating app at Tavern. I got stood up and ended up talking to a woman at the bar. It was Elliott."

"Okay." The word was long and drawn out, like, *Keep talking.*

"She ended up coming along to the baking class I'd reserved for the date I was supposed to have. We walked around downtown and talked, too, and we actually have a lot in common. Back then, I didn't know the reason, but I never saw her again after that. Now I know it's because she had the transplant. So a few months ago, when she came to The Patriarch . . . I remembered her."

"Wait." Confusion marred her tone. "But you acted like complete strangers. Both of you. Why didn't you say anything?"

This was the part he'd never be able to explain. "I don't know, I was surprised, and—"

"*Wait,*" she said again.

He stopped short.

"Holy shit—are you the guy? *The* guy? The one Tiffany told us about that kissed Elliott and who she pined over the whole time she was in the hospital?"

A dull ache pounded between his ears. "It was me," he whispered.

"Are you *kidding* me?"

"I'm sorry. I'm sorry I didn't say anything. That was wrong of me, but you and I weren't together the night I met her. We had a good time and we kissed, and months later, when I'd heard nothing, I assumed I'd never see her again. I moved on."

"Yeah, to *me.*"

"You're the one who suggested we get back together—"

"And you agreed! You said you wanted to try again!"

"I did." At the time, it had been true.

"Only because Elliott disappeared on you, though, right? Only until she popped back up into your life. Oh my God, you dumped me just a few weeks after she came back into the picture. You said there wasn't anyone else, but you lied, didn't you?"

He was at a loss. Nothing he said would be the right thing. "I didn't break up with you *for* Elliott." That much was true. "Her presence brought some clarity and got me thinking about things, yes. I started asking myself what I wanted from a relationship, and if I could be the man you deserved with her around. The truth is, I couldn't, and I had to face that. I refused to be that guy. But I didn't end things with you in order to pursue her. And I never made any move on her while we were together, I can promise you that."

She laughed, but it carried no joy. "What, you want a round of applause? A pat on the back for waiting a few months before going for it? Gotta wait the appropriate amount of time, I guess. Maybe I should thank you for being such a good guy and doing the hard thing in the name of integrity. Is that what you were hoping for?"

He shook his head. "No, I—"

"You're just like your dad, aren't you?"

It was worse than a physical blow. His lips parted as all the air whooshed from his lungs and an ice-cold sensation trickled down his backbone.

"Why did you even agree to get back together this time when you so obviously still had a thing for this woman?" Her voice rose as she went on. "It's like you used me as a prop to fill the time while waiting for her. For years I've listened to you say you wanted to be different, but that move right there—it's a total Rick Sullivan move, through and through."

The room started a slow spin around him as deep unease settled in his gut. Was she right?

His heart hadn't been in it when he and Carly got back together after Elliott, but at the time, he'd honestly thought Elliott was gone for good. What was he supposed to do? Never try with another woman ever again? That had seemed ridiculous and a little pathetic, and he'd thought moving on was the right thing to do. That it was the way back to his normal.

But he'd known Carly didn't make him feel the same way Elliott had. Was Carly right? Had he used her as a distraction or as his second-best option when his first no longer existed?

It had been a mistake.

Maybe calling her today had been, too.

"I'm so sorry." The words felt hollow and useless, but the damage was done, and an apology was all he could offer her. "I never wanted to hurt you."

"If that was true, you would have been honest with me from the start."

He forced a swallow down his parched throat. "I should have been."

"I'm done with this; I have to go. Good luck with Elliott. Actually, I should wish her good luck, because who knows how long it will be before you find someone fresh and new to move on to. You might have been late to the game, but it's the same one all the men in your family play. I guess you've finally joined the team."

The line went dead, and he stared at the screen, eyes burning. He tossed the phone to the side, sudden exhaustion leaving him with a strange emptiness, and dropped his head into his hands.

CHAPTER THIRTY

Elliott

Elliott thought about Jamie all afternoon. She'd left after lunch, allowing him privacy for the conversation with Carly.

She was just as much a part of this as he was and had wanted to deal with it together, but he and Carly's history went back several years. There might be things he'd want to say without her listening in. Part of her had hoped he'd ask her to stay, anyway . . .

He hadn't.

So now it was past dinnertime, and she hadn't heard a word. Surely they'd spoken by now?

Were they still talking? Maybe he hadn't gotten ahold of her at first and she'd only just called him back. But what if the call had ended hours ago and it had gone so poorly he was upset? What if he needed her?

She tucked her hands between her knees, staring at her phone for a few long seconds before she grabbed it and called him. It rang once, twice, three times. Once more and then his deep, friendly voice asked her to leave a message.

She ended the call and texted him instead.

Elliott: Thinking about you. I hope everything went okay.

When he didn't reply, she opted to get out of her apartment and away from the ass-size indention she'd made worrying on her couch for the last several hours. She passed his truck in the lot near his building on her way out.

She went to Target for a few groceries, taking a couple of extra laps around the leisure wear and candle sections when he still hadn't responded to her text. She stopped by a coffee shop for hot tea, then went back to their complex.

His truck was still there.

The clock on the dash said it was almost eight thirty . . . Screw it. She pulled into the spot next to his building and put her car in park. Right before she got out, her phone dinged.

Jamie: Hey, sorry. I had my phone on silent. I'm pretty exhausted. Heading to bed early tonight.

She frowned at the screen but stayed put, abandoning her plan to show up at his door.

Elliott: Are you okay?

Jamie: Yeah

Elliott: Did you talk to Carly?

Jamie: Yeah. Let's talk tomorrow, okay?

No, she wanted to say. *Not okay.* What was going on, and why didn't he want to talk to her about it?

But she'd respect his request, as difficult as it would be. Something had obviously happened, but there'd been times when she wanted to be alone to process something, too. She wouldn't push him tonight, but tomorrow would be a different story.

She gave him until 9:00 a.m. She'd tossed and turned all night, thinking and worrying about him. And about Carly.

He said they'd talk today, so by 9:07 a.m. she stood on his doormat, still in her pajama pants and tank top. She knocked.

Nothing. Not a single sound came from inside his apartment.

She frowned and knocked again, louder this time. Not even a bark from Hank.

They hadn't been at the dog park when she left her building—she'd checked before making the trek here. She slipped her phone from her pocket, but just as she hit the "Call" button, the door to the stairwell at the end of the hall opened.

Hank bounded out, panting and drooling everywhere, followed by a shirtless, sweaty Jamie.

Elliott knelt to greet Hank but kept her eyes on Jamie's face. His flushed cheeks, damp hair, and troubled eyes.

He stopped beside her. "Hey."

"Hi."

"Sorry about last night." He swiped his wadded-up shirt across his face, then pulled a key from his pocket. "Come on in."

She followed him inside, scanning the apartment as she went. Everything looked normal. A vase of aging flowers on the table, Hank's toys scattered around, several books stacked beside the couch. Even the cereal bowl in the sink was a usual finding on a weekend morning.

Hank collapsed on the kitchen tiles. Jamie filled a glass with water and sat at the kitchen table like he always did after a run, not wanting to get the cushions all sweaty.

On the surface nothing seemed out of the ordinary.

But something still felt off.

Maybe it was the tension in his shoulders that a run hadn't even loosened up, or the downward tilt of his lips. Maybe it was the way he wouldn't look at her.

"Good run?" she asked, like a complete coward.

"Fine." He chugged half the glass and wiped the back of his mouth with his hand. He finally met her gaze for a few seconds, then dropped his eyes to the table, dropping his face to his hands.

"Oh, Jamie." She sat beside him, her hand on his back, not caring that his warm skin was damp. His ribs rose and fell underneath her touch. "Was it that bad?"

The pained sigh he released was so heavy she felt it in her bones. Suddenly, she dreaded hearing what he'd say.

He glanced up, the green in his irises darker than usual. "I told her everything."

She kept her hand on him, sliding her palm up and down. "By 'everything,' you mean . . . ?"

"How we met before your transplant. That I knew who you were at The Patriarch. That I'm the guy Tiffany brought up that night in front of everyone. Well." He blew out a puff of air. "That last part she figured out on her own, but I wasn't going to lie when she asked me point-blank. Figured by now we've kept enough secrets already."

Elliott nodded her head slowly and tried to stay calm. She hadn't expected him to tell Carly so much.

As if he could read her mind, he went on, "I wasn't planning on all that. I started off just telling her we were together and asked if she wanted to talk about it. I fucked up and said I was in love with you, and she asked how that was possible when we'd just met. I didn't know what else to do. So I just told her everything."

Her heart snagged on his referring to loving her as fucked up but didn't linger there. He hadn't meant it that way, probably, and was obviously distressed by this whole thing—and he hadn't even told her Carly's reaction yet.

"How'd she take it?"

"She was . . . shocked. Got pretty upset. Assumed I broke up with her for you, which is . . . only partly true." He bowed his head and gripped his hair, tightening it in a fist. "I tried to explain it wasn't just that, but we both knew it was a big part. Because even though we were just friends first, I *would* have. Left her for you if you'd so much as given me a hint of interest. No questions asked." He lifted his face once again, expression miserable. "What kind of man does that make me?"

Elliott reached up, slowly, and pulled his hand away, threading her fingers through his. She didn't know what to say in this moment. Everything felt wrong. "Whatever kind of person you are, so am I."

He offered her a sad smile, the equivalent of *Thanks for trying to make me feel better. It's not working, though.*

"I'm so sorry, Jamie. I'm sorry Stephen and Tara saw us and that you had to tell her like this. I'm sorry it didn't go well. But don't you think with time, things might change? That she might . . . get past it, maybe?"

"I don't know. If she does, it doesn't seem like it will be anytime soon."

"Should . . . should I call her? Maybe if I talk to her, too—"

He shook his head. "That would probably make it worse. I think it's best for you to just stay out of it, for now." He straightened, pulling his hand away from hers. He leaned back against the chair and crossed his arms, staring at the table.

Elliott regarded her empty hand and frowned. She understood he was upset, but she hadn't expected the distance. He might as well have been across the room.

"Do you still love her?" she asked quietly.

"What?"

She told herself it would be okay if he did. If talking to her yesterday and the emotions that came with it revived prior feelings. "Do you still love her?"

"No. Not the way I love you. I just hate that I hurt her."

The tightening in her throat loosened a little. "I do, too."

"I'm sorry I'm . . . so off. I just don't know what to feel right now. Or do. I'm all over the place."

She wanted to touch him again. Wrap her arms around him or scoot closer, at least. Whatever happened they'd figure it out together, and eventually things would even out.

But he'd pulled away once and now had his arms crossed over his chest, forearms rising and falling with each breath. It apparently wasn't what he needed right now, something she tried not to read anything into. Yes, ever since the day she'd walked in and kissed him, he'd had his hands on her at every available opportunity, but this was also the first time she'd seen him deal with something tough like this.

Maybe this was normal for him. *Carly would know,* a tiny voice reminded her, and she jumped to her feet. "Let's go somewhere."

He eyed her. "Where?"

"Anywhere. Somewhere fun, where we can forget about this and just be together for a little while. Take a break to smile and laugh. What about an arcade? Mini golf? I'm so awful you'll be laugh-crying after the first hole, I promise."

He finished off his water and rubbed at his jaw. "I think I'd rather just hang around here. Is that okay?"

She sat back down. "Sure. Want to watch movies? Cook something? I could go grab some books, and we could sit on the balcony."

Jamie's brows pulled together, and he tucked his lower lip between his teeth before he spoke again. "I sort of want to be, um . . . on my own for a bit. Alone. I'm still processing some of the stuff she said, and I just think I need to sit with it. Is that okay?"

Oh. That was unexpected and hurt more than she cared to admit. She stood again, feeling ridiculous with all the up and down, but mostly for misreading the situation so badly. Yes, it was a completely reasonable request, and he wasn't being unkind. He'd said he loved her multiple times throughout the conversation and referred to how much he cared about her.

So why, then, did she feel like she was back in eighth grade, watching the guy she liked walk right by without even sparing her a glance?

"Sure, that's fine." She grabbed her phone and keys and whirled around to rub Hank's ears to hide the tears welling beneath her lids. "I'll just see you . . . later, then."

His chair scraped the floor as she went straight for the door, and suddenly his warm, gentle hand was on her arm, pulling her back and against his chest.

"Thank you," he whispered into her hair. He kissed her just above her ear. "I'm sorry."

He released her and she didn't look back, opening the door and letting it fall shut behind her. Maybe that final hug and kiss should have made her feel better. Given her some sort of confirmation everything was okay. That they'd be okay. But it didn't.

It only made it worse.

The rest of Sunday sucked. Monday morning, too.

Elliott was completely worthless and unable to focus on anything. Maybe if she'd had a client into dark colors and serious themes, like a Halloween event or a therapist's website, she'd have been in the right headspace. But no, her current clients boasted bursting, bright businesses that required positive creativity and vision, and she didn't have it in her right now. Not when she had this sense that something terrible was looming.

She hadn't heard a single thing from Jamie since she'd left his place yesterday. After weeks of being with each other so much she'd wondered if they should just move in together and get it over with, the solitude was unnerving.

Lonely.

Quiet.

She couldn't shake the feeling something was wrong—really wrong. She and Jamie had just hit their stride, finally finding a rhythm together, and things had been almost perfect. But something was really bothering him, and he wouldn't talk to her about it. Not only did she wonder what Carly said to cause this reaction in him, but the fact he'd pulled away instead of opening up to her was the biggest red flag of all.

Were they . . . over? Her heart cracked, just thinking about it.

There was also the fact Carly's reaction meant she was hurt by what Jamie'd told her. Which was completely fair—they'd lied to her, and Elliott might never forgive herself for not pushing harder back then, demanding she and Jamie come clean from the start.

But like Jamie, she couldn't find it in her to regret being with him in the end. From her point of view, he was *it* for her. He'd said it was the same for him, that he and Elliott together was the kind of thing people move mountains for.

Even so, was it possible the collateral damage would prove too much? Would it linger between them forever, a constant reminder of who they'd hurt in the process of finding happiness?

The questions cycled through her mind that morning as she went for her monthly surveillance labs, which she belatedly realized she hadn't even been worried about because she'd been so caught up in the situation with Jamie and Carly.

Her brain didn't even conjure the possibility that something could be wrong until she stepped out of her apartment that afternoon before going for a run, hoping to clear her head in the fresh air. Her phone rang before she hit the stairwell, and she frowned at the screen.

It usually took a few days to hear from the oncologist's office.

"Hello?"

"Elliott? It's Dr. Varghese."

She tightened her grip on the phone.

She couldn't remember the last time he'd called her himself. Ninety-percent of the time she spoke with his nurse or the medical assistant. These calls were usually three seconds long. *Everything looks perfect; we'll see you next month.*

"I got the results from the labs we drew this morning. Do you have a second to talk?"

She was in the middle of the hallway, but her legs didn't seem capable of moving just now, so it was as good a time as any. "What is it? Is the leukemia back?"

"I'm not sure," he said carefully. "There's no evidence of that, but your blood counts have been trending down over the last few months. I've been watching them closely, and while they'd been steadily dropping, they'd still been normal. This time they weren't."

A wave of dizziness hit her, and she sat right in the middle of the floor so she didn't pass out. "What does that mean?"

"It can mean several things, and I don't want to make assumptions yet. I'm going to send it off for more cytology, which I'll probably get back tomorrow, but I think we'd better schedule a bone marrow biopsy to get a closer look. I can get you in first thing Wednesday morning at eight. Can you make that work?"

"Yes." She was scheduled at Starbucks, but she'd find someone to cover.

"I know it's easier said than done, but try not to worry until we have more answers, okay?"

"Okay. I'll, um, see you Wednesday."

She took several deep breaths, in through her nose and out through her mouth. Shaking, she stood and turned back to her apartment, struggling for a few seconds to unlock the door. As soon as it closed behind her, she sank back to the floor. She tucked her knees to her chest and stared blankly into her living room.

She remained there for several minutes, heart racing and mind spinning. *It's back. It has to be. I thought I was done with all this—the chemo, the weekly labs, the symptoms and side effects. And now I have to do this all again.* Hot tears spilled over, and she wept until she had nothing left.

Drained and overwhelmed, she picked up her phone and dialed the first person that came to mind.

"Can I come over?"

CHAPTER
THIRTY-ONE

Jamie

"Dude. What's wrong with you?"

Jamie looked up from the pots of yellow and orange chrysanthemums. "What do you mean?"

"You've been watering the same flowers for twenty minutes," Ian said. "That pallet's gonna have to go to the clearance section if you keep that up. Can't sell plants with root rot."

Jamie blinked and glanced down. Sure enough, water was spilling over the rims, the soil too saturated to absorb more. "Shit, sorry." He switched off the sprayer and tossed the hose aside, wiping his hands on his jeans. "I guess I'm a little distracted."

Ian crossed his arms and leaned against a table packed with ornamental cabbage. "You've been quiet all day. Everything okay?"

"Just a lot on my mind, I guess." A nonanswer.

"Anything I can do to help?"

"Nah, but I appreciate it. Just some personal stuff I need to work through."

Apart from his sister and mother, Ian was the only person Jamie'd told about Elliott. He didn't know the whole story, though—just that they'd recently started dating—and despite his longstanding friendship with Ian, he didn't want to get into the details right now.

Ian nodded. "Want to take a break? I could use some coffee and one of those chocolate croissants from Blythe's."

"Do you really want a croissant, or are you giving me an excuse to visit with my sister-slash-therapist?"

"Does it matter?"

"I guess not." He clapped Ian on the shoulder, giving it a squeeze of *thanks* as he passed. "Be back in a bit."

Melt My Tart was only ten minutes from the nursery, and Jamie was lucky enough to snag a parallel spot right in front of the bakery. He'd come in the middle of the afternoon lull, and the café was empty, except for one of the college students Blythe had hired sitting at the counter.

"Hi, can I help you?"

"Yeah, is Blythe here?"

"Sure, hang on a sec." She disappeared around the corner and returned with Blythe on her heels.

Blythe raised a brow. "Ian send you to pick up his afternoon coffee and pastry?"

"Jeez, does he come in here that often?"

"Almost every day." She grabbed the tongs and bagged a croissant before turning to the coffee pots.

Jamie snorted. "I hope you charge him extra."

"He's your boss, brother. His coffee's always free."

"He was my friend first. You don't need to do that."

Blythe grinned. "Yeah, but when I do, he tips way more than I'd make on the coffee."

Jamie took the items she offered him, then glanced at the girl who'd taken her seat again near the register. "Could we chat for a sec?"

"Sure." His sister followed his gaze and waved him behind the counter. "Why don't you come back here? I was just about to make some cookies."

He sipped the coffee as he followed her back, figuring he'd get Ian a fresh cup on his way out. He settled onto a stool, and Blythe slipped on an apron before she stopped in front of a sink to wash her hands.

"Sorry I couldn't talk yesterday," she said. He'd called her yesterday afternoon for this very reason, but she'd been at her in-laws.

"No worries. We can work out a schedule later so you're always available when I need advice."

"Seriously, what would you do without me?"

"I seem to remember being the advice giver for most of our teenage years. It's my turn."

She arched a brow, giving him that. "You did keep me away from some assholes. But don't you have Elliott now? I bet she's a great listener."

He shifted, crossing his arms. Blythe was right, Elliott would be great to talk with about most things. In fact, she was arguably the most important person for him to open up to about this very issue, but . . . he hadn't. Like an asshole, he'd pulled away, too confused and mixed up to think straight. "It's . . . sort of about her."

Blythe's demeanor shifted in an instant, and she glared at him. "Did you screw things up already?"

"What? Why would you say that?"

She just shook her head, ponytail swinging. "You're finally with the right person, and you barely make it two mon—"

"Will you let me explain?"

"Fine. What did you do?"

He rolled his lips between his teeth. "I . . . told Carly. Everything." At her confused expression, he started from the beginning, explaining what happened at the bookstore and why he'd called Carly in the first place. He told Blythe about their conversation and how he'd accidentally revealed he loved Elliott, which inadvertently led to the whole truth about when he'd first met her. "It was bad."

"That's . . . damn. I'm sorry, Jamie. Telling her yourself was the right thing to do, and I think down the road you'll be glad you got everything out in the open. But I know that wasn't easy."

He rubbed at his eyes and took another long drink of coffee.

"So Carly's upset, which I get. But what happened with Elliott?"

He regarded his sister, the only other person in the world who would know the weight of what he was about to say. It was the main reason he'd wanted to talk to her and only her. No one else would understand, not really. "Carly said I was just like Dad."

Blythe stilled, a bag of flour in her arms.

"She said I'd just used her to pass the time until something better came along. And when someone did, when Elliott did, I cast Carly aside for the newest thing. Just like Dad does." His voice trembled on that last part. *Does*, present tense. Cycling through women was their dad's pattern—past, present, and future. He'd never change because it was who he was.

Jamie had spent the last two days asking himself if that's who he was, too.

His sister set the bag down gently and came toward him. She put her hands on his shoulders and dipped her head, looking him straight in the eye, her expression as serious as he'd ever seen it. "That's not true. Tell me you believe that."

"How do I know that? What Carly said was one hundred percent true—I did move on when a new woman came into the picture." The thought he could possibly feel more for someone than he did for Elliott seemed impossible. Beyond his heart's capacity to love. But he hadn't even known this feeling existed before her, so what did he know?

If Elliott felt for him even a fraction of what he did for her, he couldn't bear the thought of hurting her like his dad hurt his mom. He'd watched his mom suffer at the hands of the emotional turmoil his dad caused, and even after all this time, he didn't think she'd ever fully recovered. The chance he might be capable—predisposed, even—of treating Elliott that way had sent him in a downward spiral of fear that he didn't deserve her and she was better off without him.

"You're not in the right headspace if you're really comparing your situation with Dad's. He hops from woman to woman, avoiding intimacy and commitment. You haven't had many relationships, and of the ones you did, most of them lasted at least a year. That already sets you apart. So you found your one person and experienced that life-altering feeling while you happened to be with someone else. You ended the first one as gracefully and honestly as possible. You weren't looking for the next high; you were staying true to your heart."

She made a good point: by this point in his dad's life, he'd probably burned through two dozen women. Still, though. "I guess hearing her say it out loud freaked me out. She said it was only a matter of time before I move on and do the same thing to Elliott that I did to her. And I just started thinking . . . what if she's right?"

Blythe looked tempted to slap him. "Can you imagine someone else fitting you better than Elliott?"

"God, no." If he'd allowed it, Elliott's gray eyes and beautiful smile would have been forefront on his mind every day for the last year and a half. "But I've been wrong before. What if I fuck up and hurt her, too?" Elliott had been through enough in her life already. He'd never forgive himself if he broke her heart on top of it.

Blythe pinched the bridge of her nose. "When you were with Carly, did you see a future with her? Did you think about your life together down the road?"

He frowned. "Not really. But we first started dating in college. We were young."

"Well, you're not young anymore, old man, and you still didn't make plans because you weren't really in it for the long haul. Elliott or no Elliott, you'd have figured that out. Carly's just lashing out because you caught her off guard, and maybe she's a little jealous because she's human. I think if you let it sit for a bit, things will blow over."

"Maybe." He hoped she was right.

"Do you see a future with Elliott?"

If a future with Elliott meant lounging on opposite ends of the couch reading and swapping books until they were too old to see, then yes. Running together, maybe training for a few 10Ks and comparing times as they moved up in age groups? Yes. Getting a house with a yard, planting trees and flowers, maybe adopting another dog or two to fill their house with love and laughter? Definitely.

Still waking up next to her well after her hair had turned gray and lines had begun framing her eyes? He couldn't think of anything he wanted more.

His chest tightened. "I could picture it almost from the moment I met her."

"Then I never want to hear you compare yourself with Dad again. He doesn't see past the next gala with these women. He's constantly thinking ahead, planning his next move and what he needs to change in order to stay on top. If that means a new relationship, so be it. If something gets hard or doesn't fit what he needs, he won't hang around. Dad's instinct is to run away. Yours is to lean in and ask how you can help. If Dad had been in your shoes, he'd have broken things off with Elliott the second it looked like he'd have to face Carly. That kind of drama and responsibility-taking isn't his style, and no woman is worth a slice of his pride. But you faced it head-on and had the difficult conversation because what you have with Elliott is worth it. You're worth it, okay? You're worthy of her because you're willing to fight for her. Even when things get tough."

He slid his hands down his thighs to his knees, letting her words sink in. It made sense, and he wanted to believe her. Wanted to have the same confidence his sister seemed to have that he was a good man and would always do his best to do the right thing.

"I want to hear you say it," Blythe said in the don't-talk-back tone she used on her son. "Say 'I'm not like Dad.'"

He squinted at her. "I don't think—"

"*Say it.*"

God, sometimes she was terrifying. "I'm not like Dad."

"Now, I want you to believe it."

"You can't make me do that one."

She tilted her head, regarding him with the same hazel eyes he knew reflected back at her. "You will. It might take time, but something tells me this thing with Elliott will prove you'll be a one-woman man for the rest of your life. You'll look back on this conversation and whatever fear you're letting take hold of you and laugh. You'll wonder how you were ever such a dumbass."

He stared at her, unblinking. "Jeez."

"And I'll say I told you so."

She would, too. His sister never passed up an opportunity to rub being right in someone's face. That reminded him: he couldn't wait to witness the cheesecake showdown between her and Elliott. Because if Blythe was right, which she usually was, and he could convince Elliott to forgive him for ghosting her this weekend, that conversation was definitely in the imminent future.

He stood up and hugged her. "Thanks, sis."

"For . . . ?"

He laughed and lightly pushed her away. "For letting me barge into your workplace, drink your coffee, and lay my deepest fears at your feet. For helping me see the big picture, and for not laughing at me."

"I laughed on the inside, but only because you're being such a lovesick fool."

"I won't argue with that."

"It's about time, brother. Now get out of here. I've got work to do." She shooed him away. "Get Ian a new coffee so I don't have to hear him complain tomorrow."

He complied, and his phone buzzed in his pocket. He tossed an "I love you" over his shoulder as he reentered the café, looking at his phone screen.

The rush of relief when he saw Elliott's name was palpable. He smiled and swiped to answer but stopped short when someone on the other line spoke first.

"Where the *fuck* are you?"

CHAPTER
THIRTY-TWO

Jamie

Jamie cut through the store and didn't speak again until he was on the sidewalk, balancing two cups of coffee and a pastry bag in one hand. "What? Who is this?"

"Yuka. Elliott's in the bathroom and I swiped her phone, so we don't have long. You'd better tell me what's going on and why the hell you're not here before I send someone to kill you and make it look like an accident."

It might not have been the best idea in the world to ask for space this weekend, and he didn't plan on doing it again, but he'd told Elliott what he needed and she'd seemed fine with it. Had he totally misread her? Was she so upset she'd called Yuka? "I—wait. What you do mean, why I'm not there? And you're on her phone . . . Are you with her? Where is she?"

The other end was silent for a beat. "You don't know, do you?"

A chill shot down his spine. "Don't know what?"

Seconds later, two cups of coffee splattered across the pavement, and he was running.

Jamie had made the drive between Omaha and Lincoln several times over the years. It always took him about forty-five minutes to make the commute.

Today he made it in thirty-six.

He went straight to Elliott's parents' house, parking behind Yuka's Hyundai. He was in such a hurry he was halfway out of his seat before he sat back down to turn off the ignition. His heart was in his throat as he knocked on the door, shifting on his feet.

Elliott's mom opened the door. "Hi, Jamie. Come on in."

"I'm so sorry. This weekend was . . . I just . . . I didn't know. She didn't call me," he rambled as she put a gentle hand on his back to urge him fully inside, closing the door behind him. "I'm sorry I wasn't with her; I can't believe she was alone. I'm so—"

"It's okay," Mary's calm voice interjected. "She called Yuka and came here. She's not alone."

He dropped his chin to his chest, worried and ashamed. Her tone wasn't accusatory. On the contrary, she seemed to be trying to comfort him. But still, he should have been with Elliott. Should have known what was happening. He would have been if he hadn't—

"Yuka's in the kitchen with Elliott's dad."

He lifted his gaze to Mary's, the soothing smile on her lips not quite enough to cancel out the worry line between her brows.

"Is Elliott . . . ?"

Mary tipped her head toward the stairs. "She's in her room."

He nodded his thanks and took the stairs two at a time. Elliott's door was closed, and he knocked softly before easing it open. "Elliott?"

The switch was off, but natural light filtered in through the window. He swallowed as memories flooded him of the last time he'd been in this room, laughing and making love to her in the dark of the night, trying to be quiet so her parents wouldn't hear. His eyes searched the room—the desk, the chair in the corner, the bed.

That's where he found her. Curled on her side, facing him, watching him silently with red-rimmed eyes. He could do nothing but go to her, and he hoped she didn't ask him to stop or stay back. He didn't know what he'd do if he couldn't touch her.

She said nothing, so he kept moving, toeing off his shoes and putting one knee on the bed. He reached out to stroke her hair with a trembling hand. Still no reprimand, and when she closed her eyes and a tear slipped down her cheek, he nearly broke.

"Baby," he whispered, lowering himself down fully and curving his body around hers. She burrowed into his chest, and he wrapped his arms around her, panic and love warring for a stronghold in his chest. He couldn't hold her tight enough, couldn't wish hard enough he could take this from her.

She cried in earnest now, and he just held her, rubbing her back and sliding his fingers through her soft hair, trying to make up for the hours he hadn't been beside her to hold her up. His insecurities about becoming his father seemed so meaningless compared with what she was going through.

"I'm so sorry." His voice cracked.

"I—" She started, then paused to take a breath. "I don't know if I can do this again."

Yuka had told him the basics—that something was wrong with Elliott's lab results but they didn't have a definite diagnosis yet. Relapsed leukemia was on the list, but it wasn't the only possibility.

"I hope you don't have to," he said. "But if you do, you can. You're the strongest woman I know, and I won't leave your side. I'll be there the whole time if you want me to be."

"Of course I want you there."

He kissed her forehead once, twice, and slid his hand underneath the hem of her shirt, just a little, so he could feel her skin. "I'm so sorry I wasn't there today." He was sorry he wasn't the first person she'd called. He wasn't sure if it was because he hadn't become her person yet, or if he had but his actions this weekend had made her hesitate. "I'm sorry I pushed you away."

She inched back to meet his eyes, eyelashes wet. "Why did you?"

He shifted his head on the pillow to see her better and slid his hand a little higher up her back so his entire palm was against her body, nothing between them. The gesture wasn't sexual, he just wanted to feel her warmth and her breath. Feel her living body next to him. "Something Carly said hit on a deep-seated fear I have of turning into my Dad, and it just . . . got to me. I don't know why. I'd just done something that hurt her, and I started thinking about if anything like that ever happened with us. And then, while I was insistent on working through it on my own when I should have just been open with you in the first place, I wasn't there for you when you needed me."

"Don't worry about today; it was just a few hours. I still have a support system here. It's what I'm used to."

"I'm glad you have them, but I want to be part of it, too."

She nodded, but a question remained in her eyes. "Are you sure?"

"I'm sure." As he said the words, he realized how deeply he meant them, and how they only solidified what Blythe had said today about him leaning in. The fact that he was here, ready to do whatever Elliott needed from him, no matter how hard, was proof he wasn't his father. "I won't disappear on you again. I promise."

She sniffled. "Okay."

"Promise me you'll call me next time? I don't care if I'm at work, asleep, we're in a fight, or we're doing perfect. I need you to talk to me, too."

"I promise." She slid her hand up and down his back. "Yuka called you?"

He cracked a grin. "It was more of a threat than a call, but yes."

"She's small but mighty."

"She is." He cataloged her features as they lay there. Her gray eyes, the freckles splashed across her cheeks. The slight puffiness in her eyelids that he hated because he couldn't stand to see her cry. The strands of blond hair framing her pretty face. "God, I love you," he whispered, pulling her closer against his chest.

She pressed her lips to his throat. He wanted her in his arms and to have her lips on his skin forever. "I love you, too."

After a few minutes of silence, he asked, "What's the plan? Were you going to stay here tonight?"

"I didn't really think—I just came here. It's where I've always been when I got bad news. I didn't bring anything to sleep in."

"We can fix that if you want. I can go grab something for us at Target."

"You'd stay with me?"

He pressed his fingertips into her back. "You couldn't get rid of me if you tried."

"What about Hank?"

"I already asked my mom to go grab him. I didn't know what you'd need, and I wanted to be available."

"Oh." She thought for a moment. "I kind of want to see him."

"Hank?"

"Yeah."

He chuckled softly. "He's been missing you. We can go back if you want. Stay at my place or yours, whatever you want."

She nodded, her hair brushing his chin. "Yeah, okay. Let's go home."

CHAPTER THIRTY-THREE

Elliott

She asked Jamie to drop her off first so she could shower while he went to grab Hank from his mom's. When she'd cleaned up and knew he was back at his place, she made her way across the complex.

She stepped off the elevator and the comforting, sugary smell of baked goods assailed her senses. It got stronger the closer she got to Jamie's apartment, and by the time she opened the door, she had a huge smile on her face.

Jamie had his back to the door. The clash of a wire whisk against a metal pan muffled the sound of her entrance.

She dropped her keys on the table, and he whipped around.

Elliott cocked a brow. "Whatcha doing?"

A sheepish blush crept across his cheeks. "It's a surprise."

"One that smells awesome."

"That's good because without a severe schoolmarm watching over me, I'm not sure I'm doing this right." He turned back to the stove and after another minute of whisking, stepped back. "The first batch looked a little weird, so I started on another while that one cooked, just in case." After stuffing his hands in red-and-white-checkered oven mitts, he bent down to pull a tray out of the oven. He slid one of two bright-red ramekins onto a plate, then presented it to her like a Christmas present.

"Actually . . ." He took the plate back and set it on the table, then pulled her into his arms. "This first." He pressed his hand to her back and bent her backward as he kissed her, eliciting a laugh from her throat.

"What is all this?" she asked when she was upright. "Why the surprise?"

His brow furrowed and his gaze caressed her face, tracing across her eyes, cheeks, lips. "The last few days have been hard. For a lot of reasons. And I don't really know what to do. I guess I just wanted to recreate one of the best nights of my life. Which, incidentally, is the same night I met you.

"I hoped maybe we could go back in time for a little while and just forget everything. Everything but us."

This man. "I love that idea."

"I love you," he said, his expression pensive. "I'm sorry I didn't show that this week."

She pulled one hand from his grasp and laid it flat on his chest. "You're allowed to have bad days. You're allowed to hurt and be sad. We both are. We just have to be there for each other on the good days and the bad ones." She paused. "Especially the bad ones."

He closed his eyes. "Promise?"

"Promise."

He crushed her against his chest, hugging her tight. She loved the feel of his strong arms and his large, warm body around her. He pressed his lips to her hair, breathing deeply while she did the same.

She helped finish the soufflés he was working on, and while the second batch were more visually appealing, both went down just fine. As far as Elliott was concerned, if it had butter and sugar, and was chocolate-free, she'd eat it. Jamie refused to let her help clean up, so she settled onto the couch and found a new romantic comedy on Netflix. After he joined her, though, it didn't take long to lose interest in the movie.

It started with his hand in her hair, fingers working their way down to her neck. She leaned into the massage, and he shifted to settle her between his legs so he could reach her shoulders better. His thumbs rubbed slow, deep circles along her muscles, sending her entire body melting into him, her lower back in the triangle of his thighs. His hands curved over her shoulders, gently caressing the space below her collarbone, just above the curve of her breasts.

It felt so good, and yet all she could think about was his hands moving lower.

"Relax," he said into her ear. The tender yet commanding way he said it, combined with the press of his skin on hers, did the exact opposite.

"I can't," she said, voice low. She shifted, hoping to find some relief, and felt him hard against her spine. "Not when all I can think about is where else I want your hands."

One of his hands snaked up to gently grab her jaw. He angled her face to the side and leaned up to brush his nose with hers, pausing with his lips a breath away. The fierce look in his eyes sent a rush of heat curling from her belly to her toes. Her breathing became shallow, yet she felt every rise of her chest against her shirt, her nerve endings lighting up like matches.

Keeping her eyes locked on his, she put her hand on his thigh, and the second she touched him he moved. His hands dropped to her waist and he flipped her onto her back, stretching his large body over hers. He slid off his glasses and set them on the end table before his lips came down on hers, tongue slipping inside her mouth. A light burst open in her rib cage, sending shimmers of glittering rays into every corner and crevice of her heart where doubt had crept in.

When he arched his hips against hers, she sucked in a breath, followed by a moan with her exhale. "Jamie . . ."

"I've missed you," he breathed into her neck, kissing along the column of her throat and the curve of her shoulder. "I want you so much."

"Yes. *Please.*"

His hands were everywhere. She yanked at his shirt at the same time he tugged her pants down her legs, one arm under her lower back to lift her up. When all their clothes were on the floor and his warm, strong body was poised above hers, he tipped his head forward to softly kiss her cheeks, her forehead, and finally her lips.

"I'm here," he whispered. "Always."

She nodded, her voice thick with emotion. "Always."

On Wednesday morning, Elliott and Jamie sat silently in the waiting room fifteen minutes before they were called back to the exam room.

Her oncologist knocked and entered a few minutes later. Dr. Varghese was a man with graying black hair, though he only appeared to be in his forties. His job probably led to a lot of sleepless nights.

After she was treated the first time, Elliott briefly considered going into the medical field, figuring it might be a good path based on what she'd gone through. But the thought of all those science classes made her stomach turn, and her true love was in the arts. Photography, design, and creativity.

She also hadn't wanted people's lives in her hands. How on earth did Dr. Varghese do this every day?

"Hi, Elliott. Thanks for coming on such short notice."

"Thanks for getting me in so quick." She leaned forward in her chair. Well, as far as she could with Jamie's death grip on her hand. "I, um, brought my boyfriend, Jamie." The men acknowledged each other with nods. "Did you find out anything more from the labs?"

Dr. Varghese sat on the stool in the center of the room. "Nothing definitive. There are still several things that could be going on. It could be a virus, or it could be the leukemia has returned and is attacking your bone marrow. Or it could simply be your donor cells are losing their effectiveness."

Elliott blinked. Relief hovered just out of reach at the thought it could be something other than cancer. But the other options didn't sound great, either. "Can that happen? The transplant cells can stop working after all this time?"

"It's not common, but it's possible. The bone marrow biopsy will give us more answers."

There was a time she'd dreaded the procedure, but by this point she'd had so many it was old news.

"Then what will the plan be?" Jamie asked.

"If it's cancer, we'll have to have another conversation. It will depend on how extensive the disease burden is. We might need to do a little more chemo first, and then we could try a donor lymphocyte infusion, or DLI. Think of it like a stem cell boost. That's also what I'll recommend if there's no cancer and it looks like the original donor cells are losing their hold."

"A stem cell boost?"

"Yes. If your first donor is able and willing, we'll ask her to donate again. Sometimes that's all it takes to get everything under control."

The same lightheaded sensation she had on Monday crashed through her again. "The first donor?" she whispered.

"Yes." Dr. Varghese consulted the papers in his hand. "She was a perfect match. I'll be surprised if the cells are losing function, but like I said, it's possible. You did so well after the transplant, using the same donor will be the best thing."

She might need more cells from Carly. She never would have imagined that was a possibility. How could she even ask such a thing, after everything that had happened?

She glanced at Jamie, wondering if he was having the same thoughts she was. His skin was a little pale as he met her gaze, but his expression was unreadable.

"Do you have any other questions right now?"

Elliott sat in silence for a long moment, thinking. She'd learned not to hold back during office visits, and to take advantage of having the doctor's undivided attention when they were face-to-face. He'd always been responsive when she called in between visits, but he had other patients to take care of, too. The time blocked off for them to sit in this room together was hers and hers alone.

"What—" It came out almost like a whisper, and she paused and swallowed before trying again. "Um. What if she won't donate a second time?"

Jamie's grip on her hand firmed up again.

"That's not usually an issue, but we'll cross that bridge when we come to it, okay? There are other options. That one's just my preferred one." He stood. "I'll go get the medical assistant, and we'll be back to do that biopsy."

The door clicked quietly with his exit, and Jamie immediately pulled her into his arms. Hot tears streamed down her cheeks.

"It's okay," he said, rubbing circles on her back. "Shh."

Her throat ached and her eyes burned. "I thought I was done with all this." She broke down again, and with one arm still around her, Jamie leaned to the side to grab a box of tissues.

"I'm so sorry." He hugged her tighter. "But I'll be here, no matter what happens. You're not in this alone, okay?"

Sniffing, she nodded. "I'm glad you're here."

"I wouldn't be anywhere else." He wiped her cheeks with a tissue and kissed her hair.

Elliott wiped her nose and tipped her head back. Jamie's lashes were damp, and he brushed his thumb across her cheekbone.

"Carly . . ."

Jamie smoothed her hair back, gripping the back of her head gently. "Don't worry about that."

"How can I not? She hates me."

"She doesn't hate you. She's hurt and probably pissed, but mostly at me. I'm the one who did wrong by her. You were an innocent bystander I happened to fall in love with."

She didn't agree, and more tears slid down her cheeks. She didn't deserve to be absolved for what had happened.

"We don't know what the plan is yet, either. That might not even be on the table. Let's take this one step at a time, okay? Get the biopsy results and face it, then."

Wiping more tears, Elliott nodded, then pulled away and stood.

"What are you doing?"

She used the lever on the side of the exam table to adjust the height and climbed onto it, laying stomach down. "Getting ready for the biopsy."

Jamie moved from the wooden chair against the wall to the rolling stool, scooting near her head. He took her left hand in both of his, stroking each of her fingers with his thumbs, his eyes filled with concern. "Does it hurt?"

"Nah. They numb it first." She turned her head to look at him, the paper crinkling, and rested her cheek on the table. "But if you're not good with blood and stuff, maybe don't watch when they do it."

His eyes went wide.

"It's just a big needle, is all."

His chest rose with a deep inhale, and she almost laughed at the look on his face.

"You don't have to stay." She'd done these plenty of times by herself.

"The hell I won't."

She shrugged. "Okay. But if you pass out I'm not carrying you out of here."

That got a tiny smile out of him.

Dr. Varghese returned with a young woman in scrubs carrying a package of equipment. She laid everything out on the counter, and Dr. Varghese started the procedure.

Jamie kept his eyes on her face or his ministrations with her hand, staying stock-still, as if he were afraid to jostle her.

When he was finished, the doctor said he'd call her as soon as he had results and discuss next steps. Elliott and Jamie walked to the car together, and he looked over at her before he turned the truck on.

"What now?"

She leaned her head back. "Will you take me to your trees?"

CHAPTER THIRTY-FOUR

Jamie

When they got home that evening, Jamie ordered food to be delivered. Elliott hardly ate, and he saved the leftovers for tomorrow, then rejoined her on the couch.

"How are you feeling about everything?"

"Fine." She huffed out a wry amused breath. "You know what's funny? This whole year, I've been terrified of every little ache, pain, or quirk I felt, worried it was leukemia. But these last few weeks, I've felt perfect. All that worry, and it showed up when I never expected it."

He brushed his knuckles across her cheek and kissed her forehead. "Life is so fucked up sometimes."

"Yeah, it is."

"What do you need? What can I do?"

"Nothing. This is the worst part. Waiting for answers." She tilted her head as she looked at him. "Are you okay?"

He was terrified. "Don't worry about me."

"Of course I'm worried about you. I've done this before, but this is your first go-around."

How many office visits had she sat through? How many blood draws, needle pricks, chemotherapy treatments? "I'm so in awe of you."

"Don't be. I'm not saying I do it well. I just do what I have to."

He shook his head. "Don't do that. You're a complete badass, and you deserve to hear it."

One corner of her lips tipped up. "Okay. I'll allow it."

They got into bed a short time later, and he tucked her into his chest, planning to just hold her after everything that had happened today. But when she started kissing his neck and slid her hand inside his boxers, he couldn't stop his body from responding.

"Elliott, we don't have to—"

"I want to." Her tongue traced his earlobe, and he groaned into her hair. "Please."

She rolled on top of him, and he caressed her body with his hands, loving the way she responded to him, even now. He tried to think only of how much he loved her instead of how terrified he was. Knowing her fear must be ten times what he was feeling, he wanted her to forget about it just for a little while.

"You're so beautiful," he rasped. His chest was tight, like a fist gripped his lungs. He slid his hands up her thighs. "Your legs make me insane. And your breasts fill my thoughts far more than what's appropriate, I'm sure."

She giggled, and even that tiny smile on her face loosened the pressure in his chest. He continued on, moving his hands all over her body. "This collarbone, your shoulders, your perfect lips . . ." He sat up and traced each part with his tongue. Burying his fingers in her hair, he nipped at her earlobe with his teeth. "Your hair is so soft and sexy. I loved it when I first met you, and I'd love you without it. But the fact that I can do this—" He wrapped the midlength strands around his fist and gently pulled back, exposing her neck. "It drives me wild."

A moan slipped from her throat. Her hands gripped his shoulders, and she dragged her nails down his chest. Scooting forward, she clamped her strong runner's legs around his waist. Her position put her face several inches above his, and he tilted his to catch her lips in a deep, open-mouthed kiss. His eyes slid closed, and he focused on the feel of her warmth, her affection, and her need for him.

All he wanted was for her to feel wanted, loved, and *safe*. Safe from everything outside these walls, this bed, their bodies. Even if her blood was failing her, he'd move mountains to do whatever it took to see her healed.

Two days later, the call finally came. He and Elliott had just finished dinner and were about to take Hank to the dog park when her phone buzzed.

Elliott lunged for it. "It's Dr. Varghese." She put the phone on speaker before she answered, and Jamie appreciated the gesture to include him. "Hello?"

"Hi, Elliott. It's Dr. Varghese. Is now a good time? I'm sorry it's so late."

Jamie sat on the couch and held out his hand. Elliott sat beside him, holding the phone flat in her palm. "Yes, now is fine. My boyfriend's here, so you're on speaker."

"I'm calling because I have the biopsy results. The good news is there's no leukemia."

His head dropped back with relief. *Thank God.* Elliott remained where she was, head bowed, one hand holding the phone and the other gripping her neck.

Jamie quietly scooted closer and put his palm on her back, reminded of his inexperience with calls like this. Her cancer wasn't back, which was worth celebrating. But still, something was wrong, and they had to find a way to fix it.

"The bad news is the engraftment studies showed the donor cells are very low. I want to proceed with the stem cell boost, like I mentioned on Wednesday."

Elliott let out a shaky breath. "Okay."

"We've already tried reaching out to your original donor. We haven't gotten ahold of her yet, but we'll keep trying. As soon as we can get the procedure set up, I'll let you know. You won't need to be in the hospital like last time. We can do it in the outpatient infusion center, and it won't be more than an hour."

"What happens if you can't reach her?"

"Let's not go down that road unless we have to," Dr. Varghese said. It irritated Jamie that the man kept hedging the question, but he forced himself to keep quiet and let Elliott handle it how she wanted. "That's really the preferred option, and we only made the first attempt yesterday. We have plenty of time. Nothing on your lab work was emergent. That's why we check them so often—to catch things early and give us time to plan."

"Okay. So now . . . do I just wait?"

"I'm afraid so. I hope we can get this set up within the next two or three weeks. We'll be in touch as soon as we have new information. Reach out to my nurse if you have any questions or issues in the meantime, okay?"

"Okay. Thank you."

Elliott set the phone on the coffee table and looked at him. "You're as pale as when I got the biopsy," she said. "Come here."

She wrapped her arms around him, and he hugged her back. "Please tell me this is comforting for you, too," he said into her hair. "Because that's the most important."

"It definitely is."

"I'll call Ca—"

Elliott pulled back. "No. You won't."

He frowned at her. "Elliott, she has to do this."

She leaned back again, her gaze steady. "She will. She's a good, kind person. And even if she was *that* upset about us being together and didn't want to give me another part of her body, that's her prerogative. I think she'll agree, but I want it to be through the regular channel. I don't want her to be guilted into it by you or by me. That's not how this should work."

He knew she was right. "I know I sound like an asshole. It's just . . . Her part is easy, right? It's not dangerous. I'd never expect her to put herself at risk for you, even if I'd do it a thousand times over."

"I know you would."

He just wished he could do something to fix it, but he was completely helpless in this. "I wish our bodies weren't so complicated. I wish I could give you mine."

She smiled softly. "Are you in the registry?"

He nodded. "I signed up in college, the same time Carly did. There was a big table set up by some organization every year at the student union."

"Well, if you were a match for me, they'd already know." She patted his knee as if to say that was that. She seemed surprisingly okay with the news she'd just heard, but then again, she'd been doing some version of this for more than a decade. "It's only been a day. Let's just give her some time, okay?"

"Yeah, okay." He leaned over and kissed her softly. It was a chaste kiss, yet his stomach flipped over as if she'd driven her tongue into his mouth. Maybe it was the way her fingers slid through his hair, pulling him in. "Hey, Elliott?" he said against her mouth.

"Yeah?"

He lifted his head to look at her. "I do take issue with something you just said."

"What's that?"

"Our bone marrow might not match, but everything else fits perfectly." He was being cheesy as hell, but her smile made it worth it. "In every other way, I'm your perfect match. And you're mine."

CHAPTER
THIRTY-FIVE

Elliott

When a week passed without word about more cells from Carly, Elliott's optimism dwindled. Jamie never seemed to have much to begin with. Despite Dr. Varghese saying they had options if the stem cell boost wasn't possible, Elliott knew anything after the preferred choice wasn't good. She'd lost her battle to stay positive and started wondering what would happen if her blood cells stopped working. In a way, it was like having leukemia again, but instead of sick blood cells that didn't work right, she just wouldn't have any at all.

Not having blood cells didn't seem compatible with life, so . . . Not great news.

She was restless and Jamie seemed uptight, and their conversations were stilted and brief. They often went on runs together or read silently on opposite ends of the couch. During the day, they were like ships passing in the ocean, careful not to disturb the wake and knock the other off-balance.

Then came the nights. When the lights were off and she couldn't see his eyes, Jamie made love to her with desperation and determination. As he drove her body to the brink, he breathed his devotion into her skin and whispered love into her heart. He held her close to his body as they slept, as if he were afraid she'd slip away.

Another week came and went.

No news.

Anger had been her primary emotion the entire first two months of her initial diagnosis, and then again for months after the cancer came back.

But by this point she was resigned. Things would work out or they wouldn't. The idea of not being able to grow old with Jamie made her want to curl up in a ball and weep, but letting it show would only make things worse for him.

If she'd learned anything over the last few months, it was that she needed to try to let go of things she couldn't control.

Her feelings.

Other people's feelings.

The intricate inner workings of her body.

She could try to manhandle them all she wanted, but it would only lead to frustration. And sometimes failure. The only things she could control were her actions and response to things. She and Keri, her friend from the support group, had talked about that a lot. About letting go of certain things (worry) and focusing on what they could change (life goals—even short-term ones). Especially things they could change for the better.

Elliott wanted to leave this world better than she found it. She wanted to share positivity and creativity and help people's dreams come true, and she hoped she'd have the chance to keep doing that.

The following Monday she called the oncologist's office. She couldn't handle the silence, and asked the nurse to leave a message with Dr. Varghese, asking him to call her so they could discuss other options.

So that afternoon, when her phone rang while she was working alone in her apartment, she didn't even register the unfamiliar number, assuming it was the doctor calling from somewhere in the hospital.

"Hello?"

"Elliott? It's Carly."

Shock froze her muscles for a few seconds, her brain's jaw on the floor.

"Are you there? Sorry to surprise you like this."

"I'm here," Elliott blurted, too loud. "Sorry. I just . . . wasn't expecting it to be you."

"Yeah, I know." She paused. "I'm so, so sorry. I got a phone with a new Oklahoma number recently, so I had no idea your doctor had been trying to reach me. I guess I had my mom as my emergency contact, and they finally called her. I was freaked out at first, when she said who was looking for me. I thought something had happened to you."

"Oh. Well, I guess something did, but not like that. Just my body jerking me around like it does every few years."

Carly let out a surprised laugh. "That . . . honestly really sucks."

"It totally does. If I could trade for a new one, I would. Though I sort of did once, because of you."

"I'm sorry it didn't work like it was supposed to."

"Me too."

"Anyway, I just wanted you to know I wasn't, like, trying to avoid this. I'm happy to donate again. It's already been set up. I know if I were you I'd be a mess if it took two weeks to find me, so I wanted to apologize. I never even thought about it when I changed my number."

Elliott let out a slow breath, and her muscles loosened after weeks of built-up tension. "Don't apologize. I wouldn't have thought about it, either." It had been a couple of days since she'd cried, and she wanted to keep the streak going. "Thank you, Carly. So, so much for doing this again. There's literally nothing I'll ever be able to do to repay you for what you've done for me. And I don't just mean with the stem cells. You were so kind to me, bringing me into your life and sharing your friends with me when I was a stranger in Omaha. You were the most selfless person, and then I—I—"

Shit. She was crying.

"It's okay," Carly said. "I know what you're about to say, and don't. I'm not going to pretend I was happy about it, but I've made peace with it. The fact is, I moved on, too, so who am I to judge? Would I have appreciated honesty? Yeah, but I can understand it was a weird spot for you to be in. Jamie, too, probably, and he and I weren't meant to be anyway. We both knew it, but neither of us wanted to admit it. I overreacted when Jamie told me, and I'll call him soon—when I'm ready—and have a better conversation with him about it, too. But just know I'd never let something like that stop me from helping you again. Okay?"

"You're a really, really good person. I hope you know that. And I am sorry, truly. For how I handled it all."

"Well, I have you to thank for something, too, you know. If it weren't for you, I don't think I'd have taken this chance in Oklahoma City, and it's turned out to be the best thing I've ever done."

"Really? It's that good, huh?"

"I love it."

"That's great to hear. I'm happy for you."

"Thanks," Carly said. "I've gotta get going, but I just wanted to touch base about everything. I'm thinking good thoughts for you, and I hope this second round of cells does the trick."

"So do I. From the bottom of my heart, thank you for everything."

"You're welcome. Oh, and Elliott?"

"Yeah?"

"Take care of Jamie, okay? He's one of the good ones."

By the time Jamie got home from work, Elliott thought she'd composed herself well enough to head over to his apartment, but the tears started up again as she walked down the hallway to his door. He took one look at her face and pulled her into his arms.

"What's wrong?"

"J-Jamie—"

His fingers brushed her hair and neck, his eyes sweeping her face. "What happened? Did the doctor call?"

She nodded and sniffed. "Sort of." Not the doctor, but same difference. "They'll have the cells."

He sucked in a sharp breath. "Did she . . . ?"

"Yes. They're Carly's."

He let out a shaky exhale and whispered a thank-you. Then his arms wrapped around her waist, and he picked her up, swinging her around the kitchen. She laughed through her tears, and he smiled up at her, his eyes lighter than she'd seen them in weeks.

She scattered kisses all over his face, even catching his teeth with one when she tried to kiss him as he smiled. A blur of color on the kitchen table caught her attention and she pointed.

"What are those?"

His gaze didn't leave her face. "Flowers."

"For me?"

He shook his head.

"For . . . Hank?"

"Nope."

"Jamie, did you buy yourself flowers?"

He chuckled and lightened his hold, allowing her body to slide slowly down his front. "What if I did?"

"I'd think that's pretty adorable."

He met her gaze, reaching up to straighten his glasses. "They're for us."

She tilted her head a little.

"I know you love flowers, and they're mostly for you because the thing I love most in this world is seeing you smile. But I like them, too, and I love that it's something we share. Every time I see them, I'll remember how happy they make you, and I'll also remember how perfect you are for me."

Her fingers slid up his neck to brush his thick hair. "I am?"

"I never thought I'd find someone like you. I didn't think you existed."

"Maybe I don't. Maybe I really am a unicorn."

Laughing, he pulled her close. "No. You exist, but only a few people know about you. You're the best kind of secret."

"What I'm hearing is I'm actually a narwhal."

His eyes glittered with mischief and love. "I don't care what you are, Elliott Holland, as long as you're mine."

EPILOGUE

Elliott

Two and a half years later

Elliott cleared her throat and smiled. "Hi, everyone. Most of you know me, but I see a few new faces tonight. I'm Elliott, and I'm a four-year cancer survivor."

She told the members of the survivors' group her story and listened intently as each person went around the room, talking about their experience and triumph over their cancer diagnosis. Keri sat to her right, hands folded over her hugely pregnant belly. Elliott had slipped several cookies from Melt My Tart into Keri's purse earlier, and Keri had immediately announced Elliott as this child's godmother.

An hour later, Elliott pulled into the driveway of the house she and Jamie had purchased six months ago. It was an older ranch-style home that needed a little updating on the inside, but the yard and back patio had ultimately swayed them. The prior owners spent a lot of time outside, and when the Realtor stepped out to take a call while showing them the home, Elliott and Jamie had sat on the back porch for a few minutes. He'd said he loved the trees shading the backyard, and she'd said she could see herself relaxing out here with a book every night, even in the winter with the built-in fireplace.

The decision was pretty easy after that.

Elliott smiled when she saw Jamie's truck was already there. He'd been gone for a couple of days at a tree-climbing competition, and she'd missed him terribly.

Hank was at the door, tail thumping the wall when she stepped inside.

"Hey, handsome," she crooned, scratching his head.

"Talking to me or the dog?" a masculine voice asked from her left.

She smiled and took the single step down into the sunken living room. "Both."

He met her in the middle of the room and slid his hands around her waist, pulling her in. His hair was slightly damp from a recent shower, and his sexy smile, along with the crisp, fresh scent of his skin, sent her heart racing.

She hugged him tight, running her hands across the long, hard muscles along the length of his back. "Welcome home."

His lips searched along her temple and down her cheekbone, and she tilted her face to give him what they both wanted. Even years later, his kiss still sent butterflies swarming through her stomach.

"How'd it go?" she asked, keeping her arms around him.

"Good. Got another trophy."

"Yeah?"

He tipped his head to the coffee table, and she released him to lean down and look at it.

"Wow. It's even smaller than the last one."

That got her a light pinch on her waist. "I had a surprise for you, but now I'm thinking maybe I shouldn't give it to you."

She twisted around and slipped her hands under his shirt, running her fingers across his warm skin. Looking up at him with her best doe eyes, she leaned in. "You're the best, fastest, most impressive tree-climber in all the world."

He squinted one eye, his lips twitching. "And the sexiest?"

"Definitely the sexiest. I've never met another arborist with an ass like yours."

"You've never met another arborist."

"Irrelevant." She pressed a kiss to his scruff-covered jaw. "Please give me my surprise. Please?"

He pursed his lips and shot her a skeptical glance. He tapped his index finger against his lower lip, and she grinned, kissing him there. With a satisfied nod, he took a step back. "Okay. But it's not here."

"Where is it?"

"You'll see. But we need to leave now so we don't lose daylight."

Excitement filled her as they climbed into his truck. He entwined his fingers with hers and rested their hands on the console as he merged onto the highway.

"Blythe called while I was at the airport waiting to board," Jamie said. "Said she saw something on Instagram this morning I might be interested to know."

"What's that?"

Jamie squeezed her hand as he smiled with genuine happiness. "Carly's engaged."

Elliott sucked in a breath. "What?"

He nodded. "He's a doctor, apparently. Blythe said they looked stupid happy in the picture."

As his words sank in, Elliott's lips parted and she let out an involuntary laugh. She clamped a hand over her mouth and blinked rapidly. "I'm just . . . I don't think I've ever been so happy for another person."

"I know." His voice held a sense of wonder. "It's like part of me is relieved for selfish reasons, like I finally feel sort of absolved of the hurt I caused her. But more than that, I'm just happy she's happy. That she found someone who's so much better for her than I could have ever been."

Elliott lifted their joined hands and kissed the back of his. "That's such great news. I'm glad Blythe told you."

"Me too."

He exited the highway and she looked around. "Are we going to the trees?"

"Yup."

"That's not a surprise."

He gave her the side-eye. "Can you just trust me?"

"Fine."

Once they reached the field, he pulled into the grass and parked in his usual spot, then helped her over the fence. They walked hand in hand to the bench underneath the arching canopy of the oaks, like they'd done dozens of times before.

"Sit," he said, then added, "Please."

She did as instructed.

Jamie remained standing, and as he shuffled on his feet in the grass, she admired the long, lean muscles of his forearms and the way his chest and shoulders filled out the fitted shirt. His hair had dried and was a little messy and windblown from the drive over, and it looked positively delicious. As he lifted a hand to adjust his glasses, she nearly reached out to pull him down with her.

"Do you know what today is?"

She searched her brain for the significance of this day but couldn't think of anything.

He smiled softly and stopped moving. "We met four years ago today."

Mentally calculating backward from her transplant date, which was one she'd never forget, she realized he was right. How could she have missed that?

He dropped to one knee before her.

At the simple gesture, goose bumps swept across Elliott's skin, and the breath whooshed out of her. Within seconds, tears were streaming down her cheeks, and she scooted forward, framing his face with her hands.

Gently, he took her hands and brought them down. His fingers trembled slightly, but his eyes were determined and steadfast. "My life was never the same after that night. From the second I saw you at that bar, I knew you were special. I'd been hoping for an excuse to talk to you, and when you brought up the ridiculous notion that cheesecake is a pie, I had my in. I almost jumped off that stool and whooped with joy."

She choked back a laugh. "And yet you interrupted and mansplained instead."

Uninhibited devotion shone in his eyes. She couldn't tell how much was his and how much was a reflection of her own. "Got me a few more hours with you, didn't it?"

Pressing her forehead against his, she whispered, "It got you a little more than that, I'd say."

"Hours, days, years." He swallowed, his voice thick. "Marry me, Elliott. Every second with you has been worth it, and I won't be happy with anything except forever."

She kissed him softly, her knees bumping the one he had extended. She smiled against his lips. "I will if you admit I was right. Cheesecake is a pie."

His breath brushed across her face as he laughed. "Just don't tell Blythe, okay?"

"I swear."

"Elliott Holland, love of my life. You were right. Cheesecake is a pie, and will you please marry me?"

"Gladly." She launched herself at him, and he fell back into the grass with a grunt. Laughing, she kissed his face, tears mixing in with the insistent movement of their lips.

His arm pressed her close to his chest while he buried his other hand in her hair. "I have a ring in my pocket," he said into her mouth.

"Mmm," she murmured. "Is it big?"

"Size is subjective."

"I disagree." She put her hands on his chest and lifted herself up a little. With a sly grin she slipped her hand into the front pocket of his jeans. "Is this it?"

"Nope. That's another surprise, that needs to wait until we get back to the truck."

Heat rushed through her like a lit fuse, but she stayed on task. With a wiggle of her eyebrows she shifted her hand until she felt a small piece of metal. "This is definitely smaller than the other thing."

He huffed out a laugh. "Shit, Elliott. This is supposed to be serious."

"No it's not."

His hazel eyes slid back and forth between hers. "It's not?"

She shook her head and pulled out the ring. "Love is happy. And fun. And wonderful." Light caught on the beautiful round diamond on its simple gold band, and fresh tears fell from her eyes. "And so very beautiful and perfect. I love it, Jamie."

She looked down at his handsome face then, and his lips were tight in that way when he was trying not to cry. His chest rose and fell with each breath, and he looked at her like she was everything.

He took the ring and slowly slid it onto her finger. "I love you."

Her heart couldn't handle it. "I love you more."

ACKNOWLEDGMENTS

Any author who has been consistently writing for at least five years has a COVID book, and this one's mine. I don't remember exactly when I started it, but the bulk of it was written during the summer of 2020. Based on conversations with other authors and my own experience, most of us would say our COVID books are a little different. Several said theirs were quieter, gentler books with lower conflict and less angst. During that time many of us wanted something comforting and as low stress as possible. For me, I don't think my COVID book is different in tone or vibe than my usual. The part that was different was that it was hard as hell to write. I don't know if it's because it's sort of a love triangle, which is a trope I swore I'd never write, or if it was my frame of mind as a health care worker serving cancer patients during the pandemic. Whatever it was, this book took many, many versions to get to where it is. We're talking major overhauls—POV changes, major plot adjustments, character changes. I even put it down, wrote a different book, then picked this one back up. But through it all, Elliott and Jamie were at the center, and their connection never wavered. I feel so lucky when characters speak to me that deeply, because no matter how big of a mess I make as I'm trying to figure it out, the characters always bring it back to the right place. I'm so, so happy with where this book ended up, but believe me when I say it wasn't an easy process.

TL;DR, I'm proud of this one.

Many people were involved in molding this book to what it is—from early feedback that led to major (needed) changes to words of praise that told me I had something in this story, which encouraged me not to give up. Admittedly by the time I'm writing these acknowledgments, it's been more than four years since some of those early reads, so if I try to make a list, I know I won't catch everyone. But please know, if you read an early draft of this book—thank you. Thank you for taking the time, especially during 2020, to read messy drafts and help me improve the story. I will specifically thank Sarah Schmidt for letting me ask you all sorts of leukemia and stem cell transplant questions—because as we all know when I went to solid tumors I never looked back. (But any onc folks who read this book—please note while I take medical accuracy seriously, I needed to take a little artistic license in places . . . so anything that might seem like a stretch is all on me.)

Thank you to my agent, Kim, for being willing to fight for this book even if it meant dipping our toe in a different genre, and for knowing me well enough to know the perfect place for this book was with someone who wanted it for what it first was—a tried-and-true romance. Which brings me to that editor, Lauren Plude, who sees and loves my inclination to tell emotional romances with medical themes and who believed Jamie and Elliott's story was worth telling. Thank you, along with Selina MacLemore, for improving this book and making it shine (please note I'm wearing skinny jeans as I write this).

Thank you so much to all the romance readers out there who love and cherish the genre. I'm one of you, and I'm so thankful to have the opportunity to not only read these books that make me so happy but write them for us, too. Thank you for your kind words and posts that make my day, and for sharing your love for books. Thank you to all the booksellers (special shout-out to Best of Books in Edmond, Oklahoma) who celebrate and sell romance. You're sharing love with the world, and we love you for it.

ABOUT THE AUTHOR

Photo © 2019 Ashley Porton

Allison Ashley is the author of *The Roommate Pact, Would You Rather, Home Sweet Mess,* and *Perfect Distraction.* She is a science geek who enjoys coffee, craft beer, baking, and love stories. When Allison is not working at her day job as a clinical oncology pharmacist, she pens contemporary romances, usually with a medical twist. She lives in Oklahoma with her family and beloved rescue dog. For more information, visit www.authorallisonashley.com.